KU-531-495

Shirley Smith was born in Yorkshire. For some time she worked as a headmistress in Manchester, and as an inspector in South Yorkshire.

TANGLED DESTINY

Beautiful heiress Sophia Winterton runs away on her wedding day, defying her Aunt Harriet and her fiancé, Lord Devenish. Still in her wedding gown, Sophia takes the stagecoach to London to seek sanctuary with her godmother. Walking to the Eight Bells coaching inn, she meets the attractive Sir Paul Maunders, who is reputed to be a rake. He escorts Sophia to her godmother's house in Islington. But Sophia's troubles have barely begun. Harriet is bent on revenge and Sir Paul is determined to have his own way. Sophia has a testing path to follow before finding happiness.

SHIRLEY SMITH

TANGLED DESTINY

Complete and Unabridged

ULVERSCROFT
Leicester

First published in Great Britain in 2005 by
Robert Hale Limited
London

First Large Print Edition
published 2006
by arrangement with
Robert Hale Limited
London

British Library CIP Data

Smith, Shirley, *1942* –
    Tangled destiny.—Large print ed.—
    Ulverscroft large print series: romance
    1. Love stories
    2. Large type books
    I. Title
    823.9'2 [F]

    ISBN 1–84617–518–6

Published by
F. A. Thorpe (Publishing)
Anstey, Leicestershire

Set by Words & Graphics Ltd.
Anstey, Leicestershire
Printed and bound in Great Britain by
T. J. International Ltd., Padstow, Cornwall

This book is printed on acid-free paper

With love and best wishes
to Paul and the dear twins,
Trudi Elizabeth and Heidi Mai,
from Shirley Smith

1

'Go away,' she said in a low firm voice. 'I never accept rides from strangers.'

'I'm hardly a total stranger,' Sir Paul said mildly. 'I am acquainted with your aunt and uncle, and your cousin David and I are old friends. I am offering assistance very respectfully, there is no offence intended, ma'am. Won't you please let me help you into my carriage?'

Sophia Winterton didn't halt for one second in her swift stride and neither did she look at him. She had long legs he noticed and the length of her stride was quite inappropriate and unfeminine for a refined young lady, particularly as she was a bride. On looking closer, Major Sir Paul Maunders had observed that she was wearing the regalia of a bride on her wedding day, though to be sure, her veil was a little awry and had allowed several strands of beautiful Titian hair to escape from its confines and float freely down her flushed cheek. He also noticed that she was carrying a valise. She continued to disregard him as she shifted the heavy valise to her other hand and carried on with her rapid walk, intent only on getting away from him.

'Miss Winterton?' he said again. Sir Paul liked to drive himself, but as she continued with her rattling pace, he threw the reins to his groom and got down from his carriage, falling into step beside her. In spite of her rapid stride, he was able to keep up with her easily. She was a tall, slender young woman and quite fleet of foot, in spite of carrying the valise and holding up the train of her gown with the other hand.

Sir Paul was all of thirty-two years old and there seemed nothing new in the world which could possibly surprise him. He'd had some difficult times fighting in Portugal and Spain and had been at Waterloo, which had been by far the worst. Nevertheless, his army training had always been the framework of his actions and he'd always known what to do in the dangerous conditions of war. Things were different now. The situation which was confronting him on the Cottleton road for instance, made it difficult to know what action to take. He'd been gazing almost mindlessly in front of him until suddenly, what he'd thought was a heat-haze, was in fact Miss Winterton, the niece of one of his neighbours, dressed all in white and positively racing along a road which was little more than a cart track. The last time he'd seen her she'd been but a girl and now she was a young woman.

He noticed the determined jut of her chin, her tightly closed lips and consciously averted eyes as she walked on rapidly, as though to put as much distance between herself and Cottleton as possible. He felt a spurt of irritation that she should so patently wish him elsewhere when he had merely wanted to be helpful.

Sir Paul set his jaw. He was unused to being crossed in anything he wished to do. As the loved younger son of doting parents, since his brother's death, he had become the heir. Flunkeys, fond mamas, and simpering debutantes alike, leapt to do his bidding and habitually gave way to him. Everything he did was right and everything he said was right. 'Yes, Sir Paul. Of course, Sir Paul' were the words he was used to hearing. In no way was he familiar with the curt order to, 'Go away', especially from a young woman.

He tried again, politely but insistently. 'May I at least assist you with your bag, ma'am?'

Sophia wished he'd leave her alone. Hadn't she enough problems without this determined Sir Galahad? Although she'd no intention of slowing down, she couldn't help noticing that his sophisticated drawl was pleasingly deep and cultured, not that a pleasing masculine voice cut any ice with Sophia Winterton, definitely not . . .

But even so, she was obliged to slow down because of the uneven road and eventually, still without even glancing at him said, 'I thank you, sir. I need no assistance.' She firmly adjusted the train which had been trailing in the dust and made to move on, her face still averted and all her nerves quivering with resentful impatience.

'Let me at least escort you back to your family,' he said.

'Never.'

At that moment, a huge friendly drover with a cartful of hay, passed them with difficulty on the narrow road. He stared at them curiously.

'Miss Winterton, is it? Want any assistance, ma'am?'

'No, thank you,' she said shortly, but he stared dubiously at the fine gentleman with the splendid carriage and Miss Winterton in her wedding gown, walking unchaperoned along the dirt road.

'You sure, Miss?' he said, and spat on his huge spade-like hands. 'Can I help you, ma'am?'

'No. Please. I am quite all right.'

He passed by slowly, staring at her all the while and for the first time, Sophia began to look uncomfortable and discommoded at her position. To make matters worse, a couple of bare-footed village lads with home-made fishing rods ran by, scuffling and chasing each other as they sped past her.

'Yonder's Miss Winterton,' one of them said.

'Yeah, she'm our Sunday schoolteacher,' his friend replied. 'What on earth be she doin' out 'ere, like?'

They stood stock still in the road, gazing at her and grinning, nudging each other and scuffling about in the dust trying to summon up the courage to speak.

'Good day, miss,' they both chorused at last and Sophia felt more uncomfortable than ever. She waited for them to pass and then finally turned reluctantly to speak to Sir Paul. The coachman meanwhile, was tactfully walking the horses along and making out that he was oblivious as to what was being said between his master and the young lady he had encountered on the road.

Sighing, she put down the heavy bag for a moment, shivering in spite of the hot August sun and glared at him, her hands clenched in anger.

'Kindly leave me, sir. This is intolerable. An

impertinence which no decent woman should have to endure.'

She shook her head impatiently and a few more strands of red-gold hair tumbled free from her bride's tiara and caressed the creamy skin of her cheek. 'I must be on my way. I would ask you to drive on, sir, and stop troubling me in this ridiculous fashion.'

Her cousin David, he recalled, had always declared that Sophia Winterton was beautiful, but, as Sir Paul observed her at close quarters, he decided that her cousin had been mistaken. For a start, her chin was a shade too firm for most tastes, almost square in fact. Her lips were too full and sensual, the lower one jutting most stubbornly as she frowned at him angrily. Despite that, even with the covering of her bridal veil, her vibrant hair seemed to exude a radiance all its own and with that particular colouring, went the creamy porcelain complexion which most women of the *ton* would die for. But it was her eyes which were her most arresting feature. Wide hazel eyes, with thick curling lashes, which were sending out bright green sparks of anger as she tried in vain, to brush him out of her way.

His dark brows made a straight black line as he frowned at her. 'Let me ask your destination then, ma'am,' he said. 'Do you intend to walk all the way to Norwich?'

'Of course not,' she snapped, but he felt it was a fair question. After all, it was obvious that she was dressed as a bride on her wedding day. Surely she must have given some thought as to where she was running, instead of merely concentrating on escape? He'd heard rumours that her aunt Harriet had arranged a marriage for her with Lord Devenish.

She seemed somewhat at a loss at his question. Forced to confront her intentions, she seemed not to know where exactly she was going.

He let the pause lengthen somewhat and then said delicately, 'I suppose you could make for your cousin David's house in Dersingham.'

Her head jerked round immediately. 'My cousin is at Aunt Harriet's at the moment as one of the wedding guests. I'm on my way to get the stagecoach at the Eight Bells. Anyway, what do you know about my cousin David? I do not even know your name.'

He gave a snort of amusement at that and she added irritably, 'I do wish you will go away, sir, and leave me alone.'

He bowed, but kept his eyes on her face. 'It must be very frustrating for a gently reared lady to stand quarrelling on the highway with someone who has not been introduced. I am Paul Maunders, ma'am, at your service.'

'Sir Paul Maunders?'

'Yes, you seem to know my name.'

'Er . . . yes I think you are a neighbour of ours.'

'Yes, when I'm in the country, that is. Thankfully, I do not have to visit the family seat very often.'

In fact, he rarely visited Norfolk, but Wilkinson, his estate manager had requested an interview regarding the purchase of some land on his south boundary and, as a conscientious landowner, he'd spent a good three days at Cottleton Hall going through the figures and negotiating the new boundary of his extension. He'd never liked the country and was pleased when his business was completed and he was able to return to his London town house. It was a hot August day and working in the estate office with Wilkinson had been, to say the least, sticky and uncomfortable. Still, he thought cynically, he'd never expected to see such a sight as a fleeing bride when he'd agreed to Wilkinson's request.

Aloud, he said, 'As I've already mentioned, your cousin David Winterton is an old friend of mine and I knew your uncle Charles when he was alive. He would be most concerned about you. I must beg you to consider the outcome of your actions. Let me escort you home to your family.'

He knew that Sophia Winterton had been orphaned at a young age and had been brought up by her aunt and uncle.

'Never,' she retorted. 'My uncle Charles died last year,' she added quickly. Suddenly she remembered some of the disgraceful stories of Sir Paul's scandalous conduct that had circulated when she'd shared dancing lessons with two of the vicar's daughters in Cottleton. They'd told her of the type of weekend parties for which Sir Paul was famous and which were mostly frequented by members of the muslin company as guests. None of these tales was fit to be repeated if any adults were present and looking at him, Sophia could believe that even the most outlandish ones were all true. He looked so rakish and so devastatingly attractive she was sure he was capable of anything.

He was still standing patiently before her.

'Your cousin David, never mentioned your wedding,' he probed gently.

'There isn't going to be any wedding.'

Her fair skin was stained by a fierce blush which started at her neck and rose to her high pale brow.

'I'm sorry.'

She had the idea that his drawled remark hinted that he was laughing at her and she scowled at him.

'I know you said you didn't want a ride, but it's quite a long walk to the Eight Bells, especially in your wedding apparel.'

For the first time, the full implications of her actions seemed to dawn on her and, as he continued to look at her, he noticed that she gave a little shiver of nervousness.

'Are you still set on taking the stagecoach to London?'

'Yes . . . I . . . my godmother, Miss Fitzpatrick, lives in Islington. I shall visit her there.'

His dark brows met in a frown. 'And what of your groom?' he asked gently. 'I take it there was going to be a husband in your wedding plans?'

Now she knew he was laughing at her, but she was past caring. Tight-lipped, she replied, 'Yes, indeed. Lord Devenish will probably never forgive me for leaving him to cope with Aunt Harriet and a hundred wedding guests waiting in the rose garden at Winterton Manor.'

He smiled openly at this and immediately his rather saturnine face was transformed into that of a much younger and more humorous man. 'That's no doubt a sin against the Holy

Ghost and you'll never be forgiven either on earth or in Heaven.'

Her sudden laughter burst out of her with all the freedom of youth. This unaffected joyous sound struck at some long hidden chord inside him and he revelled in it for a moment and then frowned again.

Almost immediately she was serious and said, 'Aunt Harriet will go to bed with hartshorn and water. It's what she does when she has an attack of the nervous vapours. Lord Devenish will no doubt be obliged to deal with the guests and the wedding gifts, on his own.' She glanced back down the road towards Winterton Manor, as though expecting to see her betrothed pursuing her with a hundred guests.

He followed her glance and said sympathetically, 'A difficult time for all concerned. His Lordship will be understandably disappointed.'

'Yes. It was only what he deserved though, but you are right, it certainly is a difficult time.'

As for Sir Paul, he knew something of Devenish, who was forty-five if he was a day and a confirmed roué, on the look out for a wealthy bride. He could well understand a young woman's reluctance to fulfil the role. He made a hasty mental calculation. Sophia Winterton could be no more than twenty-four he decided, beautiful, wealthy, and by no means at her last prayers, but he kept these thoughts to himself and said, 'Well now, Miss Winterton, ma'am. You seem to have burned a good many boats today, but what's done is done. So, are we agreed? Shall I convey you to the stagecoach at the Eight Bells?'

For a moment, her strong determined glare softened into a much more vulnerable expression and she looked so much younger than twenty-four, that he was moved to add, 'You may count on my discretion. I promise that I won't divulge your whereabouts to the avenging hundred strong horde who will be pursuing you.'

Once again, she was obliged to smile. 'Yes, very well. I thank you, sir.' Even while he was basking in the warmth of that artless and brilliant smile, Sir Paul was aware that he still had to run the gauntlet of his groom's opinion of the wisdom of picking up young females on a lonely country road. Sir Paul knew that Morgan was fully aware of his reluctance to start coaching untried milksop maidens in the pursuit of love. Sir Paul had always preferred to dally with females who were already skilled in the art of love-making and knew how to please him. He never tampered with innocent virgins and was impatient of time wasting. He enjoyed his bachelor freedom and had no wish to be involved with inexperienced chits or leg shackled in matrimony.

As they approached the carriage, Morgan gave his master a stern look and declared, 'Sir, I hopes and prays as you'll have nothing to do with conveying this 'ere young lass to London. She'm trouble, sir, as sure as eggs is eggs. You don't usually spend your time and trouble on such young chits.'

'Nonsense, Morgan. I am, in fact, only assisting Miss Winterton as far as the Eight Bells. She will be travelling on the stage-coach.'

'Has she a ticket then, sir? Has she booked an inside seat? Has she an abigail or some respectable female what's accompanying her? What's her relations goin' to say when they learns of what you've done?'

Both Morgan and Sir Paul were aware that these were rhetorical questions. The answer to the first three was a definite 'no'. As to the reaction of the relations, Sir Paul smiled and said lightly, 'Good Lord, Morgan, I'm not abducting the young lady and no doubt you'll be able to speak for my good character, if the relations complain.'

Sir Paul had always appreciated Morgan's straightforward approach. He liked and trusted him. Morgan always said what he meant and meant what he said. Now, Morgan glared ahead of him mulishly, not wishing his beloved master to commit any such social solecism and Sir Paul, equally stubborn, compressed his lips and refused to discuss the propriety of assisting his neighbour's ward to abscond on her wedding day.

'I only hopes as none of the interested parties'll think that George Morgan had any hand in this business.'

'If you mean her betrothed and her aunt, I'm sure they won't,' Sir Paul said gravely, then, seeing the funny side of it, he burst out laughing and clapped the groom on the shoulder. 'Come, what do you say, Morgan? You can act the abigail and the chaperon for Miss Winterton and be our careful driver. Between us, we're bound to see her safely to the Eight Bells. After all, what would you have me do? I cannot abandon a young lady in distress and surely you wouldn't wish to see her married under duress?'

Morgan muttered deeply into the collar of his smart livery, but said no more. He helped Miss Winterton into the carriage and when she'd arranged her rather crumpled lace and satin gown to her satisfaction, he took his seat, staring straight ahead, deliberately poker-faced, then took up the reins and urged the horses into a trot.

The soft scent of her in the warm air filled Paul's senses with the delightful perfume of cottage garden flowers, scents he'd almost forgotten during his years in the army. He was reminded of his country childhood and in those first few moments of their drive to the Eight Bells, of a younger, more innocent and carefree Sir Paul Maunders.

Much against his intellectual judgement, he was drawn to her, attracted by her spirited independence as well as her vulnerability. Mentally, he shook himself. This was no way for a mature man to think. He was no longer a callow youth, but a wealthy landowner with all the responsibilities that his position entailed. His first and most important responsibility, however, was to get his unwanted protegée back safely to her family, but this idea had been killed stone dead by the lady herself. A sudden thought struck him: Miss Winterton was of age, wasn't she? She had every right to refuse a marriage which was unacceptable to her. If the idea of returning to her aunt's home was anathema, at least he could see her safely on her way to London.

He cleared his throat and said, 'We have to pass through Borwell on the way. Would you like to stop and make any purchases for your journey? It would be no problem to halt the horses for a while, if there's anything you need?'

'That won't be necessary,' she said shortly. She sat in the opposite corner of the carriage to himself and appeared to be keeping as far away from him as possible. With a flash of insight, Sir Paul realized that the confident and spirited young lady was in fact, rather nervous. He'd heard that her uncle's second wife was a difficult woman. Perhaps she still didn't feel safe from the dragon-like aunt or the irascible Lord Devenish.

None of these thoughts was reflected in his expression as he said equably, 'Just as you wish.'

'I have some clothes and toiletries with me, also my writing-case. Anything else I can buy when I reach my destination.'

This was only partly true. Sophia had to acknowledge to herself that her main consideration was to put as many miles as possible between Winterton Manor and herself. She was still nervous about anyone catching up with her.

After the way she had destroyed Aunt Harriet's plans for an advantageous marriage with Lord Devenish, an occasion which had taken weeks of planning on her aunt's part, she was loath to risk meeting either her relations or her rejected bridegroom.

She sat on the edge of her seat, willing the driver to go faster, to get her to the Eight Bells and freedom as speedily as possible. Morgan had stowed her luggage under the seat, but she fingered the little cream brocade reticule, dangling from her wrist and felt secure in the knowledge that at least she had more than enough money with her for every eventuality. She removed her lace gloves and, as she moved to push them into the reticule with the money, the diaphanous wedding veil fell across her cheek. She struggled briefly with the long hair pins holding her tiara in place and then tossed the fine lace veil to one side. Even while Sir Paul watched in admiration of her graceful figure, he could almost feel the heat of her impatience as her fiery hair was now revealed in all its burnished glory.

He glanced down at his fob surreptitiously. Damn. Five twenty-five. They'd be hard pressed to get the stagecoach now. He shouted to Morgan to let them rip and then resumed his scrutiny of Sophia Winterton.

She seemed lost in thought and gave an involuntary soft shuddering sigh as she gazed out of the window. No doubt she was thinking of all she'd left behind. It would be more than her private possessions, he thought, but also all that remained of her

17

family and the friends who'd been invited to the wedding. She must now be feeling utterly alone.

'One day, you'll be able to tell your grandchildren about this,' he said sardonically. 'As the little ones gather round your knee, you'll say, 'My dears, I ran away from my own wedding', and the little darlings will gasp, hardly able to believe you.'

A slight smile curved her lips but that was all. They'd reached the Eight Bells and she started up eagerly waiting for Morgan to open the door, impatient to be gone.

Her hopes were dashed as the landlord confirmed what was obvious. The stage had left a good five minutes earlier. 'In any case, sir,' he said, 'you'm be better waitin' for the next one, there bein' no room like, even atop. Full to the gills, sir, it were.'

Miss Winterton went pale at this and Sir Paul asked when the next stagecoach was due.

'Six tomorrer, sir. I can put you and the young lady up for tonight, wi' a tasty supper in the private parlour.'

He looked more closely at Sophia's crumpled dress and dishevelled hair. 'Be you goin' far, sir?'

'No. It's of no moment,' Sir Paul snapped, and he quelled the landlord's nosy questions with one look from his dark, arrogant eyes. This was worse than he could ever imagine even in his darkest nightmares: stuck in some dead or alive hole in the middle of nowhere with a chit dressed in a dusty wedding gown, who seemed not to know what she wanted and didn't even have a maid to attend her.

'We'll get back in the carriage while we consider our position,' he said, in a low voice. His face was utterly impassive. It wouldn't do for him to reveal how he felt about the enormity of her situation. Sophia nodded, her face white and strained. Morgan opened the doors resignedly and they got back in. Then he stood pointedly staring at nothing in particular, while they conferred with each other.

'What do you wish to do?' Paul asked, without preamble. His face was stern, almost angry-looking.

'I . . . I have funds enough to stay at the inn,' she said, staring bleakly at the back of Morgan's head.

'That might be uncomfortable without an abigail, or any respectable female to keep you company.'

'It would only be until six tomorrow.'

'Long enough for your reputation to be ruined in this neighbourhood.'

'And for the horde to catch up with me,'

she said bitterly. 'But I've no choice.'

'I could escort you to — where was it? — Islington? To your godmother, if you wish.'

There was no warmth in his invitation, it was merely a statement of fact, delivered in a flat uncompromising tone of voice. Take it or leave it was what he implied and for the first time, Sophia felt a rising tide of panic at her situation.

One of the ostlers sauntered by the carriage, staring in, trying to see the occupants. A frisson of fear skidded up her spine and she wished she'd changed from her wedding dress before escaping from the house.

When she didn't answer, he said, 'There's always your cousin David.'

'No,' she said. 'No.' David had always been the companion of her childhood, more her brother than a cousin. It would be infamous of her to embroil him in the family quarrel with Aunt Harriet.

'What, then?'

For the first time, she seemed to detect genuine concern in his curt voice. She tilted her chin. Her tawny brows drew together in a frown line and she squared her graceful shoulders. Her face had a ludicrously young and stubborn expression. She drew a deep breath and made her decision. 'Very well, thank you, Sir Paul,' she said at last. 'I would like to accept your offer.'

He groaned inwardly. He was stuck with her now and would have to work out some plan for explaining her situation at every inn they stopped at *en route*. Just for the moment though, at least it should be possible for her to change into something less conspicuous.

'The landlord has offered us the chance of some refreshment and the use of a private parlour before our journey to London,' he said. 'You might wish to take the opportunity to change into more suitable clothes.'

He could see that she was alarmed at the prospect of emerging from the privacy of the carriage and appearing in full public view inside the coaching inn, but he made his suggestion so diffidently, that Sophia was reassured. She inclined her head graciously and said, 'That seems a capital idea, sir. I shall do so immediately.' She stepped down from the carriage and walked confidently into the parlour with her valise. In spite of the difficulties of changing her dress unaided, she was determined to exercise all her ingenuity in managing the small buttons down the back of her gown and the tapes and hooks on her travelling dress. When she finally emerged she was wearing a travelling dress of dark-green silk and matching shawl and avowing that there was no need to provide any refreshments for her. She was unable to eat a thing.

He bowed his acceptance of this and handed her into the vehicle in silence. Then he ordered Morgan to whip up the horses and they set off. They were bound for London.

Sophia closed her eyes and leaned her head back against the seat. She could still hardly credit the enormity of what she'd done, but she couldn't regret it. She'd tried for years to please her Aunt Harriet, but she knew it was impossible. She wasn't really her aunt, Sophia reflected, merely the wife of Sophia's beloved uncle and guardian. To please him, Sophia had been very punctilious about calling her 'Aunt Harriet', and had done her best to love her. All to no avail. Having got over the funeral of Sophia's uncle, Aunt Harriet's next project was to be rid of his niece by engineering an advantageous match for her. Sophia would never forget the shock and horror of Aunt Harriet's reaction to her announcement this morning that she would not — could not — marry James, Lord Devenish as planned. Aunt Harriet had railed against the wicked ingratitude of her, screeched at her to remember how much effort she, Aunt Harriet, had put into the task of bringing his lordship up to scratch. The small fortune spent on bride clothes, invitations, food, flowers. The army of workmen who'd been employed to polish up the rose garden and the formal knot gardens below the terrace, the reshaping of the ornamental lake, overseen by one of the top garden designers of the day.

The list was endless. Her aunt's diatribe had ended in a scream of pure hatred and hysteria. When she'd finally swooned, overcome by strong emotion, Sophia had seized the moment and grabbed her few indispensable items, stuffed them into her valise and fled. She sighed as she thought of all she'd left. It was a great deal more than clothing, books, personal possessions. It was twenty-four years of her life and history, her childhood friends, her cousin David. She wondered what he would say when he knew what she'd done. She hoped he would understand how impossible it was for her to go ahead with marriage to a man who'd told such lies, who'd betrayed her so treacherously. Her only regret, she told herself, was that she hadn't personally ducked the perfidious James Devenish into the ornamental lake, before she left.

When her beloved Aunt Maria had died and Uncle Charles had remarried within a couple of years, Aunt Harriet had been all that was civil and polite, but Sophia felt the emotional distance between them. She knew life would have been easier if she'd been prepared to go along with Aunt Harriet's wishes, but in the end, she had not been able to bring herself to do so. Instead, she was now embarking on a completely new life. She opened her eyes for a moment and looked at her travelling companion. Not only was she starting a new life, she was travelling in the company of a man who was as disturbing as he was attractive.

2

They were both silent as they continued on their way to London. Sophia noticed Sir Paul glancing at her and she relaxed against the squabs with her eyes closed. Already, she felt some of the tension draining out of her and was now content to lie back and think her own thoughts, as they rapidly increased the distance between herself and her aunt Harriet.

She was still brooding on the unhappy past and she was unable to free herself from the images which kept appearing in her mind's eye. Lord Devenish had inherited his father's wealth when he was all of forty years old. He was already deeply in debt but had immediately embarked on a life of dissipation and depravity, and only his desire to continue in this style had made him reach the decision to seek a wealthy wife. If she could also prove decent, biddable and from a good family so much the better. He would no doubt be able to produce an heir if he managed to win a youngish bride. Unfortunately, aided and abetted by Aunt Harriet, he'd fixed his sights on Sophie Winterton, an orphan, who, at 24, must in his opinion, be at her last prayers, although he was well aware that she was very beautiful and would come into a fortune on her twenty-fifth birthday. As this was only a few months away, he knew that his creditors would wait once they knew he'd landed a wealthy heiress.

Aunt Harriet had stepped in briskly at this point and reminded Sophia that Lord Devenish was a considerable catch. Although he was no longer young and his figure had become somewhat portly, he came from a long and aristocratic family line with an impeccable pedigree. She could do a lot worse than a lord, however impoverished he was. His mother was still living and the family was well respected in the neighbourhood. As Lady Devenish, she would be the mistress of a beautiful stately home and with her exquisite taste and her fortune, would be able to refurbish it to her own liking. Lord Devenish would give her free rein to make any improvement or modernization she wished. He would take her to his London house for the Season and introduce her to the *ton*. Wasn't that better than mouldering away in the country, teaching in Sunday school and doing good works, until her youthful bloom had quite faded and no one would offer for her?

Reluctantly, Sophia had acquiesced, allowing Harriet and her future mother-in-law to plan a wedding which had nothing to do with the joyous celebration of a marriage between two people who loved each other, but everything to do with a society event that would add cachet to both families and considerable wealth to Lord Devenish himself.

That had been almost a year ago and Aunt Harriet had been able to prevail upon Mr Shaw, Sophia's man of business and one of the executors of her father's will, to release substantial amounts of money as the plans for their nuptials had gradually become more lavish and extravagant. Weary with it all, Sophia had learned to close her mind to Aunt Harriet's excesses and had tried to distance herself from the whole affair.

The wedding was to have taken place in the ancient church of St Andrew in Cottleton village and the reception for the wedding guests was to be in the formal gardens behind her aunt's imposing residence. The rolling green lawns and box hedging were manicured to perfection, the roses almost artificial in the beauty of their blooms and buds. Aunt Harriet had even hired huge stone urns, as tall as a man and filled with riotous summer blooms, to ornament the terrace and impress the guests with their magnificence. A hundred small gilt chairs, with satin covers were hired to be set out in the conservatory and on the terrace. They were grouped round little circular tables, so that the honoured guests could partake of the refreshments in comfort. The imposing marquee was sheltering serving tables covered in white damask cloths and groaning with exquisite food and large wine coolers, filled with bottles of champagne. At the front of the tent, Aunt Harriet's butler presided over rows of sparkling glasses, polished in readiness for the guests. On a special table, was displayed the bridal cake, set on an imposing silver stand and decorated with cupids and pink sugar rosebuds.

'What overweening pretentiousness,' Sophia muttered to herself, at the remembrance of Aunt Harriet's insufferable bad taste.

'Your pardon, Miss Winterton. I didn't quite catch your remark,' Paul said. 'What did you say?'

Lost in her unhappy thoughts, Sophia hadn't realized she'd spoken aloud. Startled, her magnificent eyes opened wide, seeking his.

She found herself looking into a dark and strongly handsome face which appeared to have no trace of any softness in its expression. His skin was the sort of colour which suggested long exposure to the sun and covered high cheekbones and a strong, unquestionably aristocratic, nose. His mouth she noticed, was shapely and finely moulded, although at this moment, it seemed turned down with either disdain or disappointment, she didn't know which. His hair was black as night and worn fashionably long at the back, overhanging the collar of his beautifully tailored jacket. Curious, she raised her eyes to his. They were of the deepest and most sparkling dark brown that Sophia had ever seen and set under straight black brows which almost met over the craggy nose. His face was strong rather than beautiful. His hands were his most attractive feature. They looked both capable and sensitive, as tanned as his face, the fingers long and shapely. Most of the fashionable bucks Sophia knew would be using all manner of ploys to show them off. Sir Paul Maunders didn't wear any jewellery, except one thick gold signet ring.

She was so engrossed in her observation of him, she'd forgotten what he asked. What had he said to her? Oh yes, she'd been thinking about Aunt Harriet and had spoken aloud.

'My Aunt Harriet went to unprecedented lengths in entertaining the wedding guests to an unreasonably sumptuous reception, that is all,' she muttered crossly.

He smiled at Sophia's cross expression and said, 'But it's of no moment now, unless you are going to change your mind yet again.'

She looked crosser than ever. Her head came up and her eyes sparkled at the challenge in his voice. 'Sir, you are offensive: I am not in the habit of making important decisions so lightly.'

She heard the anger and indignation in her voice and feeling slightly ashamed of being so ungracious to the man who'd helped her, changed the subject, pulling her thoughts back from feelings of regret for her unhappy past.

Abruptly, she asked about the journey and he answered her courteously enough.

'We shall reach Bury St Edmunds about dusk,' he said. 'We shall put up at the White Lion which is a fairly quiet hostelry and where the landlord is discreet.' He cleared his throat and said, 'If you agree, Miss Winterton, I shall pass you off as my sister. For the sake of propriety, you understand.'

'Yes, very well,' Sophia said in a small voice.

She was suddenly overwhelmed by loneliness and wondered if what she'd done would reverberate in her mind forever. If only she'd been able to take one of the maids into her confidence and have a female companion on her journey. At least she could then have had some semblance of respectability. As it was, she would somehow have to ride out the disgust and disapproval of mine host and his lady, when they reached the inn. She was fully aware of Morgan's rigid disapproval at the whole sorry venture. The very shape of his body and posture expressed his thoughts and feelings at this disgraceful departure from decent convention on the part of his master and Miss Winterton. Miserably, she closed her eyes again, trying to blot out the unhappy present.

A few hours later, they drove into the inn yard of the White Lion. She was unable to guess the time, but there were still fingers of light in the summer sky as Sir Paul helped her down and the disapproving Morgan pulled out her valise and his master's luggage. They walked across the silent yard towards the inn. A little breeze disturbed the balmy summer air and it ruffled her hair, and stirred the skirts of her green travelling gown and, quite suddenly, Sophia's mood changed completely. After a whole year of oppressive despondency, she felt suddenly, gloriously, lyrically free. For the first time since her betrothal to James Devenish, she was able to think positively about her future. She would see her godmother soon and would request an interview with Mr Shaw, with a view to purchasing a house of her own. Sophia faced the wind head on, enjoying the feel of it against her face. It made her feel gay and almost light-hearted.

'We should make our way to the inn,' Paul suggested. 'Soon it will be dark and Morgan needs to oversee the stabling of the horses.'

Sophia's attention was caught by a couple of puppies, playing near their mother. The mother cuffed them when they became too bold and they wrestled and nipped each other in the gathering dusk, with all the exuberance of young creatures. It made Sophia feel young also and she was prepared to linger a little, enjoying their playful antics for a bit longer.

'It will be warmer in the inn,' Paul suggested again.

'That's true,' she said. 'But it wouldn't be such fun.'

Fun had been noticeably lacking in her life, ever since her aunt Maria had died and she'd been at the mercy of her uncle's second wife. The only real fun she'd had was in the company of her uncle Charles and cousin David. Even that was ended, now that Uncle Charles was dead and David had disappeared to live his own life. When David had returned home for the wedding, they'd seemed constrained and unnatural with each other.

His open, honest face, so like her own, had expressed concern and an emotion she couldn't recognize. It was as though he'd wanted to mention something to her privately and yet had been unable to find the right opportunity. Perhaps he didn't approve of Aunt Harriet's matchmaking. Perhaps he disliked Lord Devenish. She never found out. Perhaps now, she never would.

Sighing, she turned to follow Morgan as he led the way across the inn yard with the luggage. The sun was now a fiery ball behind the squat silhouette of the White Lion and the air was suddenly chill. Paul continued to watch her with an interest, which he told himself, was entirely due to his concern for her safety. He was fascinated by all the different expressions on her beautiful mobile face as she gazed around her, enjoying the last of the sun which was now sinking rapidly.

The innkeeper came out immediately and his small pleasant wife hovered behind him, wiping her shiny red hands on her immaculately white apron. They were stocky country people with genial faces, obviously used to providing rooms and serving food to weary travellers.

Sir Paul bespoke two rooms, one for himself and one for his sister and arrogantly outstared the landlord's wife when she darted forward and said, 'Let me take your luggage to your chamber, ma'am and that of your abigail, of course.'

Sophia blushed, but Sir Paul said smoothly, 'My sister's maid has broken her leg, but we only had time to make arrangements for her care before we left Norfolk. We hope to appoint a replacement maid — '

'Of course, of course,' the landlord said, equally smoothly.

Sophia knew that he didn't believe them. He must have seen all sorts of travellers, rich and poor alike, she reflected. She was sure that he would have recognized immediately that Sir Paul and she were Quality and were wealthy and only pretending to be brother and sister. She was grateful that he didn't reveal his doubts, but bowed, rubbed his hands and showed them to a private parlour where they could wait until their rooms were ready. Although it had been a warm day, it was cool inside now and his wife sent in the maid to light a fire and bustled herself about to make them a very decent supper.

She sent her own young daughter, named Polly, upstairs to attend the young lady and Sophia was pleased and grateful for the hot water and scented soap as Polly helped her to prepare for supper. She had only one more gown apart from her travelling outfit and no curling tongs or extra ribbons for her hair, but Polly was more than helpful and Sophia came downstairs feeling both refreshed and hungry.

He was waiting for her in the parlour and, as soon as the landlady had laid her best fare on the table, he dismissed her, saying they would serve themselves. They were alone and he poured them both a glass of wine and carved the side of succulent ham into slices. Sophia ate eagerly and then reached for a wedge of steak pie, while he watched her with some amusement. He served himself and they ate for a while in silence. But that didn't stop him from observing the lovely soft sheen of her cheeks, coloured by the evening breeze, or her thick luxuriant hair, tidied now after the ministrations of Polly. It was of a vibrant fiery colour and texture such as he'd never seen before. Even her cousin David's good looks were but a pale imitation of those of Sophia Winterton, he thought, although the family resemblance between them was very marked. In the soft light of the candles, her beautiful hair glowed and shone as if it could burst into flames at any moment.

'It is very displeasing for a lady when you stare so rudely,' she said irritably, helping herself to another piece of pie.

His sudden smile at her aggressive words seemed to Sophia to be both arrogant and insufferably male.

'I do beg your pardon, Miss Winterton. Your displeasure quite unnerves me.'

It didn't matter that the smile which accompanied his words was so charming and lit up his handsome face in the most attractive way. In spite of her brief feeling of liberation in the inn yard, Sophia had been through a most trying and difficult day. His irony touched a raw nerve of repressed anger and fury which she'd had to stifle ever since her late uncle had wed Aunt Harriet. Her eyes flashed and he found himself fascinated by the hidden fire, of the passion underlying her outward appearance of English rose perfection.

'So it should,' she snapped. 'Your conduct is most unbecoming for a gentleman, sir.'

Her cousin David had the same quick temper, he reflected. Perhaps it ran in the family like the red hair. She continued to glare at him and he raised one black eyebrow. 'Unbecoming, you say?'

He stood up and moved round the table. 'You know, Miss Winterton, there is a great deal in your own conduct that might be deemed unbecoming. Unladylike even,' he drawled with deceptive mildness. 'You are very like your cousin David when you are angry.'

She jumped to her feet and faced him indignantly and he let his eyes rove over her insolently from the top of her red-gold curls to the dainty satin slippers peeping out from under her dress. 'Except,' he said, still smiling, 'that you are so much prettier.'

The temper again leapt into her eyes and he took a step towards her. He was now so close that she could feel the male warmth of him and smell the scent of his cologne. She was very tempted to slap his face, but instead gave him a glare such as Aunt Harriet would be proud of, hoping to distance herself from him. He was unabashed and stepped even closer, invading her private space, his long legs in their immaculate unmentionables and polished Hessian boots, brushed her skirt. She drew herself up sharply and frowned at him, but although she was tall, her head was still only on a level with his shoulder. She knew he was going to touch her and gave an involuntary gulp, but proudly refused to step back and give way to him.

'I warn you, sir. I often carry a pistol in my reticule. My uncle Charles taught me to use it and . . . and I am . . . I am an excellent shot.'

Ignoring her scowl, he reached out and

touched her hair very gently. 'Miss Winterton,' he said gravely, but his eyes were smiling, 'pray do not be angry. Your hair is coming down.'

She jumped back and feverishly tucked up the straying locks of hair and fixed the hairpins more securely. He watched her, amused. She was so attractive and appealing and he liked her brave spirit. Damn the woman. The last thing he wanted was to develop a *tendre* for her.

He told himself that he was content with his life. His bachelor existence was in perfect balance. He considered that his wealth and responsibilities as a landowner and his interest in physical sports on the one side, and discreet recreational activities with his current mistress, added up to a civilized lifestyle. All right, his mama constantly urged him to find a suitable bride and he must apply himself to that decision sooner or later. But, definitely later, he told himself. He'd be glad when Miss Winterton had been safely delivered to her godmother. He must just concentrate on that and think of her merely as a responsibility to be discharged as soon as possible. He walked round the table back to his own place. Frowning, he sat down and resumed his meal.

'I shall be glad when we reach Islington,'

he said aloud. 'Your cousin David always said that you were a firebrand. Now I know what he meant.'

She tried to stay angry with him, but at the mention of her beloved childhood companion, her eyes softened and she became nostalgic. 'He is quite a firebrand himself,' she said. 'How did you meet him?'

'There is a disparity of four or five years in our ages,' he said, 'but David was old enough to belong to the same London club as myself, before the army that is. Since my brother . . . since then . . . we have met occasionally in town.'

She was silent. She wanted to ask what had happened to his brother, if her cousin was happy in his life since his beloved father's death, whether David had met the right young lady yet, all the questions that she'd had no opportunity to ask when David had arrived all on his own, for the wedding. Instead, she said, 'When do you think we will reach Miss Fitzpatrick's house?'

He gave a careless shrug of his elegant shoulders. 'We might reach St Albans tomorrow evening, if we make good time. Then, less than one more day's travel should bring us to journey's end and we shall be at the parting of the ways.'

He saw the shadow that flitted across her

face and she said wistfully, 'I've never been to London. Aunt Maria was really too ill at the time when my come out was planned and then, my uncle . . . well, he married Aunt Harriet and the time passed. When he died, the very thought of a Season in London seemed trivial and . . . and . . . inane, somehow.'

'And then of course, there was the betrothal,' he said thoughtfully.

'Yes. Oh, that . . . '

He saw the involuntary shudder and decided he was on dangerous ground.

'Yes. Lord Devenish asked Aunt Harriet if he might pay his addresses and she agreed. She thought it a good match . . . '

Hell! She looked so sad. What wouldn't he give to hear that peal of laughter coming from her lips again. But he seemed compelled as though by some force beyond his control, to probe more deeply.

He was amazed to hear himself asking, gently, 'Did you love him?'

'James? No. But as Aunt Harriet pointed out, one may grow . . . grow to love each other in an arranged marriage . . . ' Suddenly, she burst out with, 'And I did so long to be free and have a married life with . . . with . . . little children to love . . . ' Her voice tailed off again and she was silent.

He kept his eyes on her face. 'So, like a lot of young ladies, you yearned for a romantic attachment. I understand that.'

Once again, she felt a sudden spurt of anger. 'You understand nothing about me,' she said irritably. 'We've only just met and you don't even know me.'

'That's true,' he smiled blandly. 'But I gather from what you've told me that you were somewhat . . . disappointed? Disillusioned?'

'I was unable to go through with it,' she snapped. He could almost feel the heat of her rising temper as she struggled to control her anger at Devenish.

Maunders was still watching her carefully. He poured out some wine and offered her yet another morsel of the steak pie on the edge of the serving knife. She sighed and accepted it almost mechanically, her thoughts still elsewhere. He registered both her anger and the sigh. Sophia Winterton was a complex young woman, he decided. He would do well to remember that.

He raised his glass. 'Well, here's to journey's end and our safe arrival in London,' he said.

She raised her own glass silently and took a sip of wine. For some inexplicable reason, Sophia didn't appear to find the idea of journey's end or the parting of the ways to be very appealing. Her mouth drooped a little and she put down her knife and fork not wishing to eat more. She glanced up and noticed he was still looking at her very keenly, his brilliant dark brown eyes questioning.

'Are you having doubts about visiting your godmother, Miss Winterton?'

'Not at all,' she said defiantly. What an insufferably arrogant man. Some women might find him attractive, but not she. As soon as she reached the haven of dear Miss Fitzpatrick's modest town house, she need never see him again.

'I should like to retire now, sir, if you will excuse me,' she said.

He stood and bowed slightly as she left the room and then remained drinking his brandy moodily.

When she reached her bedchamber, Polly appeared almost immediately and tapped on the door. She'd obviously had no experience as a personal maid because she didn't bother to wait for a request to enter, but burst into the room breathlessly.

'Ooh, miss, Ma says as I got to help you get ready for bed, but I ain't never been a lady's maid before. I don't know how to go on. It were all right doin' your hair and such, because I often does my friends' hair for 'em when they wants it, Miss. I've put your night rail out and can bring water, should you be wanting to wash . . . '

Her conversation lacked any coherence, being merely a string of disjointed remarks and observations, but Sophia found herself warming to the landlady's daughter and smiled at her, prepared to be friendly.

'Thank you, Polly. If you will kindly hand me my nightgown and take away my dress to be smoothed . . . no, not now this instant,' she laughed, as Polly made a bolt for the door, with the dress over her arm. 'It is usual for a lady's maid to brush out her mistress's hair before she retires.'

'Oh, yes, miss. Sorry, miss,' Polly gasped, very flustered.

She had the same stocky build and tow-coloured hair as her parents, but her face was quite pretty, flushed as it was with anxiety. Obediently, she began to remove Sophia's hair pins and to gently brush out her luxuriant hair.

After listening to the stream of chatter for some time, Sophia interrupted her gently, 'A real lady's maid always uses a lady's full name, or even 'ma'am' never just 'miss', Polly.' She decided to take a calculated risk and let Polly know she was not 'Miss

Maunders'. She doubted if Polly moved in the sort of social circles that would pose a threat to her reputation.

'Oh, yes, miss . . . er . . . ? Ma'am . . . '

'Miss Winterton. Thank you, my dear.' Sophia climbed into bed and, as Polly picked up the dress once more, she said, 'I am ready to retire now. One more thing, Polly, a real lady's maid always waits until told to enter. You may go now.'

'Yes, miss . . . ma'am . . . Miss Winterton. Good night, ma'am.'

Long after Polly had left her and she was waiting for sleep in the old-fashioned four poster, Sophia thought of all that she'd done that day and, as she closed her eyes, saw in her imagination, a picture of the uniquely attractive face of Major Sir Paul Maunders and with it, all the boats that she had so irrevocably burned.

The object of her thoughts was still toying with some of the innkeeper's smuggled brandy. His mind remained on his encounter with Sophia Winterton for a long time. As he absently swirled the brandy round in his glass, he reflected on all that had happened between them. She might be infuriating like many of her sex, but Maunders didn't find her small-minded or unintelligent. Rather, her fighting spirit and combative attitude were a welcome change from the milk-and-water misses he constantly met in London. It was refreshing to find that her challenging personality was totally different from most of his women. Most of them? He gave a cynical smile. He never kept a stable of them. One at a time was how he normally ordered his life and he knew that once he was married, he would remain faithful to his wedding vows. He wondered idly what repercussions there might be from Harriet Winterton after her failed attempts to get her niece married off. He remembered the absurd plans that his own mama had made when she was casting around for a suitable bride for his brother Anthony, but his mother was warm and affectionate and he knew that she would treat any bride that Anthony had chosen exceptionally well. It was to no avail because Anthony Maunders had died suddenly in a hunting accident and Paul had become the heir equally suddenly. As a younger son, he'd originally taken the conventional path and joined the army, but on his brother's death he'd resigned his commission and returned briefly to the family home to offer support and comfort to his parents and hoping vaguely to take up his romance again with his former sweetheart. But it was not to be. As a seasoned soldier, after two campaigns with his hero Wellington, he'd learned the hard way that nothing is for nothing. His hoped for marriage plans had gone awry because his childhood sweetheart had tired of waiting for him and had found love elsewhere. Then, after his father's untimely death, he'd become a model landowner and an exemplary employer, accepting gracefully the chagrin and disappointment when his former love married someone else.

Sir Paul Maunders would never be content with a marriage of convenience. He would never marry without love and would want a wife who was equally as committed as himself. He frowned. There would be plenty of time to think about his mama's desire for him to be married and start his own nursery when his life returned to normal. And his life would return to normal, he thought grimly, just as soon as he'd safely delivered this angry and difficult young woman to Islington.

3

Sir Paul Maunders had decided that they must make an early start and had bullied Morgan into setting the horses to and packing the luggage almost at the crack of dawn. Reluctantly Sophia emerged from her room, just as he began to pace up and down the parlour and scowl at everyone within scowling distance. Polly and the landlady deposited the breakfast dishes on the dining-table and disappeared hastily to the kitchen. Morgan, glaring almost as ferociously as his master, donned his travelling coat and went to the stables, still carrying his succulent piece of bacon on a slice of freshly baked bread.

Sir Paul met her in the breakfast parlour and for some reason he didn't understand, he seemed to resent her fresh-as-a-daisy appearance and her cheerful smile.

'Have you had your breakfast?' he asked curtly.

'Why?'

Hell and damnation. Did she have to question everything he said? How on earth could that lily-livered old roué, Devenish, have thought he was ever going to get mastery of this woman?

'Because we have a long drive ahead of us and can ill afford a delay if you start to swoon from hunger.'

'I'm not in the habit of swooning, sir. In fact, to the best of my memory, I have never yet done so.' She looked at him with her incredibly wide hazel-eyed stare expressing absolute disdain and he had the grace to look away.

'Mrs Dawkins, the landlord's wife, has prepared a hamper of food for us for later,' he muttered. 'If you haven't yet broken your fast, you must eat something before we depart on our journey.'

He looked again into her eyes and at her fresh full lips. Her hauteur was maddening and he had a sudden insane desire to kiss her and destroy her cool female confidence. As she read the unmistakable message in those hot brown eyes, Sophia felt a sudden shiver and was overcome by a feeling of breathlessness. She mustn't give way to his obvious male attractiveness. Especially not now, when she had no intention of exchanging one cage for another.

'Sir,' she said, as repressively as she could, 'I am an adult and quite capable of deciding whether I wish to eat breakfast. Merely because you are kindly escorting me to my godmother, does not mean you have the right to direct me in any aspect of my life.'

She looked so magnificently haughty he was obliged to grin and said mischievously, 'But there is an old Spanish proverb which says that once you have rescued someone, their life belongs to you.'

'Sir, you have not rescued me. You have merely taken me up in your carriage and agreed to convey me to Islington. My life does not belong to you, nor ever will.'

'That's true,' he said softly. 'I should have left you on the road from Cottleton and let the horde catch up with you.'

She thought briefly of Aunt Harriet and James Devenish and dismissed the idea that they might be giving chase. The idea of the horde amused her though and she was obliged to smile. 'Odious man! Come, sir. Let us proceed if we wish to be in St Albans before nightfall.'

As she continued to gaze at him defiantly, he was now seized by an irrational impulse to touch her soft, peachy cheek. He clasped his hands firmly behind his back, and said, 'Very well, let us be on our way then, Miss Winterton. The sooner we start the sooner we shall be there.'

Her defiance left her and she said eagerly,

'Yes. I am so looking forward to being with my godmother.'

She looked so young and enthusiastic, so optimistic with all the hope of youth, he succumbed to temptation as he'd feared he might, and, almost with no conscious decision on his part, his hand touched the soft downy skin of her cheek and stroked it gently from the high bone near her eye to the firm classic curve of her jaw. As his fingers gently touched the contours of her lovely face, her skin was suffused with a burning tide of red and her body felt prickly with annoyance and tension.

'Sir, will you kindly stop touching me?' she snapped angrily, between clenched teeth, her hazel eyes stormy with temper.

He smiled lazily. 'If you insist, ma'am,' he murmured. 'But you are very touchable.' He looked at her determined mouth and firm chin. 'And very kissable,' he added, almost in a whisper.

'How dare you? This is no way to treat a lady, sir. If you don't keep your distance . . . '

He raised his hands in mock surrender. 'I know. I know,' he sighed. 'Your unerring aim with the dreaded pistol that you always, sorry — *usually* carry in your reticule.'

Angrily, she raised a hand to brush him away and found her hand suddenly caught in his. His long fingers were surprisingly strong and his clasp cool and gentle. Their eyes met for a long moment.

I must be firm with him and give him a real set down, Sophia thought.

Paul thought, I must stop this at once, it isn't at all what I want. If I give way to my feelings and kiss her, I shall be utterly lost.

As though drawn by some irresistible force, they moved closer and then immediately, stepped back from each other, both of them wary of the danger that such proximity could hold. The early morning sky was pearly with the pink glow of sunrise. The horses were ready, Morgan was in his usual place gazing ahead stoically. Mrs Dawkins had agreed that Polly could go with my lady and be her replacement maid until they reached London and the girl had already packed her bags excitedly and taken her place inside the carriage. They were ready to go.

He moved away from her and silently helped her to take her place at the side of Polly. Both of them were shaken, neither of them was prepared to admit it. They sat opposite each other and set off for St Albans in silence. Sophia refused to let herself think of the clasp of his strong cool hand, the warmth of the expression in his deep eyes. Instead, she gazed out of the window at the golden fields and low-roofed cottages bathed in the hot shimmering August sunshine. She was acutely aware that he glanced at her frequently, but she was determined not to look at him, preferring instead to think of her beloved little godmother and only answering when she was spoken to.

'Islington is a long way from your home in Cottleton,' he remarked. 'Have you been able to keep in touch with your godmother over the years?'

Reluctantly she came back from from her reverie.

'Yes. Oh yes. She only retired to Islington when my uncle ... when my uncle remarried.'

'So she is not a native of Cottleton, then?'

'No. She is, in fact, a distant cousin of my mama.'

This was the first time he had heard Sophia Winterton refer to her dead mother and his voice softened somewhat as he said, 'I take it then that she has always been a single lady.'

'Yes,' Sophia said stiffly. 'She's never married and was our governess when David and I were children.' Sophia didn't mention that all Miss Fitzpatrick's life had been devoted to the family because she'd also been nurse to Sophia's beloved aunt Maria in her last distressing illness. When they were children, she and David had always called her 'Fitz'. It seemed impossible to remember a time when there had been no Fitz. And Sophia still missed her. She turned her face away from him again and looked out of the window remembering happier times when they'd all been together as a family.

Paul sat still, glancing frequently at the lovely profile turned so determinedly towards the window. Her cousin David was right, he reflected; she really was a beautiful woman. The August sun glinted through the window, making her fiery hair gleam with a myriad of shimmering lights. Her exquisite profile was etched with a golden line of sunlight. She was more desirable than ever. He thought of the tender softness of her cheek and gave a deep sigh and forced himself to look away from her. He'd no intention of falling prey to emotions he had kept in check for years. When he had safely delivered this attractive firebrand to her godmother, his duty would be discharged. He would disclaim any further responsibility.

By midday, they'd reached a quiet country road bordered by woodland and trees. Paul called up to Morgan to halt the horses and then he got out of the carriage and held the door for Sophia.

'Miss Winterton, should you wish to get

out here and have some of the refreshments that Mrs Dawkins has put up for us?'

'Yes, sir. I should like that very much.'

He held out his hand to help her down and she was obliged to take it, blushing furiously. He gathered a rug from inside the carriage and led her to a shady spot in the little wood. He spread the rug on the ground and said, 'How will this suit, Miss Winterton, ma'am? The grass is bone dry after all this sunshine. I trust this is shady enough for you.'

'Yes. I fancy this will do very well. Thank you.'

He went to fetch the covered basket himself, while Morgan walked the horses. Then Paul produced glasses and wine and linen napkins, setting out the picnic as though he were a servant rather than a wealthy aristocrat. Methodically, he wrapped two large wedges of pork pie and a hunk of bread and cheese in one of the napkins and gave it to Polly with some ale to take for Morgan and for herself.

'Well, now,' he said, when Polly had disappeared. 'What would be your pleasure, ma'am?'

For some reason that she was unable to fathom, Sophia blushed again. She was leaning back against the wide trunk of a tree, stretching her legs luxuriously in front of her,

54

feeling relaxed for the first time in days.

'A little ham, I think,' she said, suddenly shy. 'And perhaps some bread, if I may, sir.'

In all her life, Sophia had never been served and waited on by a man, not a wealthy or aristocratic man, that is, only by the likes of Aunt Harriet's decrepit old butler. It was a novelty, being served this al fresco meal by such as Sir Paul Maunders. He knelt before her on Mrs Dawkins's rug, his head bent in concentration over the food and wine glasses. The sunlight gleamed on his glossy dark hair and she noticed the smaller shorter black hairs at the nape of his neck, which offset her previous impression of the impenetrable harshness of his appearance and made him look suddenly vulnerable.

At that precise moment, he presented her with a piece of succulent pink ham nestling in the snowy napkin and looked up at her. The hazel eyes were suddenly no longer shooting out green sparks of anger and aggression. They were gentle and luminous. She looked so young and defenceless in the bright open air, her lips no longer disdainful and haughty, but soft and slightly parted.

Inwardly, he cursed James Devenish and Harriet Winterton, for the distress they had caused her, but he let none of this show as he asked, 'May I offer you a glass of wine, Miss Winterton?'

When she smiled and accepted, he pretended to clown the role of butler and put a napkin over his arm saying, 'Would moddom care for another slice of ham?'

He was delighted when she laughed out loud at this and he poured them both some wine, keeping one hand behind his back in a very butler-like fashion. It was so wonderful to hear that laugh, he would have been prepared to keep up his clowning all day, just to hear it again. Instead, they settled down in companionable silence to do justice to Mrs Dawkins's picnic hamper. He offered her every choice bit of food first from the basket, before taking any himself and replenished her wine as soon as she'd finished the first glass, until Sophia suspected that he was just an old-fashioned chivalrous gentleman, instead of a rakehell as she'd first supposed. After being betrothed for a year to a selfish boor like Lord Devenish, she found herself fascinated by the differences she'd observed between the two men.

She refused a third glass of wine, covering her glass protectively with a graceful hand and saying, 'I thank you, sir, but I am not used to strong drink and I fear the wine is going straight to my head.'

They ate in a comfortable silence. Maunders was content just to look at her, at the changing shadows on her lovely face as the slight breeze disturbed the leaves on the tree above her. With a sigh, she wiped her lips and put down her knife and fork.

'That was excellent. Mrs Dawkins has done us proud.'

It was now her turn to look at him. She leaned back luxuriously against the gnarled old bole of the tree and adjusted her travelling dress modestly. She studied the firm jut of his chin and the compressed lips of his shapely mouth. What had been his intention, she wondered, when he'd insisted on taking her up into his carriage? She assumed he'd at first determined to return her to Aunt Harriet. She guessed Sir Paul Maunders was not the sort of man to bend for anyone. His sardonic smile and the set of his strong wide shoulders proclaimed the utter confidence of the upper-class, privileged male. She gave a little grimace of amusement as she thought of her pathetic attempt to boast of her prowess with the pistol. She couldn't even remember now where she had put it. She knew it was not in her reticule at this moment. As if he would care, she thought. Instinct told her he was proud as well as strong, somewhat lonely, perhaps.

Whatever he was or he wasn't, Sir Paul Maunders would not be an easy man to know. He'd make a good friend, but a dangerous enemy, she decided. Well for her then that after Islington, they would be at the parting of the ways and she need never see him again.

At that moment, he raised his dark unfathomable eyes from his plate and gave her a probing look. With a shock, Sophia realized that he had been utterly aware of her scrutiny all the time and the realization brought the deep colour flooding into her face.

'There is one thing I'm rather curious about, Miss Winterton.'

'Oh?' She raised her chin defiantly and forced herself to meet his slightly mocking gaze.

'Yes. Tell me, did you never love him, even at the beginning?'

Polly returned at that moment and began to tidy up the remains of the picnic basket. Sophia waited until she had removed the basket to the carriage and then said, 'No. Not at all.'

'And yet you were going to marry him?'

'Yes. I was going to marry him.'

'And what brought about your change of heart?'

She was angry at his impertinent question and, looking into his confident face had a sudden impulse to slap him and wipe off his arrogant expression, but instead, she said coolly, 'I have no wish to discuss any aspect of my betrothal to Lord Devenish with you. As for yourself, sir, you have been less than specific about your own motives and intentions when you were so insistent on taking me up in your carriage.'

She could tell by his change of expression that her counter attack had had effect. He drained his wine glass and stood up without answering. He held out a hand for her and Sophia stood also. As he took her hand in his and helped her to her feet, he linked their fingers together and stared down in silence at their joined hands. He stared for a long moment, at the slim white fingers entwined with his strong brown ones, as though trying to memorize them.

Then Polly returned and folded up the rug and they all got back into the carriage.

4

Now that she had Polly, who was at least a fair approximation of her abigail, Sophia was feeling noticeably more secure and relaxed in Sir Paul Maunders' company and even began to positively enjoy travelling with him.

'I can't tell you what a pleasure it is for me to be to be travelling to London,' she said impulsively. 'You see I have never travelled at all . . . since . . . my mama's death. My aunt and uncle were very quiet, and restricted their visiting to nine or ten families in the county with whom they were friendly.'

'But surely, you are out, Miss Winterton?'

'I'm old enough, sir, but I have not enjoyed a formal coming out and a Season in London.'

'And do you regret being much too old for such a frippery occasion, ma'am? Are you disappointed?'

She flushed and looked up angrily at what she thought was his usual sarcastic humour at her expense, but found, somewhat to her surprise that the dark eyes looking directly at her were full of warmth and kindness. Since they'd met, he'd never looked at her like that and for the first time in her life, Sophia Winterton had a definite inclination to lean on someone who could take on some of her worries. He was certainly strong enough to bear them, she thought, taking note yet again of his broad shoulders and firm chin.

'You need not mock my disappointment, sir.'

His voice softened at this and he said gently, 'My name is Paul. I can assure you, Sophia, that is something I would never do to you. I can guess that you have had too many disappointments in life already.'

Sophia was a little shaken at his use of her name and the change from his usual sardonic remarks and said meekly, 'No . . . no, not at all . . . You mustn't think . . . in fact I have always been thoroughly spoilt and indulged.'

'Perhaps, when your aunt and uncle were alive, but I fail to think of anyone close to you now, who could support and advise you.'

She smiled slightly and said with a return to her old spirit, 'Spare me your compassion, I beg you, Paul, or you will have me breaking down in tears.'

She was surprised at how easy it was to use his first name.

He smiled with her and said, 'No, the last thing I want is for you to burst into tears. Someone is bound to come by and wonder what I am doing to you.'

She laughed out loud at this and he said, 'My guess is that Miss Sophia Winterton is not the weeping sort and is not the kind of young lady who is given to attacks of the vapours.'

'No,' she said ruefully. 'Due to my upbringing with my cousin David, I am more inclined to do some unladylike swearing.'

Keeping his voice admirably serious, but with his eyes smiling all the while, he said, 'I hope you will not feel at all restricted or inhibited by my presence, Sophia. Please feel free to let out as many curses as you wish. I assure you, there are very few that I haven't heard already.'

She gurgled with laughter and said, 'Odious man, don't be so provoking.' He raised his hands in mock surrender and promised that he wouldn't.

They chatted away and Sophia continued to be interested in the passing scene, sometimes craning her neck to look at a particularly quaint cottage or to wave to friendly children who came out to stare at the unusual spectacle of a carriage going through their quiet village and Sir Paul was content to watch her and enjoy her enjoyment.

They made excellent time to St Albans and the organizing of accommodation at the

Falstaff Arms was a much less uncomfortable experience for Sophia. Polly was inexperienced, but she was young and lively and to Sophia's mind, was almost convincing as a lady's maid. As soon as Sophia had been shown to her room, Polly had run downstairs for hot water for her mistress and had whisked away the much worn green travelling dress, returning it half an hour later, sponged, pressed and remarkably fresh. She ironed Sophia's embroidered ribbons and borrowed some curling tongs from the innkeeper's wife and by the time Sophia came downstairs for supper, she looked as though she'd just stepped out of a band box. She had been happy for the last hour while Polly had been helping her, and she also realized how happy she'd been on the journey, enjoying a different, more relaxed side to Sir Paul Maunders. In spite of the limitations of her wardrobe, she was looking forward to her dinner and felt she was in her best looks.

Someone else thought so too, because as she stood hesitating for a moment in the gloomy passageway of the inn, not quite knowing which room was the parlour, she was aware of a cold prickling along her spine, as though someone was pouring cold water down her back. Her hand was already poised over the latch of the old pine door which she thought must lead to the parlour, but she turned round quickly. Close to her, only a couple of feet away, was a man, bulky and breathing noisily with whistling hoarse breath, which seemed to resonate eerily in the confined space. For such a big man, he moved very quietly and she had not heard him approach. Brave, spirited Sophia Winterton, who usually had nerves of iron, was suddenly and uncharacteristically, frightened. The cold feeling in her spine, ran down her waist and settled in the pit of her stomach, turning her legs to jelly.

'Why, what have we here?' he said, in a strange cracked voice and as soon as she heard that peculiar tone, she recognized him immediately. Even in the gloom, she could see what expensive clothes he was wearing and identified immediately the stale smell of whisky on his breath. He might be a fine gentleman, but as she was pushed into a dark corner she knew that he was half drunk and very amorous.

He was William Baggett, another member of her cousin's club and well known to both David and Lord Devenish. In the half light and in his drunken state, he didn't seem to recognize her, but as soon as she'd heard his distinctive rather reedy voice, Sophia had recognized him. The high voice and his portly, almost womanly, figure were well known to her. He also had an insolence, a trace of cruelty in his high-pitched voice which was especially noticeable when he gave his habitual nervous titter.

'Why, what have we here?' he said again, pawing her shoulder. 'What an attractive jade, to be sure. A little kiss wouldn't come amiss, sweetheart.' His words were now slurred and he lunged at her, pulling her towards him and beginning to slobber.

He was uncomfortably close to her, and she was pressed to his soft plump body in a most unpleasant fashion. Sophia could still feel the cold feeling of apprehension along her spine. She was suddenly panicked and raised both hands and tried desperately to push him away from her, looking round quickly for help. None was forthcoming. In spite of his less than athletic appearance, Baggett held her in a steely grip and pressed his wet mouth to hers, sickening her, but she was still unable to loosen his grasp. He drew back for a moment and said in his sibilant whisper, 'Hold hard, my dear. Don't thrust me away like that. Let's have a look at you.'

He began to tear drunkenly at her gown and although Sophia fought heroically and silently, she was no match for his weight and the sheer heavy strength of him. In spite of her terror, she was still capable of coherent and logical thought however, and whatever the shame of being found in this compromising situation, she decided she could be silent no longer. If might frighten her attacker away if she were to shout for help and then face the embarrassment and exposure which would inevitably result. She drew a long shuddering breath and opened her mouth to let out a piercing scream. The swaying silent struggle had carried her backwards to the foot of the stairs and with inexpressible relief, she heard the sound of slow deliberate footsteps. Baggett's cruel tearing hands fell away and Sophia snatched at the edges of her gown, straightening her clothing and adjusting the neckline more modestly. Coming down the stairs at this moment, before he had even realized that it was Sophia struggling silently in the passageway, Sir Paul Maunders heard her gasp, 'Please unhand me at once. You are no gentleman, sir. Let me go . . . '

Now he recognized her and seized her attacker from behind, pulling him away from her and drawling, 'Do as the lady says, sir, or it will be the worse for you.'

William Baggett whirled round and snarled in his peculiar broken voice, 'Get away, this is none of your concern, this game little pullet is mine.'

'I think not,' Maunders said, and ducked swiftly to avoid the blow that was aimed at his head. It missed him and he sprang back, the better to assess his opponent and decide how to deal with him. Baggett was no stranger to the art of fisticuffs. Like many wealthy gentlemen, he regularly enjoyed boxing sessions and in spite of his unfit appearance, he loved a mill.

Not recognizing Maunders at first, he put up his fists in the classic boxing pose and said, 'Come on then!'

And Sir Paul Maunders did come on. All the pent-up frustration and anger of a very taxing few days with the difficult Sophia Winterton was released with a powerful left and a right to Baggett's jaw. His opponent's head went back and he gave a grunt of pain. It didn't knock him out, but it made him pause long enough to see that not only was the other fellow a gentleman of equal status to himself, but could actually box and he recognized Sir Paul Maunders as a member of his own club. His confidence gave way to chagrin as he also recognised the young woman he'd molested. He attempted a laugh and a sneering remark to cover his humiliation.

'I beg your pardon, Maunders,' he tittered, in his high-pitched voice. 'I hadn't realized I was poaching on your own preserves when I attempted a kiss from the young lady. No offence intended, my dear sir.'

He made a mock formal bow to Maunders and gave Sophia a searching glance before disappearing back up the stairs.

What a confounded nuisance the woman was, Maunders thought. Every memory of his delightful journey with Sophia and the pleasure he'd had in their conversation was wiped out of his mind by the encounter with Baggett. He'd be glad when she'd been safely delivered to Miss Fitzpatrick. There was no knowing what sort of rumours Baggett would spread about her now.

Aloud, he said, 'Just as well he has gone. Are you all right, ma'am?'

'Yes, I think so,' she said with a shudder.

His face was unreadable. 'Then let us go into the parlour for some refreshment.' He offered her his arm and could feel her hand trembling through the stuff of his coat and realized how nervous she was. After all, in spite of the unconventional escape she'd had and the idyll of their journeying together, now that they were nearing London and the real world, he too, felt the weight of Society's rules beginning to press in on him. He was furious with himself for not taking greater care of her. He'd never had a sister, but imagined his anger would have been just as great if someone so close were subjected to Baggett's insulting behaviour. Unreasonably, he was angry with Sophia Winterton as well as Baggett, merely for being in the wrong place at the wrong time, even though he knew that logically, this was unjust. Most of all, he blamed himself for putting a respectable gentlewoman in such an intolerable position. But why did she have to be so damned beautiful and independent?

She was silent during dinner and every time he glanced at her covertly, her beautiful head was bent and her eyes lowered. It was obvious that she was toying with the food that had been provided by the innkeeper and talking blandly about nothing very much, Sir Paul sought to calm her jangled nerves. He filled her wine glass and after a few sips, he was pleased to see her expression gradually relax and she slowly began to respond to his conversational overtures. Neither of them mentioned the incident with Baggett and by the time she excused herself to retire to bed, she had even managed to eat a little cheese and a morsel of bread.

They set off on the final leg of their journey very early the next day, driving along on a perfect dew-fresh summer morning. The horses were lively and high stepping, Morgan was marginally less disapproving, Polly was cheerful and seemed without any trace of homesickness for Mrs Dawkins or the White Lion. Sophia was looking forward to her reunion with Miss Fitzpatrick. All seemed well with the world and she succeeded in putting Baggett to the back of her mind. Not long now, she thought. She had enough ready cash to make a contribution to Fitz's modest funds and in a few months, she would receive the inheritance due to her from her parents. Her late uncle had been the trustee of her fortune and now dear David was the one she would be able to turn to until she was twenty-five. Suddenly, with all the exuberance of youth, Sophia felt life was at last looking good. There had so far been no repercussions from Lord Devenish and no sign of any pursuit. She had dismissed the episode with William Baggett because she'd convinced herself that he had not even recognized her. He'd probably thought her a country wife, travelling up to the town, she thought unrealistically. She even felt well disposed to her rather complex travelling companion, who was gazing silently out of the window, his eyes hooded, his lower lip jutting thoughtfully. He seemed quite a different person from the charming companion who had chatted so easily on their journey yesterday.

Major Sir Paul Maunders was certainly not an easy man to know, she reflected; he would probably not be an easy man to love. Yet she doubted that there was a woman anywhere who would be able to resist his rugged, dangerously good looks. Apart from herself, that is. Thank goodness, she thought, with a rush of satisfaction, that they would soon be parting forever.

There was no conversation between them but even so, he had noticed her secret womanly smile and against his better judgement was intrigued by it. He waited until the maid seemed to be engrossed with some grey-looking knitting and then said softly, 'Did you know that fellow?'

'William Baggett, you mean? Well, I finally recognized him. He is rarely in the country, but I know my cousin David sees him sometimes in town. I doubt he recognized me, or he would not have behaved so, I am sure.'

'Quite so,' he murmured, unconvinced by her optimistic assessment of the situation. In his experience of rakes like Baggett, Paul knew that in spite of his set down, the man would merely wait for another opportunity to seduce such a beautiful young woman. He knew Baggett to be a grinning sadist and an unprincipled seducer of young girls. It was rumoured in London that he and one of his cronies had kidnapped a respectable young girl and had abandoned her naked in the street when they'd finished having their pleasure with her. It was a good job that he'd been near when Baggett had attacked Sophia.

Although half of him admired her unquenchable spirit and the way she challenged him unremittingly, the other half of him knew with certainty that she was trouble. Her tall slender figure and the seeming fragility of her beauty, the grace of her every movement, her eyes, her scent, could easily drive a susceptible man to the brink of obsession . . .

He pulled his thoughts back with difficulty and said with deliberate banality, 'We shall soon reach Islington and then you will be reunited with your godmother.'

She nodded, not speaking and for some reason, he could not fathom, he decided to probe further. 'I expect you will have an opportunity to confide in her as to what went wrong with your betrothal,' he hinted delicately.

'Yes. I'm sure I will eventually be able to talk about it,' she said. 'But not at the moment, especially not after . . . ' Her voice faded as she recalled once again, Aunt Harriet's response to her refusal to go through with the wedding. Her aunt had insisted that Lord Devenish's perfidious actions were merely the behaviour of all normal gentlemen and that she would do well not to repine on it too much.

The truth was that she had found out from a friend that Lord Devenish had been paying court to Squire Winfield's daughters over in Dersingham. It seemed that both of the young ladies had lived in hopes of a declaration because their papa had made it known that he would provide a generous marriage settlement for the lucky girl. After dangling after both the sisters for over a year, it seemed that he was going to fix his interest with the elder one, Miss Amelia Winfield. When he realized that Sophia Winterton was a bigger prize, he had no conscience at all in jilting Amelia and fastening his attentions on Sophia. The spiteful rage of the Winfield girls and their mama knew no bounds. They put it about the neighbourhood that Sophia Winterton had tried to persuade him to marry her and that he had rejected her. That this was patently untrue would be evident in time, but the damage was done. His disloyalty was obvious when he made no move to deny the gossip and the ugly rumours continued to circulate for months.

Living as he did in London, Sir Paul

Maunders knew nothing of this when he had supposed she would confide in Emma Fitzpatrick about her broken engagement. Now, looking at her stricken expression, he was aware that all the sunshine had left her face and he despised himself for his crass questioning. 'I do beg your pardon,' he said in a low voice. 'That was a tactless remark on my part.'

'If that's an apology, sir, I accept it,' she said, and to his relief, a smile appeared once more.

They stopped at an inn beside the river for luncheon and Maunders himself brought out ale for Morgan, with some refreshments for Polly. What a considerate employer he was, Sophia reflected, but a man of such contradictions. Would anyone ever be able to understand him?

No sooner was she seated on an old wooden bench overlooking the mill stream, when a couple of rustic labourers passed and then lingered, eyeing her in a very particular way, one that Sophia recognized. Sir Paul Maunders chanced to reappear at that moment and scowled so ferociously at the two lads, they went on their way hurriedly, with no backward glances. He was carrying bread and cheese and a bottle of wine with glasses. His scowl was now turned on Sophia and she was faintly amused.

Was Sir Paul Maunders a little jealous? She could hardly credit that thought. At first she'd been surprised by the obvious male interest of the two young men and then dismissive. They were yokels, their horizons limited to the few village wenches they met in their neighbourhood. It was natural that they would stare at a lady born and bred, who was sitting alone by the river. She was slightly diverted and shrugged her shoulders as he approached her.

'Damned bumpkins,' he said. 'Why did you not tell them to be on their way instead of simpering like that?'

'Simpering?' she said indignantly. She was still inclined to take the incident lightly and was more than a little amused by his primitive response.

His mouth tightened at her expression and he sat down next to her on the bench expressing disapproval and anger in every line of his powerful body. As he unwrapped the bread and poured out the wine, Sophia was seized by such a devil of mischief that she hadn't experienced in a long time. She leaned towards him provocatively, her full lips pouting a little.

'Surely, they are just yokels, sir,' she said softly. 'They meant no harm. They were just . . . just looking.'

She gave a wicked little smile and his scowl became blacker than ever. The minx. She was laughing at him. For one angry moment, Sir Paul Maunders wished he might have the taming of this subversive chit. Wished he could kiss her, possess her, be responsible for her, make her do as he wished. She raised her glass provocatively and gave him a mocking smile.

'To journey's end,' she said.

'Hmph,' he growled, but Sophia saw a faint smile hover in his dark eyes and then it inevitably reached the corners of his handsome mouth and he was obliged to smile.

'Baggage,' he admonished her, and Sophia laughed aloud.

'Nothing so interesting as that,' she said, still smiling. 'I am really a rather boring, well-brought-up young lady, whose only wicked deed was to defy my aunt and run away from my own wedding.'

He looked at her sparkling intelligent face and his eyes moved to her smiling lips and back to her eyes again, lingering there for a few intense seconds. She didn't look away, but met his gaze openly and fearlessly. Knowing he was on dangerous ground, but unable to resist, he wiped away a tiny spot of red wine from the corner of her mouth, with one gentle finger and now, she did look away and blushed. He was drawn to the pink softness of those full tempting lips and had a compelling desire to kiss them. Too risky by half. He pulled himself up short. That would only lead to desperate trouble.

Hastily, he finished the last of his wine and stood up. 'I'll see if Morgan's ready to put the horses to,' he muttered abruptly, and strode round to the inn yard. Polly came up at that moment and they were soon travelling the last few miles, all of them silent as they reached the City.

Sophia was amazed at the size and bustle of London. The buildings looked huge and there was such a diversity of carts, carriages, equipages of all sorts and sizes crowding the busy streets. She marvelled at the contrast between the smart curricles and heavy lumbering brewery drays and humble carts and yet there were ragged children playing among the busy squalor of it all. The atmosphere was tremendously exciting and, as they got nearer to their destination, the style of the buildings gradually changed. Some were obviously private homes of graceful elegance, with here and there, taller, narrower buildings, smart offices and some which were downright shabby and had seen better days. It was already gloaming by the time they reached 28 Charles Street, where Eliza Fitzpatrick lived. It was one of a modest pair of semis, neat and trim with a green front door which sported a bright brass knocker.

The carriage stopped with a tremendous lurch and Morgan suddenly appeared at the window peering in anxiously. He opened the carriage door and Sir Paul Maunders helped Sophia and Polly out. They approached Miss Fitzpatrick's house with eager anticipation and Morgan obligingly used the brass knocker to alert Miss Fitzpatrick to their presence.

Sophia felt that the echoing noise of the rat-a-tat-tat had an eerie quality, as though there was no one at home. They waited while Morgan knocked again, slightly more assertively. Still, there was no response. Then an identical door in the next house opened, revealing a cosy hall lit by a candelabra. A tall buxom woman with a kindly face, appeared suddenly and stood before them, hands clasped in front of her and smiling a greeting. 'I'm Mrs Betty Soames. Was you seeking Miss Fitzpatrick?' she asked in a quiet voice.

'Why, yes. I am her goddaughter you see,' Sophia answered. Suddenly, she felt a shudder of nervous apprehension.

'I'm sorry, miss, but Emma, Miss Fitzpatrick that is, is visiting her sister, Richmond way, she being taken with a bout of the ague, like. Unable to keep a limb still, she was. Emma don't expect to return before Friday. I hope it wasn't anything urgent, miss but I can tell her you called.'

The four of them looked at each other in dismay. Not at home? Not back until Friday? Today was only Tuesday. Sophia had never thought of Miss Fitzpatrick not being at home when she'd spoken so confidently of going to her godmother.

Silently, they retired to the coach to confer at this latest setback and Mrs Soames, smiling still and waving good night, went back into her house.

5

Morgan and Polly tactfully disappeared inside the carriage while Maunders and Sophia moved into the shadows at a little distance from the house, both of them considering the implications of Sophia's predicament.

She was silent, feeling distinctly unsure and more than a little nervous. The seriousness of her situation was now brought home to her very forcibly. Firstly she had nowhere to stay, even for three nights until Miss Fitzpatrick returned from Richmond. Secondly, she had very few clothes. Her bridal gown was ruined, her travelling dress had been worn so consistently that it was looking creased and slightly soiled. She had made herself responsible for young Polly's welfare and must see her safely returned to Mrs Dawkins at the White Lion. She was with a man who was not her brother or any close male relation, but a dangerously attractive rake. She wondered bleakly if at this moment, Aunt Harriet and Lord Devenish were to appear, whether she would tamely capitulate and go home meekly to Cottleton and a boring married life. But no doubt, Devenish would no longer want her.

She had definitely burned her boats.

Characteristically, her chin came up and she gave him a straight glance, saying quietly, 'I have sufficient funds with me to stay at a hotel, if you could give me direction to one that is suitable.'

She expected him to be harsh with her after the trouble she'd been to him, but he answered equally quietly, 'You have had a very difficult time of it and I'm persuaded you should return with me to my house in Manvers Square. Polly could accompany you and my mama is at present in residence.'

When she didn't answer, he continued in the same gentle tone, 'This is not how you envisaged spending your wedding night, Miss Winterton. You have already tasted the effect on a certain sort of upper-class male of a beautiful woman travelling alone.'

'William Baggett, you mean?'

He nodded. 'In days gone by, I would have been obliged to call him out.'

She was diverted for a moment. 'A duel, you mean? But why would you feel you had to? I wouldn't expect it of you.'

'But I would expect it of myself,' he said softly. 'It would be a pleasure to dispatch such a predator and also do my duty as your protector.'

'My protector?' Her voice was still low, but

cold and haughty. 'I appreciate your concern, sir, but I would rather protect myself.'

'I take it you would even be able to fight your own duel, Miss Winterton. With your famous pistol, perhaps?'

She was delighted with his irony, used so expertly and with such an admirable lightness of touch and she tried a smile, but it was a weak one and once more, he was torn between irritation at her ridiculous pride and admiration at the way she had of overcoming overwhelming adversity. As her cousin David had told him, she certainly had spirit.

He waited for a moment as Miss Winterton finally gave up on the smile and lapsed into her former expression of dismayed disappointment. Then he remarked delicately, 'You said that at present, your cousin David is in Norfolk. Please allow me to take care of you. It would only be until Friday, when I can see you safely to Miss Fitzpatrick and meanwhile you could send a message to your cousin to let him know where you are and that you are safe. My mama will lend countenance to your presence in Manvers House so your reputation need not be compromised in any way. It will only delay your meeting with Miss Fitzpatrick a little, that is all. If, by any unfortunate chance, the . . . horde should catch up with you, they're bound to be impressed by my mama as a respectable and quite formidable chaperon.'

The time for hesitation was past. She had no wardrobe, nowhere to stay and even the money she'd brought with her wouldn't go far in an expensive city like London. He might be insufferably arrogant, but he was right. It wouldn't do to have her reputation ruined and he offered a sensible way out.

'Very well, sir. I thank you.'

With a sigh, she put her hand on his arm and they walked back to the carriage. Being beholden to Sir Paul Manvers was getting to be a habit, she fumed to herself. She was glad that she was a woman of independent means. Once she was with dear Fitz, she would see Mr Shaw and obtain enough money to replenish her wardrobe. She had every intention of buying her own house and choosing her own servants. No one could stop her once she attained her majority and had control of her fortune. As he handed her into the carriage, she wondered briefly what Sir Paul's mama was like. Probably as arrogant and domineering as he was himself, she thought, as she subsided wearily against the padded upholstery.

When they arrived, Manvers House was fully awake and fully lit. Sir Paul's mama was in the green drawing-room and he went in to pay his respects and inform her of the circumstances of Miss Winterton's unexpected arrival at his town house. His explanations were received politely by Lady Maunders who, noting his seeming concern for this unknown chit from the country, wondered privately whether his affections were engaged in that direction. If they were, she thought, it was obvious that he was so far oblivious of it. He stressed that Miss Winterton was a well-brought-up young lady and worthy of every consideration as a gentlewoman. He sketched briefly the circumstances of their meeting, glossing over some aspects of it and painting a portrait of Sophia as wronged victim rather than the perpetrator of such a serious social solecism as to run away on her wedding day.

The servants were soon directed to organize the rooms for Sophia and Polly who was now firmly established as Sophia's personal maid. They were too late for dinner, but her ladyship ordered the housekeeper to set out a cold supper in the small saloon for Sophia and some refreshments in the kitchen for Polly.

After introducing his mama to their guest, Sir Paul Maunders disappeared up to his room to change his clothes, saying that he would dine at his club and would be returning late. Lady Maunders excused herself with the hope that she would have an opportunity to speak to Miss Winterton later and Sophia was left alone.

She pushed the food round her plate in a desultory fashion for a while and then put down her knife and fork and took a sip of wine. She heard the substantial door of Manvers House close behind Sir Paul as the coachman brought his carriage round to the front steps. The sound of the horses faded gradually and then there was silence.

A slim young footman appeared as if on cue and asked politely if she needed anything further.

'No, thank you,' she answered listlessly. She felt terribly alone.

The young footman cleared his throat nervously. 'Very well, ma'am, I'll clear.'

Then he added, 'Her ladyship presents her compliments, ma'am and requests your presence in the green drawing-room, if you please, ma'am.'

She stood up immediately and he walked ahead of her to show her the way and she was ushered into a large room with symmetrical windows draped with gold brocade curtains. It was not a cosy room. The rosewood and satinwood furniture was carved in a lion's head design, the chairs and sofas were upholstered in green figured material and trimmed with gilt. There were magnificent mirrors, adorned with gold lion heads on two of the walls and the fireplace wall had pictures of various ancestors of the family. The room was well lit by pairs of candelabra with tall wax candles, resting on small gilt tables, the deep-green carpet was woven with stylized leaves of a paler green. The whole room expressed the family's wealth and privilege rather than any sense of a warm home.

Lady Maunders was younger than Sophia had expected. She was rather stout but still handsome and raven-haired, with only a sprinkling of grey at the temples. She was sitting in a large comfortable chair with a little table beside it, which held a tray of tea things.

Her eyes, so like her son's, were deep and unfathomable. She didn't rise as Sophia came into the room, but greeted her calmly and austerely and bade her to be seated.

Sophia was served with tea by the footman and sat uncomfortably on the edge of her satinwood chair, very conscious that she wasn't looking her best in her much worn and crumpled dress. Her Ladyship dismissed the footman so that they were completely alone together. Although she was punctilious in her politeness and good breeding, Lady Maunders questioned her very closely about her background, her relations and finally, observing Sophia very quizzically, with one raised black eyebrow, said, 'I understand you met my son while he was in the country on estate business, Miss Winterton.'

'Why yes, ma'am,' Sophia said quietly. In the presence of this very formidable dowager, she was conscious of the enormity of her social transgression in running away from home like that.

'And you were actually fleeing from your own wedding ceremony, were you not?'

'Yes, ma'am, but — '

Lady Maunders didn't give her chance to finish, but said, 'I expect there was a compelling reason for your untoward action, Miss Winterton?'

Sophia felt suddenly angry. How dare this proud aristocratic lady question her in this way and sit in judgement of her. 'Yes, there was, ma'am,' she spat out. 'I was being coerced into wedlock with an unpleasant man old enough to be my father. It was just unfortunate that . . . that . . . '

'That the stagecoach had gone without you,' Lady Maunders smiled. The smile lit up her face and warmed her dark-brown eyes brilliantly. Sophia was amazed at the transformation. His mother's smile was so like his that she was unable to take her eyes off her. As for Lady Maunders, she was very taken with this young woman and sympathetic to her unconventional actions. Paul had explained the situation very hurriedly and hadn't had any time to go into details. Still, she was a stunningly beautiful girl. Perhaps he already had a *tendre* for her. She must find out more about the circumstances of their meeting.

'I don't expect you to understand,' Sophia said despairingly. 'My aunt Harriet was very pressing and all the arrangements were advancing at such . . . such a pace . . . There seemed to be . . . no . . . no escape.'

No doubt Lady Maunders would bring all her influence to bear in forcing her to return to her aunt Harriet and her bid for freedom would be over. Her voice broke on a sob. Brave, indomitable Sophia Winterton was ready to burst into tears at the memory of her failed attempt to run away from Cottleton forever.

'Come now, brace up, child. Don't give way,' Lady Maunders urged her softly. She leaned across the little table and took Sophia's hand with surprising gentleness. 'I was once upon a time as young and headstrong as you, Miss Winterton. My dear parents had chosen a most worthy and respectable suitor for my hand and I was just unable to love him. I ran away with my childhood sweetheart, thinking to go to Gretna Green and marry him instead.'

'Wh . . . what . . . happened?'

Sophia was so surprised at this revelation, her tears were arrested before they even began.

'My papa caught up with us in Derby. I was taken home, but not in disgrace. I was their only child you see and once they realized that I found the gentleman so unattractive, they let me have my way. As for the childhood sweetheart, I fell out of love just as easily as I'd fallen in. Everything was hushed up, of course, and when I met Paul's father, it was love at first sight and we were married with my parents' blessing.'

Sophia was silent, thinking of Sir Paul Maunders. Most women would find it easy to fall in love with him at first sight, she thought, and her mouth drooped disconsolately.

'Come, my dear. Don't be sad,' her ladyship urged her. 'Let me get one of the maids to show you to your room. Things will look better in the morning. If you've never been far from your country village before, I can promise you that you will find London a most exciting and lively city.' She looked speculatively at Sophia, taking in the lovely face and crumpled gown. With the right clothes, the girl would be transformed, she thought. Lady Maunders had never had a daughter of her own and since her eldest son had died so tragically three years ago, she had been less and less in Society. The most devoted mother could not mourn forever, though. This young woman might be the catalyst for Lady Maunders' own return to the world, unless the relations were to be unforgiving and vengeful that is. She would have to set in place some discreet enquiries as to the girl's aunt, who, according to Paul, was not an aunt at all, being merely the dead uncle's second wife. It might be an interesting project, she mused.

Aloud she said, 'You must be tired, my dear Miss Winterton. I shall ring for the maid to show you to your room. Try not to worry, my dear, it isn't so long until Friday.'

Polly had learned quickly what was expected of a lady's maid and had already set out Sophia's night clothes and was on hand with hot water and fresh towels. She brushed out her hair and helped her into bed before disappearing to her own room. Gratefully, Sophia lay back on the pillows and closed her eyes as all the events of the day came back to her in a kaleidoscope of jumbled impressions and experiences. Sir Paul Maunders' face swam into her consciousness and she wondered what would have happened if they hadn't so fortuitously met on the roadside. Would the horde have caught up with her or would she have waited for the next stagecoach and reached London on her own? Their journey in Sir Paul's well-sprung carriage had been much more comfortable than a public vehicle. She had a sudden image of him in her mind's eye, kneeling before her, setting out the picnic, with the sunlight glinting on his hair and his dark eyes gazing into hers, before she finally drifted off to sleep.

Meanwhile, Sir Paul, having dined at White's, set off to walk to the house of his current mistress. He'd ordered Morgan to bring the carriage round to 19 Sutton Street at half past midnight and Morgan, well used to his master's habits, had merely said, 'Very well, sir. Sutton Street, half past midnight.' and returned to Manvers Square to give the horses some oats.

Maunders sauntered along, thinking blackly of his uncharacteristic action in introducing the young woman to his mama. God alone knew how he'd allowed himself to get into this tangle in the first place, or what his mama would make of the situation. He was a man who led his own ordered life and it was organized to consider his own needs and comfort, before aught else. He'd been utterly appalled at Miss Fitzpatrick's absence and angry with himself for getting drawn in to Sophia Winterton's problems. For the first time in his life, he had foolishly allowed himself to be diverted from the even tenor of his ways and to think of someone else's needs as well as his own. First he had been concerned to keep her from the dangers of travelling to London, unaccompanied. Then, it was because she was alone and friendless and had nowhere to go. It would only be a matter of time before the servants blabbed about her presence in his house and Baggett started to tittletattle in the clubs, then the whole sorry business would be out in the open. He was not looking forward to an interview with David Winterton or the rest of the avenging relations. He compressed his lips into a hard straight line. What was he about, to introduce her to his mama? Soon, she would know all the details of Sophia's flight from home and the fact that they had spent three days and nights together, with only an inexperienced country wench and a groom, to lend any respectability to the situation. He groaned aloud in the still summer air. There was no way he was going to tie his destiny to that of a friendless rebel such as Sophia Winterton however spirited and appealing she might be.

Still, her beauty and courage had impressed him and he didn't want her to have to pay the price for her brave impetuosity. None of the young ladies of his acquaintance had her strength and determination, but in spite of his admiration for her, gently reared young ladies of the *ton* definitely did not spend nights under any man's roof, especially one who was a confirmed rake like himself. Even Sir Paul Maunders was not above the laws of Polite Society. If anyone else discovered the details of their escapade, it would be hard for him to refuse to marry her. He was not the sort of man to be forced into fulfilling social obligations, even if his emotions were involved, which he told himself very firmly, they were not. He decided to leave any considerations as to Miss Winterton's situation in the capable hands of his mama, who, he felt, could turn aside any social criticism.

In the meantime, he would amuse himself with Marie for an hour and try and forget the whole sorry business for a while. He knocked on her discreet brown door, with his cane. The knock was merely a convention. Marie's maid was hovering in the hall. It opened immediately and silently on its well-oiled hinges. The maid ducked a little curtsy and took his cane. 'Good evening, sir. Madam is in her boudoir.'

Soon he was lounging at his ease, his legs crossed at the ankles, a bottle of decent claret and a wine glass at his elbow.

When Marie entered the room, she was already wearing a low-cut oyster satin nightgown and with it, a matching lace peignoir which revealed more of her voluptuous figure than it concealed. Her dark-brown hair was dressed loosely in a black ribbon and her bare feet were thrust into satin slippers. She was looking particularly seductive and she knew it. Her almond-shaped brown eyes flashed at him boldly before she veiled them with a belated pretence at modesty. Her lips were discreetly painted with carmine and her jasmine perfume filled the room. She approached his chair with a confident swaying walk and gave him her practised sensual smile.

'Good evening, sir. And how is my favourite gentleman this evening?'

It was the greeting of a common harlot, he thought, with sudden distaste, but he answered politely enough.

'Well, I thank you, Marie.'

He took a long swallow of wine. 'A fine claret, my dear,' he said civilly and twirled the stem between his fingers moodily, determined to turn his thoughts away from Sophia. He was first surprised and then appalled by this about turn in his feelings for Marie. They had always dealt amiably together and he found his sudden feeling of revulsion inexplicable.

He'd known her a couple of years now. She'd been born Mary Barnes, but had changed her name to Marie Baronne long before Paul had established her as his *fille de joie* and set her up in this small discreet establishment. Although he would never consider her as more than a mistress, yet she was far more than a common harlot. He'd been happy enough with their friendship thus far, so why was he suddenly so disgusted at her? At himself? He was so surprised at these conflicting emotions, he felt unable to maintain his usual aloof civility.

Now, she lowered her head and smiled at him, leaning forward, so as to reveal her large voluptuous breasts and the dark cleft between them. She sat on the arm of his chair and ran her index finger down the front of his immaculate evening shirt. 'Shall we go to bed, *cheri*?' she whispered, and Paul rose and followed her into her softly lit pink boudoir.

An hour later, as he was dressing, still in a moody silence, Marie leaned towards his naked back and caressed it playfully with her delicate slender fingers. She followed it with a line of kisses down the length of his spine, trying to make him forget what had put him in so black a humour. Marie firmly believed that a handsome wealthy rake like Sir Paul existed to be married to a woman like herself. Why not? she thought. She understood him. In fact, they understood each other. She was the legitimate daughter of a successful Camden grocer and since Sir Paul had set her up so handsomely in her little house, she had been most discreet when she had entertained other gentlemen and in any case, there had been very few of late, especially since James Devenish had gone abroad. She was sure Paul knew nothing about her other adventures. Greedy though she was, Marie didn't wish to jeopardize her marriage plans. She dressed stylishly, spoke nicely and felt she was worthy of becoming Lady Maunders. If only he would take her out and about with him, she would be able to prove just how worthy, but he never let her forget that she was not his social equal and they were certainly not engaged to be married.

When he'd arrived so much later than usual, she'd given up hope of seeing him this evening and had worked extra hard to try and please him, but still he seemed quiet and preoccupied. He tolerated the kisses on his back, remaining very still with his eyes closed, as though taking no pleasure in her coquetry but merely waiting for her to stop kissing him. She stepped back a little, a small angry frown creasing her brow while he put on his shirt.

She let the peignoir fall open a little and whispered, 'Must you go so soon, *cheri*? Has something displeased you?'

She saw his jaw tighten and a look of boredom appear on his face. His expression stiffened with his barely concealed impatience. She knew that look. It meant he'd had enough of her and was determined to leave. He looked away in disgust at her blatant attempt to entice him with her naked breasts and said, 'Cover yourself, Marie. I've already seen all you have on offer this evening.'

She was furious. How dare he speak to her like that? Just as if . . . Just as if she was a common prostitute. She controlled herself with difficulty. After all, it wouldn't do to quarrel with him. Not after she'd worked so hard to cement their relationship. He hadn't confided his problem, but he looked tired and strained. She must try to soothe him. She swallowed her fury and smiled as sweetly as she knew how. Marie had deliberately cultivated refined tastes and interests. She was always beautifully dressed and groomed and spent a considerable part of the generous allowance Sir Paul made her, on keeping a good table and wine cellar, as well as clothes and perfume. Like many sophisticated courtesans, she had her own box at the theatre and longed more than anything for Sir Paul to be seen as her constant companion.

'Paul, would you care to be my escort at the opera on Friday night?' she asked softly.

'I think not, Marie,' he said, and looked at her with almost contemptuous indifference.

Now she was really furious and unable to control her anger any longer. 'Why not? Aren't I good enough for you?' she shouted. 'I'm good enough for you to use as your whore.'

'Quite,' he said sarcastically, and sat down with his back to her, to put on his boots.

She was frightened now. If she let him part from her in this mood, there was no knowing if she'd ever see him again. 'Paul, I'm sorry,' she murmured. 'Please don't let's quarrel when we've been friends for so long.' She made a clumsy attempt to sit on his knee and he removed her silently, his face impassive.

'Too long, I think,' he said, and turned to go.

'Paul! Wh — What do you mean? You can't mean you wish to end it?'

'That's exactly what I do mean,' he said

coldly. 'It's over. Good night, Marie.'

This wasn't how he usually ended a relationship. It was always an amicable and friendly parting of the ways with neither party embittered or dissatisfied. Sir Paul was not in the habit of frequenting brothels and although his arrangements, by their very nature always had a commercial element, he was both generous and gentlemanly in his dealings with any dancer or actress who happened to be his current mistress. He was suddenly overcome with distaste at Marie's pretensions to a respectable advantageous marriage and her desire to take his mama's place as Lady Maunders and yet felt guilty at his own rejection of her. Why the devil was she unable to accept her position as a bit of muslin and be satisfied? After all, she was well taken care of and wanted for nothing. What the hell made her so greedy and pretentious? And what made him feel so suddenly that he might have any obligations to her?

He knew the answer to that almost immediately. He had a sudden vision of Sophia Winterton on their journey from Norfolk, throwing back her head and laughing with unabated spontaneity. It made him feel ashamed of cultivating the likes of Mary Barnes and her purely commercial favours.

He left the room, picking up his cane from Marie's maid before he stepped out into the street. He'd made sure that Marie was entitled to live in the Sutton Street house for as long as she wished, regardless of whether she was still his *chère amie*. Tomorrow, he would send round an expensive trinket as a parting gift, to underline the fact that their relationship was finished. He wasn't a fool. Very little escaped his deep penetrating gaze and he knew that Marie had played him false with other men, including Sir James Devenish, on more than one occasion. Well, they were welcome to her. The contrast between the fawning duplicity of Marie and the brave sincerity of Sophia Winterton was almost ludicrous. His face was as black as thunder as he strode towards his carriage.

Morgan was standing by the horses' heads and wished him a very civil 'good evening' before opening the carriage door for him. Paul grunted and rubbed his aching temples, his thoughts returning once more to Sophia Winterton. Damn the woman, she'd been an infernal nuisance ever since he'd taken her up on the Cottleton Road. She would only bring him further trouble. The tall beautiful creature who had so angrily raced along the road that day, was the kind of woman who could obsess his thoughts and haunt his dreams — if he let her that is. He was determined to avoid her at all costs until she could be delivered to her godmother.

After luncheon the next day, Lady Maunders sent the carriage round to her modiste with a little note saying that she required several of Madame Justine's most fashionable gowns at once and emphasizing that they were for a tall, slender young lady with unusual tawny-haired colouring.

'There is no time for bespoke gowns, Miss Winterton,' she said, 'but Madame Justine is an excellent and inventive designer and comes highly recommended. When you are settled with your godmother, you will no doubt be able to order specially made fashions to suit your own particular style. Meanwhile, she is prepared to bring a selection for your approval.'

'Why, thank you, your ladyship,' Sophia said. How kind of her, she thought. How different from the hated Aunt Harriet.

Lady Maunders had spent the morning making quiet enquiries among her close friends, having first ascertained that their discretion could be relied upon. She learned that the wealthy eligible David Winterton was Sophia's cousin and that he was often in London for the Season. All her informants spoke well of Sophia's dead parents and testified to the impeccable background and upbringing of the beautiful Miss Winterton by her father's brother and his wife. All spoke critically of the unkind Aunt Harriet. No one mentioned Lord Devenish. It was fortunate, Lady Maunders reflected, that the wedding had not been announced in the London papers. None of her friends seemed to know about it and Lady Maunders had tactfully taken care not to mention it herself.

Madame Justine arrived just after two and proceeded to display the sample dresses for the two ladies. After a few days of wearing the crumpled travel gown, Sophia was enchanted at every dress shown to her and Madame Justine, recognizing a new wealthy young client, snapped her elegant fingers at the little black-clad assistant, to bring yet another wonderful creation for Sophia's approval. Every dress was first posed in front of her before the cheval mirror and then was tried on. Three dresses needed taking in for a more exact fit and were pinned and wrapped in tissue paper ready to go back to the shop for alterations, but Sophia chose three classic morning dresses, worn only by Madame Justine's model and which fitted her perfectly and then two ball gowns, neither of which needed any adjustment.

Madame Justine, astutely kept the best

until last. It was another evening gown, made of the most beautiful deep turquoise silk with an underdress in a paler shade of turquoise satin. It was almost severe in its classic lines, but revealed, rather than hid, Sophia's beautiful figure.

'Ah. Mademoiselle Winterton you have such style. Such *panache*,' the modiste said admiringly. 'And it all is because of your so wonderful posture. You are so upright, *n'est ce pas*? A pleasure to dress.'

Absolutely no mention was made of money. Madame Justine knew the ways of the wealthy and recognized that there were rich pickings to be had in pleasing a protégée of Lady Maunders. She knew her account would be paid in full and was willing to overlook any delay because extended credit would be sure to bring further commissions.

Later, when Polly had removed the garments to Sophia's room, and she and Lady Maunders were drinking tea in the green drawing-room, her ladyship smiled and said, 'Perhaps you will have an opportunity to try out one of your new gowns this evening, my dear.'

'Oh?'

'Yes. Mrs Isabella Thornton and her husband are recently out of mourning for his mama and are having a modest dinner party for family and a few friends and when they knew that I had a . . . ah . . . young friend staying with me, they kindly included you in the invitation.'

'Young friend?' Sophia asked stupidly.

'Stretching it a little, I know, Miss Winterton, but I really feel I could get to know you, my dear and . . . and we could become . . . friends.'

Sophia looked into the handsome, kindly face of Sir Paul Maunders' mama, so like her son's and yet so different, and she was suddenly overcome with longing for her own mother. She gave a sigh and shook her head.

'What is it, Miss Winterton? Do you not feel like accepting? I can assure you they are very respectable people and you would be made most welcome.'

'No . . . No . . . It's not that. It's just . . . ' She faltered to a stop. How to explain to this affectionate caring woman, how affecting it was for her to experience such unexpected and total kindness.

'Just what, my dear?'

'It's just that my own parents died when I was but a small child and my guardians were so kind to me and now they are also . . . also . . . gone. You are so generous to consider me like this.'

'Does that mean you'll accept the invitation, Miss Winterton?'

'Yes. Thank you, ma'am.'

'Miss Winterton, may I call you Sophia?'

'Yes. Of course.'

'Does it ever get shortened to Sophie?'

'Not so far,' Sophia said cautiously. 'My aunt Harriet is rather . . . rather formal you see. But Sophie sounds very nice,' she added hastily.

'Very well then — Sophie. If you will excuse me I am going to put my curl papers in and lie down for an hour in preparation for our evening out. The carriage will be at the front door promptly at six-thirty.'

Sophia was left alone. The house was very quiet. She wondered where Sir Paul Maunders was and whether he would be at the Thorntons' dinner party this evening. Then, she decided to follow Lady Maunders' lead and lie down on the day bed in her bedroom. She'd noticed a little pile of books from the lending library in the dressing-room when she was trying on Madame Justine's gowns.

Meanwhile Polly had hung the gowns around the room and they were displayed in all their glory, ready for later. She selected a book and went to the *chaise-longue* intending to read for an hour, but the print kept dancing in front of her eyes and her mind inevitably wandered to Paul.

He was so unlike any man she'd ever met before. The romantic novel she was holding slipped out of her hand and she clasped her arms around herself thinking of his dark good looks and formidable strength. In romantic novels, falling in love was so enjoyable and thrilling, but in real life it was terrifying and overwhelming. She shivered suddenly in spite of the brightness of the afternoon outside and as she drifted between sleeping and waking, she determined that she must never do anything so foolish as fall in love with Sir Paul Maunders.

6

Once they were in Lady Maunders' very fashionable barouche, her ladyship kept up a pleasant light-hearted conversation, telling Sophia of some of the other guests that they would meet that evening. 'Paul is dining with friends before they go to White's, but you will be bound to meet one or two hostesses this evening, Sophie, who may provide more social contacts for you and, of course, there are bound to be one or two eligible gentlemen,' she smiled.

Seeing Sophia's slight shudder, she pressed her hand sympathetically and said, 'I know the situation with Lord Devenish is rather too recent, my dear, but it will do no harm to get you launched into society. Mrs Thornton has two daughters of her own to settle in suitable marriages. Elizabeth and May are twins, but they are only just out of the schoolroom and will not be having their come out until the spring.' She chuckled and said, 'Being a pair, dear Mrs Thornton had her hands full when they were younger. They were always into some scrape. The only person who could manage them and still can, is their old nurse.

Every governess appointed by their mama left sooner or later as a result of their naughty pranks, but there was no badness in them. Mr Thornton was all for sending them to one of the new seminaries for young ladies that have sprung up in the last few years, but their mama wouldn't hear of it. She said that they would only lead the other girls into mischief and then their naughtiness would be broadcast to the world. But they've never meant any harm, my dear, they're just full of youthful high spirits. Their mama wishes them to get used to being in mixed company before they are presented.

'And do not Mr and Mrs Thornton have any other children, ma'am?'

'Yes, there is a son, Thomas. He is the first born and has never given his dear mama any trouble. He is but two and twenty and is very good-looking, with his mama's fair colouring. He has recently returned from the Grand Tour. I expect he will break some hearts before he is much older.'

She sighed, thinking of her son. No doubt he had broken a few hearts too, but she wished fervently that he would choose a bride soon and start his own nursery. Since her husband and elder son had died, Lady Maunders longed above all else to be a grandmama to Paul's children.

Sophia heard the sigh and guessed the reason. In spite of her own lucky escape from the trap of matrimony, she understood entirely that Lady Maunders wanted above all else to see her one remaining son married to some suitable girl. She wondered who that girl might be. Would she be one of the young ladies she was about to meet this evening? The social circle enjoyed by Lady Maunders and Sir Paul must surely include several eligible and well-brought-up girls who would make him an appropriate bride. She had a sudden vision of him at their picnic on the journey from Norfolk. The sunlight glinting on his hair. His attractive smile. It was now Sophia's turn to sigh. Thank goodness she would soon be with her beloved Fitz and would be able to forget all about Sir Paul Maunders and her own foolish reaction to his charm and charisma.

Ten minutes later, Rodgers, the Thorntons' butler was announcing their arrival and Sophia stood on the threshold of the drawing-room being welcomed by Mr and Mrs Thornton.

Mrs Thornton's drawing-room was all that was elegant and well appointed and seemed to Sophia to be full of the most handsome and well-dressed people she had ever seen, although there were only twelve of them.

Inwardly, she thanked Lady Maunders gratefully for organizing the new dresses. The one she was wearing was a pale-blue sarsanet, with five rows of heavy lace at the hem, which made the dress hang straight down, skimming her slender figure and complimenting the deep rich colour of her hair.

As soon as Lady Maunders had presented her to the host and hostess, Mrs Thornton bore her across the room to meet the twins, who were obviously on high ropes at being allowed to stay up for a formal dinner party. As twins, they couldn't be more unlike. Elizabeth was of medium height, with luxuriant glossy dark hair done in a fashionable Grecian style. Her sister was tall and slim, with guinea-gold curls, fastened with blue ribbons and cut fashionably short at the front. Both had the most brilliant blue eyes that Sophia had ever seen, as bright and sparkling as sapphires and fringed by dark lashes. Once they'd been introduced to her, their chat was all about their dual come out and the dresses and ball gowns that their mama was planning for them.

'You both look very charming in the gowns that you're wearing,' Sophia said sincerely, for indeed, they looked extremely beautiful in their regulation white muslin dresses. They were both so fresh and pretty and absolutely artless as they included Sophia in their conversation.

'I'm the elder one, by a good twenty minutes, Miss Winterton,' said Elizabeth.

'But I'm taller,' May chipped in. 'My baptismal name is Mary but everyone shortens it to May.'

'Mama says that we shouldn't be dressed the same at the coming out ball,' Elizabeth said in a rush before her sister could interrupt her.

'Mama says that we both have different styles of beauty you see, Miss Winterton,' May was quick to point out and Sophia was obliged to smile at their youthful enthusiasm.

They were indeed both very high spirited and beautiful. Elizabeth, the dark-haired one, favoured her papa and had his firm chin and full lips, while May was as fair as her mama, with the same pretty colouring and delicate features. Both had their mama's liveliness. The dual effect of the two girls, standing together and talking animatedly, was devastating. These two will also break some hearts, Sophia thought to herself, and then she was whisked away by Mrs Thornton who presented her to Lady Elizabeth Wright, a dignified matron wearing a fashionable turban and wielding a large fan who explained that her niece, Miss Cecilia Wright, was unable to be present this evening, owing to a slight indisposition. She in turn, presented Sophia to Mr Thomas Thornton, brother of the twins and he proved to be as personable as Lady Maunders had described him. He was tall and almost impossibly good-looking with a head of golden locks which any young society woman would die for. And yet, he was in no way foppish, she thought. Although still youthfully slender, the shoulders in his fashionable coat were already broad and strong. He had the same brilliant eyes as his sisters and just as they were exceptionally beautiful, Mr Thomas Thornton was a positive Adonis.

As they chatted politely, Sophia couldn't help noticing the frank admiration in his eyes and the enthusiasm with which he spoke of his travels in Italy. 'Forgive me for being personal, Miss Winterton, but while I was abroad, I viewed so many paintings by Titian, of ladies with the same colouring as yourself. I cannot but admire it.'

Sophia smiled and disclaimed, but he was not to be discouraged and said, 'Of course, you are of a more slender beauty and are pleasingly tall for a lady. Are you interested in art, Miss Winterton? Do you sketch perhaps, or enjoy watercolours?'

'Yes to both,' she said promptly, 'but alas,

just lately, I have had little chance to do my drawing.'

'I hope later, we may have an opportunity to talk further,' he said, but just at that moment, Rodgers appeared once more to announce, 'Mr William Baggett,' and Sophia's heart suddenly contracted with nervousness.

As soon as he was announced, Mrs Thornton greeted William Baggett affably and said to her husband, 'We are all met now, Robert. I shall just introduce Mr Baggett and then we may go into dinner.'

Outwardly calm, but inwardly seething with anxiety, Sophia tried to remain as unobtrusive as possible, gradually working her way to Thomas Thornton's other side in the hope that Baggett wouldn't notice her. Her first thought had been to run away, but she dismissed it quickly. She must at all costs avoid the man who, if he chose, could ensure that she would be utterly ruined. Hastily, she pulled herself together and stood up straight, listening intently to Thomas Thornton's light chatter as though her life depended on it. Mrs Thornton was moving inexorably round the circle of dinner guests, making introductions and Sophia knew there was no escape.

'You know my son of course, Mr Baggett. Lady Wright, Lady Maunders, Miss Winterton; may I present Mr William Baggett?'

They exchanged greetings and still Sophia hung back, hoping he wouldn't notice her, trying to tell herself that he hadn't really looked at her closely as he'd grappled with her in the dark passageway at the Sir John Falstaff. Lady Maunders, noticing her reticence and suspecting incorrectly, that Sophia was attracted to him, said brightly, 'I wonder if you are related to Mr John Baggett from Norfolk, sir?'

He turned his bulky body to look at her, with an almost feminine movement of his hips and when he spoke it was in the same thin reedy voice. 'I am indeed, ma'am. He was my father; alas, he died four years ago.' He said it with an unbecoming and inappropriate titter, which appalled her.

Even though Sophia was obliged to look at him, there was something about him, about his unhealthy appearance and pouched little piggy eyes that was repellent. His tittering laugh made his apparent sorrow for his dead parent, sound hypocritical.

Even so, Lady Maunders tutted in sympathy and continued undeterred. 'Dear Miss Winterton is also from Norfolk. She is staying with me for a few days, before she goes to her godmother.'

'Indeed. And are you by any chance related to Mr David Winterton, of Dersingham?' He asked the question almost jeeringly, as though he knew something to her detriment and was having a private laugh at her expense.

'We are cousins, sir.'

'I see. And is this your first visit to the big City, ma'am?'

'It is, sir.'

She looked up at that moment and found herself gazing into a pair of cold, pale-grey eyes beneath heavy lids, no longer restless but staring at her fixedly. His florid face had once been handsome, but was now too fleshy to be attractive and although he was smiling, the smile didn't quite reach those eyes. The eyes themselves had heavy pouches, their violet tinge showing clearly against his flushed skin. It was the face she remembered, thrust so offensively into her own that evening at the Sir John Falstaff, the face of a drunken sot. She realized with a sudden shiver of alarm that his interest was engaged in a way that was not normal on first introduction. His eyes were now sharp and very focused, although he had not so far mentioned that they'd met before, thank God. There was still a chance that he didn't know her.

Mrs Thornton also noticed the particular attention that William Baggett was lavishing on Lady Maunders' young guest and when

Rodgers reappeared to announce, 'Dinner is served, ladies and gentlemen,' she did a hasty about turn for the move to the dining-room and suggested that Mr Baggett instead of Thomas, should escort Miss Winterton and that Thomas could escort both the twins.

Before offering Sophia his arm, William Baggett smirked at Lady Maunders and said, 'I hope while Miss Winterton is at Manvers House, that I may be permitted to call upon you, Lady Maunders?'

'Of course, sir, we would be pleased to welcome you.'

She smiled at Mrs Thornton as she said it. Lady Maunders was not an old tabby, she was a kind and well-meaning middle-aged woman, but she was pleased at the way her protégée had attracted the attention of one so wealthy and with such social standing as Mr Baggett. She recognized that he was not immediately attractive to a beautiful young woman like Sophia Winterton, but he was eligible and rich and it would do no harm for Sophia to be accepted in the same social circles. Baggett offered Sophia his arm with a slightly exaggerated bow which seemed to imply that he thought that she was not truly a lady, but he escorted her politely enough to her place at the dining-table with his habitual mincing and effeminate walk.

Fortunately, Mrs Thornton's reorganization of the pairings going into dinner, didn't extend to the seating plan in the dining-room and Sophia was pleased and relieved that she had Mr Robert Thornton on her right hand and his son, Thomas on her left. Mr Baggett, thank goodness, was seated further down near to Mrs Thornton and the twins. She could hear his high bleating voice as he greeted the girls and the creak of the expensive dining chair under his bulk, then she resolutely turned her attention to her neighbour.

Although he was dressed in the height of fashion and could converse in a very sophisticated way about art and artists, Mr Thomas Thornton was young and impressionable. If there is such a thing as love at first sight, this was the fateful evening when he fell head over heels in love with the beautiful Miss Winterton. As for Sophia, finding herself next to someone as personable and seemingly unthreatening as Thomas, pleased her and she didn't at first recognize quite what an effect she'd had on him. She felt easy and relaxed in his company and as the meal progressed, she gradually felt more and more secure. True, there remained the problem of William Baggett to contend with, but the incident at the inn might best remain forgotten and have no repercussions at all. She wondered what Paul would say when he knew that they had met socially and so far, Mr Baggett had not seemed to make the connection between his clumsy attempt to kiss a strange young woman in the passage of the Sir John Falstaff and Lady Maunders' guest. Her mind drifted to Paul and back to their journey from Cottleton. She wondered where he was this evening and whether he too thought of their three days together. It seemed now to have been such a halcyon time in spite of the tension of her broken engagement to Devenish. They'd had plenty of opportunity to become acquainted. She wondered what it would have been like if he'd kissed her . . . What would have happened if he'd pressed her lips with his own . . . ? If she raised her own lips to his and . . . If . . .

'Miss Winterton?'

Blinking, she realized that young Thomas Thornton had spoken to her and was waiting for her to answer. She stared at him blankly.

'I . . . I'm so sorry, Mr Thornton. I didn't quite catch what you said.' He must think her either excessively ill mannered or utterly stupid, but his handsome young face expressed only pleasant interest and concern.

'I just wondered if you would care for some wine, Miss Winterton.'

'I . . . thank you . . . Mr Thornton . . . my thoughts were wandering . . . Yes. A glass of wine would be very acceptable. Thank you, sir.'

Much encouraged, he smiled at her and poured her out a glass of wine.

'What about some fish? Should you care for a little fish, Miss Winterton?' Sophia had lived long enough to know how potently her beauty could affect the young men of her acquaintance. She looked into Thomas's guileless face and somewhat belatedly recognized the signs of his attraction to her. His frank blue eyes openly adored her and he was paying absolutely no attention to the lady on the other side of him.

Sophia's first governess had been very interested in ornithology and she recollected Miss Johnson describing some exotic bird or other whose whole courtship ritual consisted of trying to please a prospective mate by foraging for food and offering the most exquisite titbits to the female of his choice in order to secure her interest. This was exactly what Thomas was doing, she thought.

She gave him a kind smile and said, 'Thank you I'd like some fish very much.'

He halted the footman who was circulating with the fish and Sophia was served with a massive helping of poached halibut in a delicious wine sauce, far more than she could eat, much more the sort of portion to be enjoyed by a young man like himself.

'Mama has a French chef,' he said proudly. 'He is always able to procure the finest fish and shellfish for the table.'

'I will be lucky to finish all this,' Sophia smiled at him. 'I don't think I shall be able to manage any of the chicken.'

He looked so ludicrously cast down at what he thought was a crass error on his part, that she took pity on him and gave him her most ravishing smile. 'But it is so delicious, Mr Thornton, that I am willing to forgo another course later, in order to do justice to your generosity.'

He was so emboldened by her kindness as to attempt a little flirtation and Sophia was now torn between amusement at his amateurish efforts to attract someone who, he felt, was so much more mature and sophisticated than himself and guilt that she might appear to be too encouraging. Either way, at least it gave her an opportunity to covertly observe William Baggett, while pretending to be so engrossed in her conversation with Thomas Thornton that she was not able to give Baggett any eye contact whatsoever. That he was awaiting such an opportunity, she had no doubt. She was very conscious of his consistent interest in her and in spite of his polite attention to Mrs Thornton, of the glances he sent in her direction. She was determined that he should be oblivious of the fact that she was also aware of him.

Lady Maunders, observing from the sidelines was amused at the obvious delight and pleasure that Thomas Thornton was enjoying with her young visitor and smiled to herself at Sophia's success.

Sophia herself, was pleased when Mr Robert Thornton on her other side, politely engaged her in conversation and she was obliged to turn her attention to him.

'Please don't allow that foolish young pup of mine to monopolize you, Miss Winterton,' he said. 'He is maddeningly talkative on the pleasures of art since he returned to us from the Grand Tour and can be tedious as a young lady's dinner companion.'

'I shall try not to let him monopolize me, sir,' Sophia promised, but she sensed the affectionate pride that lay underneath his mock criticism of his only son and she went on, 'You and Mrs Thornton must be very proud to have such a charming and personable son.'

She couldn't have hit on a more felicitous compliment to Thomas's fond papa. He blossomed like a flower in full sunshine and forgetting any sense of modesty, said, 'Indeed we are, Miss Winterton and he is so thoroughly decent and conscientious a lad. Such a good and loving brother to his sisters, as he is. He never gives us a moment's unease.'

Still enjoying Miss Winterton's charming smile, he continued fondly, 'Unlike the twins of course. They will have their come out in the spring and that will be a lively event. Like all young ladies of their age, they can be very difficult. Being merely a papa, I couldn't possibly ever understand them.'

Thinking of the contrast between this devoted family and her hateful aunt Harriet, Sophia said softly, 'But they are so well loved, sir. No young lady blessed with parents such as you and Mrs Thornton could fail to turn out well.'

Her compliment was so patently sincere, that he positively beamed at her and the rest of the meal passed pleasantly in spite of her unease at William Baggett's malevolent presence.

Once the ladies had retired to the drawing-room, Elizabeth and May were persuaded to sing some duets and Sophia offered to accompany them at the pianoforte. By the time the gentlemen joined them, it was obvious that William Baggett had drunk too deeply of the port. He slumped into one of Mrs Thornton's elegant chairs, his toad-like eyes flickering uncomfortably towards her, and Sophia was pleased and relieved when Thomas Thornton asked shyly if he might be allowed to turn the pages of the music for her. In Mrs Thornton's drawing-room, in full view of everyone, she felt absolutely safe from William Baggett and enjoyed the company of the young Thorntons until at midnight, it was time for the carriages.

William Baggett was supported to his carriage by two stalwart and tactful young footmen, obviously used to assisting inebriated gentlemen on their way at the end of an evening's indulgence. Sophia and Lady Maunders also took their leave, with many invitations to visit again. It had been a most satisfactory dinner party.

When they were once more in the coach and on the way back to Manvers House, Lady Maunders was very enthusiastic about their evening out. 'You were a great success, Sophie,' she said, as she settled back in her seat. 'Be assured, you will receive further invitations from the Thorntons and Lady Wright.' She paused and went on, 'And William Baggett seemed very interested.'

Sophia said nothing. The last thing she

wanted was for the odious Baggett to pay her any attention.

Lady Maunders noticed her lack of response and went on tactfully, 'What a charming young man Thomas Thornton is. You've definitely made a conquest there, my dear.'

'He is very young, ma'am.'

'Quite so. And so very impressionable, Sophie. But rest assured, like all young creatures, he will grow up, my dear.'

They reached the house as the clock was chiming the half-hour and the butler was waiting to let them in. As they paused for a few moments in the hall, he bowed and bade them good night. Lady Maunders stifled a delicate yawn and said, 'I intend to retire now, Sophie. Ring for the maid if there's anything you require. We're dining with Lady Wright tomorrow and I would so like you to join us, Sophie dear.'

'Thank you, ma'am. I would like it very much. And thank you also for a very pleasant evening. Goodnight, ma'am.'

Sophia was not sleepy and went to the library to find a book that might divert her from thoughts of Sir Paul Maunders and her anxieties about William Baggett. The books were arranged in subject order and, looking upwards at the higher shelves, Sophia saw a leather-bound anthology of poetry which looked very interesting. She could dip into it, she thought, and find something to divert and soothe her. She was soon at the top of the library steps and was just reaching for her chosen volume, when she heard a familiar voice behind her.

'Miss Winterton. You seem to be a veritable night owl this evening and there was I convinced that you were the original morning skylark. Now how did that come about, I wonder? Dare I hope that you deliberately waited up for me?'

Sophia turned, startled at his voice and her foot swivelled dangerously on the polished wood of the library steps. The volume of poetry slipped from her grasp and fell noisily to the floor. Fearing she was about to fall, she clutched desperately at the bookshelf, but it was totally unnecessary. She was lifted off the steps in a pair of strong arms and set down gently on to the floor. Instinctively, she'd transferred her grasp to hold his shoulders, so that once firmly on her feet, she was still holding on to him, her face raised to his, exactly as it had been on their riverside picnic, when he'd wiped the wine from her lips and she'd been sure he was about to kiss her . . .

Appalled at where her wayward thoughts were taking her, Sophia attempted to break free of his grasp, still forcing herself to meet his intensely quizzical gaze, which held their eyes on a seemingly single thread.

'Well?' he asked.

'Well . . . what?'

'Well. Did you wait up for me?'

'Certainly not. I merely came to choose a book.'

She was acutely aware that he had guessed what was going through her mind and she wanted desperately to escape from the library to her room, before she betrayed any more evidence of her rapidly increasing regard for him. Although his hold was gentle, she was yet acutely aware of Sir Paul Maunders' physical strength and knew that if he chose not to release her, she was trapped. One half of her was determined to run away from this situation, but to her intense amazement, the other half of her didn't find the idea of this embrace in the least distasteful. In fact she rather liked the wonderful feeling of security in the clasp of his strong arms. She lowered her eyes and looked at his shapely mouth so dangerously near to her own. Held fast against him as she was, she tried to drag herself back from the intensity of her desire, but lacked the will to do so. She could feel the strong beat of his heart, or was it her own? As the moment lengthened, she was forced to look up at him at last.

She couldn't fail to register the gleam of triumph in his eyes as he drew back a little and said, smilingly, 'Well, I have the feeling that you really did wait up for me, did you not, Miss Sophia Winterton?'

Her lips parted ready for a reply, but her answer was checked by a gentle tap on the door and a soft enquiry from Polly as to whether miss was in there and whether she was ready to retire.

He raised both her hands and brushed his lips gently across her wrists, giving a rueful grin at this untimely interruption. As Sophia answered, 'Yes, Polly, I shall be up directly,' reluctantly he let her go.

'Just as well she's here, in time to remind me that I'm a gentleman and you are my guest,' he said. 'Good night, dear Sophia.'

Polly was unwontedly quiet as she brushed out Sophia's hair and slipped the nightdress over her head. It wasn't until she was ready to snuff the candle that she said with direct simplicity, 'That Sir Paul, he be a very 'andsome man, miss.'

'Yes, he is, Polly,' Sophia said, with a barely concealed sigh.

'And be you goin' to marry him, Miss Winterton?'

'I hardly think so,' Sophia replied, with an even deeper sigh than before and Polly blew out the candle.

7

The sun was pouring through the window like molten gold and although it was not yet nine o'clock, Sir Paul Maunders' entire household was already awake and busy. Polly materialized from nowhere as though she had some psychic knowledge that her mistress was fully conscious and ready to face a new day. Just as Sophia was stretching and delighting in her wakefulness, she heard a gentle tap and the little maid's cheerful face appeared round the door. Polly was carrying a jug of hot water and busied herself filling the wash basin, chattering all the while.

'Good mornin', Miss Winterton. I 'opes as you slept well. 'Ow was the supper, miss? I hopes as I did right comin' down to fetch you from the libr'y. Yer water's ready and I've put out clean linen for you. You'm better be 'ungry this mornin'. Cook's prepared a lot 'cos the master's ordered breakfast at nine sharp.'

Polly didn't wait for any replies to her exclamations and questions, but bustled across to the large clothes cupboard and asked over her shoulder, 'What was you

wantin' to wear this mornin', Miss Winterton? It's 'ot out, already. The yeller muslin's
nice and cool, ma'am.'

Sophia smiled at her. She acknowledged
that Polly had received absolutely no training
in the skills needed for a lady's maid and
didn't realize that it was *de rigueur* to remain
silent and reserved when waiting on a lady in
the morning, unless milady spoke first. Now
that she felt more at ease with her mistress,
Polly gave full rein to her natural friendliness
and chattiness. Sophia liked her exuberant
good nature and was in no way inclined to
put her right on all the formalities to be
observed by a personal servant, but equally,
she didn't want Polly to be at a disadvantage
due to her lack of formal training.

'The yellow morning dress will do very
well, Polly. I shall get up straight away. I feel
ravenous.'

Suiting the action to the words, she leapt
out of bed and stripped off her nightgown,
ready to wash herself.

It was when she was dressed and Polly was
arranging her hair, that Sophia heard the
inexorable whirring mechanism of the long
case clock in the hall and then nine clear
sonorous chimes.

'Good gracious, nine already,' she laughed.
'It won't do to keep Sir Paul waiting, if he's

stipulated nine o'clock sharp.'

Polly could see she was laughing at such a pedantic edict on Paul's part and was mocking the idea that she should obey any such rules. They both giggled, two humorous young women, mistress and servant, yet more like equals, united in their secret amusement at the pretensions of an arrogant upper-class male. Already, Sophie liked and trusted Polly as a friend. She'd miss having the country girl with her when it was time for her to go back to the White Lion. She wondered whether, if she were to arrange regular visits home for her and Polly earned enough to send some money to her mother, Mrs Dawkins would allow her to consider it a permanent place. She had a good relationship with the girl and knew that in spite of the giggles, Polly was loyal and reliable and would never gossip about what she'd observed last night. As for herself, she'd decided that she'd ignore the pleasurable interlude in Sir Paul's library the night before. Perhaps, she thought, he was a little foxed and she was honest enough to admit to herself that she, who was not used to it, had also partaken of wine and perhaps she too had been a little drunk. She drew a deep breath, determinedly quelling all the pleasurable memories of his embrace and then, with a quick smile of thanks to Polly and a last

131

look at her reflection in the mirror, she went down to breakfast.

He was alone, with just Philip, one of the younger footmen, hovering to make sure that sir had everything he wanted. Lady Maunders had not yet appeared and Philip brightened considerably when the beautiful young lady entered the room. He hastened to serve her with coffee and toast as though his life depended on it.

Sir Paul wished her a curt 'good morning' and glared at his plateful of rare roast beef sourly. For some unfathomable reason, he found Sophia Winterton's radiant energy particularly irritating this morning. He was thoroughly regretting giving way to his impulse to detain her in the library last night. It could have led to a compromising situation for both of them. He'd wanted desperately to make love to her and was determined to check any other urges in that direction, even though he was finding his decision to stay out of the beautiful Miss Winterton's way rather difficult. Having repulsed Marie, he was somewhat at a loss as to how to spend his evenings, but after all, this was his home, not Miss Winterton's. Although a fellow might sometimes feel like dining at his club, a fellow didn't want to dine at White's every evening, when he had a dashed good dining-room at home, and as for visiting Marie . . . well . . . that was the end of a chapter.

He had no regrets about giving Marie her marching orders; there were plenty more attractive and cultivated women in London who were on the look out for a wealthy protector. Sophia Winterton was a different matter. He realized that the weakness which led him to desire Sophia Winterton while she was a guest in his house, could have serious repercussions. He was already compromised by his insistence on accompanying her to London. God alone knew what had possessed him to flirt with her last night. He'd had wine and brandy, but he certainly hadn't been drunk. He was old enough to know better, he told himself angrily. Thankfully, his discomfort at her continued presence in his house would be all be over on Friday when she was reunited with Miss Fitzpatrick.

After Polly's fortuitous interruption, he'd gone to his own room and had thought about Sophia as he'd tried in vain to settle down in his very large lonely bed. In fact, he'd been unable to sleep for thinking about her; her smiles, her expressive eyes, her stern put downs, the little frown creasing the smooth creamy flesh between her tawny brows when she was angry. That sudden joyful peal of laughter when he'd pretended to be the butler . . . Her soft lips, tempting him to kiss her . . . Yet, on the way to London, she'd seemed both critical of him and resentful at his attempts to help her for the whole of their three days together. At the inns they'd stayed at, she'd been utterly reserved and formal, when she wasn't aggressively arguing the toss about every decision he made, that is. Apart from their conversation on the Cottleton Road, she hadn't allowed him to see anything of her true feelings. Yet, he'd visited Mama in her room this morning while she was having her breakfast chocolate and she'd revealed that Miss Winterton was on very friendly terms with her and had been a great success at the Thorntons, especially with the son, that gawky greenhorn, Thomas. He ground his teeth angrily at the idea of another man being attracted to Sophia Winterton, relaxing in the warmth of her beautiful smile, being approved of by her and he still couldn't forget last night when she lay so helplessly in his arms and her soft lips had been so near his own. He recalled the feel of her hands on his shoulders, the warmth of her slender body pressed so intimately against his own . . . Surely, she couldn't be totally impervious to him?

If Sophia noticed his clenched jaw and black scowl, she pretended not to and slipped into the seat opposite to him, as Philip fussed round, carving her a piece of ham, offering coddled eggs, a slice of rare beef, a portion of kedgeree, all of which she refused, merely accepting the ham and keeping her eyes firmly on her plate until Philip retired to stand by the sideboard gazing straight in front of him, not even beginning to understand the strange habits of the gentry.

When she finally raised her eyes to look at the man seated opposite her on this glorious summer day, she was painfully aware that Sir Paul Maunders was just as overwhelmingly handsome and just as potently, heart stoppingly attractive as ever. Sternly, she told herself that she must never let him realize the power of his attraction for her, especially after she'd so nearly given way to her feelings last night. During the three days they had spent together on the journey from Norfolk, he'd seemed to continually get under her guard, alternately making her lose her temper, say things she shouldn't say and at the same time, confide her private feelings to him and all the while she'd been revelling in his company and in the pleasure his dark good looks had given her. She was ashamed of herself. Thank goodness he didn't really find her in the least attractive. That encounter in the library last night must have been just a coincidence, nothing more. It had been late. If they hadn't been alone, she would never have allowed herself to acknowledge how much she enjoyed being in his arms. She'd soon forget about him and that was for the best. No doubt, other women would break their hearts over him. Sophia Winterton never would.

She was vastly relieved when he initiated some polite conversation himself and said mundanely, 'Another perfect summer morning, Miss Winterton. Do you have any special plans for today?'

'No, not really. Being new in town, I have only your mama to guide me or to introduce me to people.'

'My mama is often laid low by extremely hot or close weather and never really comes to life until the cool of the evening. Do you ride, Miss Winterton?'

'Yes. That is, I have no horse in town, sir.'

He cleared his throat. Dammit, why did he always have the idea that she was about to wrong foot him? And why was he feeling so stupidly nervous? He was convinced that she'd wanted him to kiss her last night as much as he'd wanted it himself and yet, she was so stiff and prim. He wasn't an inexperienced boy, clumsily trying to please his first desirable young lady. He was a man

136

of the world, well used to dealing with women, even women as beautiful and spirited as Sophia Winterton, so why couldn't he feel more at his ease with her? He had to admit to himself that man of the world he might be, in her beautiful, seductive presence, he was as confused as a schoolboy. He must remain cool and entertain his guest politely until the visit was over.

He looked into the luminous hazel eyes, almost amber in the brightness of the sunny breakfast parlour and for once, neither stormy nor angry. This morning her beautiful eyes were calm and tranquil, her pale brow smooth and untroubled. A man could drown in eyes like those, he thought, and took a deep breath, before asking in polite tones, 'Should you care for a drive round the park, Miss Winterton?'

'A drive round the park?' she echoed stupidly, the clear hazel eyes widening in surprise.

'Yes, round the park. The greys have had little exercise since . . . since our journey from Norfolk and it is a peach of a morning . . . '

Sophie's heart suddenly gave a leap of pleasurable anticipation and her eyes sparkled with pleasure. There was no need to guess what her answer would be. Her expressive face and large eyes revealed every nuance of her thoughts and emotions. Miss Sophia Winterton is utterly transparent, he thought cynically. She is so unspoilt and natural. What a contrast between this tall willowy girl and the devious and ambitious Marie.

He caught himself staring at her as mesmerized as a besotted boy. He pulled himself together with an effort and said, 'Well, Miss Winterton? Am I to have the honour of your company?'

'Yes . . . I should like that very much, sir. But I must first change my dress, Sir Paul.'

He stood up and bowed. 'Very well, I shall order the curricle to be brought round to the front door in ten minutes.'

Philip stepped forward and opened the door for her and she hurried upstairs to change. Sophia was well aware that a fine gentleman's mettlesome thoroughbreds must not be kept waiting and she told herself that the jelly-like feeling in her legs and her sudden breathlessness were merely the result of running up the stairs.

She changed quickly from her muslin gown and put on a walking dress of deep blue silk, one of Madame Justine's more inspired creations, which had a blue poke bonnet, lined with ruched silk in a paler shade and several soft ostrich plumes. She stood impatiently while Polly tied the blue strings slightly to one side and she was at last allowed to look in the mirror. They were both conscious that the fashionable bonnet framed her face most attractively and that she was looking her best. Polly tried to extend the pleasure of the moment, torn between pride in Sophia's beauty and disappointment that she herself was not included on this jaunt. She longed more than anything for Miss Winterton to keep her on as a personal maid. Things would be very flat at home after this, she thought.

Even Lady Maunders came out into the hall to say her farewells and offer good wishes for an enjoyable outing. She also let fall in Paul's hearing, that since Miss Winterton's success at the Thorntons' dinner party, she expected there would be more than a few visiting cards today and tomorrow.

'And of course, tonight there is a small select soirée with dancing at the home of Lord and Lady Wright. I am so looking forward to that. There will be so many nice young people there and I hope you will enjoy it, Sophie. It is in honour of Lady Wright's niece, Cecilia, who had her come out earlier this year. I expect young Mr Thomas Thornton has been invited,' she added, with a mischievous glance at her son.

To Sophie's surprise, he actually scowled

blackly at this and went to stand near to the curricle. He gave her his hand to help her up while Morgan stood near the horses' heads and then he got in himself and took his whip in his hand. Morgan let go of the horses and sprang up behind and Sir Paul spent a few seconds dealing with the restive greys, who plunged about a little before settling down under his control. Then they set off. As the spirited horses plunged forward, Sophia involuntarily clutched the side of the curricle and at last, Maunders smiled.

'Pray don't be alarmed, Miss Winterton, they are merely a little fresh.'

She was immediately reassured and returned both hands to rest on the reticule on her lap.

'They are indeed very handsome animals,' she said admiringly, looking at the horses' small proud heads and glossy necks.

'Yes, and they are beautiful beasts to handle,' he said.

He smiled again as they turned the corner at the end of Manvers Square and swept along the road towards James Street. The traffic was not particularly heavy but the horses were highly strung and inclined to be nervous. Sir Paul had to keep his attention fixed on his driving as he negotiated heavy wagons, sedan chairs and various loud-voiced pedestrians, but they finally reached the gates leading into Hyde Park with no problems and then they settled into a finely matched stride, stepping out gracefully with a proud, spirited trot.

Sophie noticed several others out for a recreational drive that morning and Sir Paul touched his hat now and then to the various occupants of phaetons or barouches who were taking advantage of the comparatively cool morning air. Sir Paul seemed to have forgotten his earlier ill temper and, gradually, Sophia began to relax and enjoy the ride.

He leaned slightly forward while turning to look at her and enquired, 'Are you quite comfortable, Miss Winterton? I notice you have no parasol with you.'

'Yes. I am comfortable, thank you. My bonnet shields me from the sun very adequately, sir.'

They proceeded in amiable silence for a while, until Sophia suddenly noticed a quartet of very dashing riders, consisting of two young ladies and two young gentlemen, cantering towards them. They glanced at Sir Paul's curricle and glanced again, recognizing Miss Winterton.

The next moment, Miss Elizabeth Thornton exclaimed, 'Why, it's Miss Winterton. Good morning, ma'am.'

The other two Thorntons, Miss May and her brother Thomas, and a young man whom she didn't recognize, reined in their horses and gathered round to greet Sophia, bombarding her with questions as though they hadn't seen her for years.

'How was she? How had she managed to be up so early after an evening with their mama? Was she attending Lady Wright's supper dance this evening? What about the opera?'

Sophia laughingly tried to answer them all, but meanwhile, looked enquiringly at the dark-haired young man.

'Miss Winterton, may I present my friend, Mr Richard Andrews?' Thomas Thornton said. He teased his friend good-naturedly. 'He is somewhat of a regular at Gentleman Jackson's, so my sisters and I all hesitate to cross swords with him.'

'Nonsense, Tom. Miss Winterton, how do you do? Thomas is a sad chatterbox, I fear. Ignore him, I beg you.'

He was a little older than Thomas, dark and good-looking, beautifully dressed and with a deceptively languid air.

'I think you already know Sir Paul Maunders, Richard?'

Sir Paul bowed. 'Yes, I have had the pleasure of Mr Andrews' acquaintance at

Jackson's. How do you do, sir?'

Sir Paul's eyes missed nothing of the admiration in Richard Andrews' glance and the openly adoring look directed at Miss Winterton by Thomas Thornton, nor the open pleasure and affection of the two young sisters.

Mr Andrews bowed and said, 'A pleasure to meet you, Miss Winterton. May I hope that we may meet again at Lady Wright's soirée? I know you mustn't keep the horses standing, sir. Your servant, Maunders. Good day, Miss Winterton.'

Taking their lead from Richard Andrews, the other members of the party took their leave with many smiles and hopes of meeting again in the evening. Sophia smoothed down her dress and faced forward squarely as Sir Paul prepared to drive on. She couldn't help feeling gratified at her obvious popularity when she had only been in town for two days.

The little smile that curved her lips did not escape his attention either. The horses had run off a little of their earlier friskiness and now they travelled a little more sedately and the other riders seemed to have all but disappeared.

He turned to her suddenly and said, 'Should you care for a walk in the fresh air, Miss Winterton?'

Sophia was only too ready to step down for

a few minutes and he offered his hand to help her.

The outlook was so pleasant with the smooth grass still not too badly scorched and the promised sultry heat of the day was as yet, only a faint haze in the distance. He tossed the reins to Morgan and offered her his arm as they walked towards a little group of trees shading the edge of one of the paths. Everything sparkled in the morning sunshine and, as they strolled along the path, even Morgan had now disappeared from view, to walk the horses up and down patiently. For the first time in many months, Sophia felt positively happy. He was smiling at her and the whole world seemed suddenly to shine. The fine skin round his deep eyes crinkled and he looked young and carefree.

'Well, Miss Winterton, you seem to be absolutely tops with your young acquaintances,' he said in his distinctive drawling voice. 'Positively the toast of the town, if I may say so. Your admirers are so thick on the ground that I shall have to pick my way carefully among them just to reach my own front door.'

She laughed out loud at his absurdity and almost by mutual consent, they paused in their stroll and looked at each other.

Just as they were feeling at ease with each

other, so their quarrel was sudden and seemed to come from nowhere.

From being pleasant and smiling, he was just as suddenly grim and said, 'But the serious side of this situation, Miss Winterton is that if you encourage these young blades to dangle after you, you may be storing up complications which may come to a head when your aunt finally catches up with you. Do you envisage either of them as good husband material, as an alternative to Lord Devenish?'

Sophia's shoulders went back and she raised her chin. 'Sir, how dare you? You are not entitled to ask such a question of me. With respect, you are neither my father, brother or husband. I have absolutely no intention of marrying anyone, ever, but in any case, my decisions are my own to make and do not depend on any opinion of yours.'

Sophia's temper was rising dangerously.

'Yet I have the right to expect that you will behave with some discretion while you are staying in my house.'

'Sir, you have no cause to even hint that my behaviour might be indiscreet.'

'I should not be surprised at any indiscretions on your part, such is your temper, madam. And it was not particularly discreet of you to leave your family and groom on your wedding day.'

In spite of the promise of the lovely summer morning, suddenly they were both now furious with one another. Sophia was too indignant even to walk away and get back into the curricle. She glared at him, her eyes flashing green anger and she saw that his were icily scathing. She felt terribly alone as she continued to gaze at him, suddenly uncertain and vulnerable.

He took a step towards her and without thinking she raised her hand, determined this time to slap his contemptuous face, but she found her wrist imprisoned in an iron grasp. Paul pulled her towards him until they were so close that they were almost touching.

'Don't you dare attempt to strike me, madam.'

'And don't you dare touch me, sir. Let me go.'

They gazed at each other silently for some seconds and then she felt her anger drain from her, leaving her feeling empty and despondent. As she continued to look into his dark unfathomable eyes, she wondered whether he felt any emotion about last evening when she had been in his arms. She desperately wanted him to kiss her, wanted to feel his body even closer to hers. She closed her eyes and almost unconsciously, felt herself leaning towards him, wanting, needing his kiss and at the same time ashamed of her need.

Nervously, she licked her lips and then suddenly, he pulled her hard against his body, crushing the wrist that he had grasped so brutally against his chest. She clung to him instinctively and he held her for a long moment before he let her go.

Now she felt utterly abandoned in the anticipation of his kiss. The ribbons of her bonnet had come loose and it fell back on to her shoulders. She was lost to all sense of decorum and propriety, conscious only of the waves of disappointment as he stepped back without kissing her. She forgot where she was, forgot Morgan, waiting patiently with the horses, forgot James Devenish, forgot everything except for the unexpected promise of his embrace and her pain and chagrin when, just as suddenly, he pulled back and she was left almost staggering with the sudden feeling of weakness in her legs.

The close embrace and her passionate response, caused Paul's senses to burn. This wasn't at all what he'd planned. He had determined not to be close to Sophia Winterton again. He felt a sudden band of tension in his neck. God help him, his desire to kiss her was, once more, almost uncontrollable. If he didn't withdraw from temptation now, he'd be lost. He steeled himself to resist her and his eyes became hard and cold as he said stiffly, 'Your pardon, Miss Winterton. I should not have spoken like that. I'm sorry. Forgive me.'

They both stood as if turned to stone, staring at each other silently. Sophia was overwhelmed with humiliation and shame. What had possessed her to encourage such liberties? How could she? How could she have responded in that open and shameless way, just as if . . . just as if . . . she were some cheap, light skirt? Shaken and ashamed, she looked away from him, replacing her bonnet and retying the ribbons with shaking hands. He stepped back from her, his head slightly bowed and they both returned to where Morgan was guarding the curricle.

The journey back to Manvers House was accomplished in an uneasy silence. He handed Sophia down from the curricle and then, in a towering rage, went with Morgan to oversee the stabling. Sophia hurried indoors to be met by Lady Maunders who was in quite a flutter of pleasure.

'Sophie, dear. How was the drive?'

She didn't wait for a reply and seemed not to notice Sophia's strained expression but went straight on with, 'Some gratifying developments since the Thorntons' dinner, my dear. Several cards this morning and not five minutes ago, a personal visit from your cousin David. He is in the library longing to see how you are going on.'

In a softer tone, she added, 'Mr Baggett called and left his card, my dear. I told him I would be at home this afternoon and he has promised to call, on purpose to see you and pay his respects.'

Still reeling from the tension of her encounter with Sir Paul Maunders, Sophia forced a smile and begged to be excused to go and change.

She was pleased and gratified that David had responded so swiftly to her note and was eager to change and go and greet him, but the idea of a visit from William Baggett filled her with apprehension. She felt unable to respond to Polly's enthusiastic chat and felt only dread at the idea of having to confront him. Thinking she had offended in some way, Polly also grew quiet but Sophia hardly noticed, she was so eager to see her cousin, the one person in the world who, she felt, held her in some affection.

When she entered the drawing-room, David was looking out of the window with his back towards her, but turned as soon as she

149

opened the door, his face alight with the joy of seeing her.

'Sophia! My dear Coz. How are you? I received your letter and it was a great relief to know you were well after . . . after — '

'After I let everyone down on my wedding day,' she said, finishing the sentence for him. She held out both her hands and he drew her into an enfolding brotherly hug, kissing her on both cheeks.

David wasn't a commanding figure. He was tall, as Sophia was, but not exceptionally so. He was slim and lithe in an elegant coat of blue superfine and immaculate beige pantaloons and polished Hessians. He was a fashionable young man of twenty-six and wore his glossy auburn hair, which was a shade darker than Sophia's own, in the modern Brutus style. Outwardly, he looked like any other well-heeled young gentleman of the *ton* but there was more to David Winterton than this. He had an air of aristocratic confidence and power, which always merited him a second glance.

His hazel eyes were more inclined to golden brown than green and they were now looking searchingly into Sophia's own, humour and concern in equal measure as she stepped back from him saying, 'Do you think

I was unforgivably hoydenish to run away as I did?'

'Not unforgivably so,' he replied gravely, but with a twinkling in his eyes that Sophia recognized of old. They both laughed aloud but then were immediately sober.

'I . . . but I am so sorry, Sophia, that it should have reached the day of the wedding before you were able to admit to such profound doubts. I know you are no flirt-gill to become engaged and then break it off on a whim. I blame myself for not taking the opportunity to discuss the rightness or wrongness of Devenish's ability to make you happy.' He took both her hands in his. 'I should have been so much more careful not to let you give yourself in marriage unless it was to someone who is exactly right for you. After all, I am the head of the family, now. Dear little sister, forgive me. I should not have trusted Harriet Winterton to agree to the marriage . . . '

Sophia's eyes filled with tears. Long ago, her cousin David had brought home a friend from Eton and had introduced her to the other lad as his 'dear little sister'. The friend had smirked at this and David's hands had clenched with anger. The presence of Sophia's governess had prevented any fisti-cuffs, but David Winterton suffered from a temper equally as fierce as her own. She knew that he was well aware of it and had come to an accommodation with it. In his dealings with his fellow men and women, he cultivated an air of gentle deliberation, and dealt with everyone in his everyday life with a courtesy and consideration far beyond what was necessary or required of him. But no amount of reason and courtesy or self-control could ever suppress that temper entirely. It was as sudden and fierce as a hurricane and, physically, Winterton was a very strong man. He could never dare let his temper have the upper hand: it would be too destructive.

Sophia hesitated before she told him the rest of the story, but he had always been her trusted confidant and she took a deep breath, still holding tightly to his hands.

'I was fortunate enough to be escorted to London by Sir Paul Maunders,' she said, 'and his mama has been all that is welcoming and hospitable in her reception of me.' She cleared her throat and continued in a less confident tone, 'One circumstance that concerned me a little was that Mr William Baggett observed me at an inn that we stayed at . . . But he was very drunk . . . He tried to molest me and fortunately Sir Paul was on hand to . . . deal with him.'

As she expected, David was incensed at

this and let go of her hands abruptly. He was both puzzled and angry at what she'd told him. He knew that there must have been a compelling reason for Sophia to act as she did and he suspected that the fault must lie with Lord Devenish. He too had heard of his lordship's dalliance with the Winfield sisters and that now Devenish was abroad. Knowing Baggett's reputation, he expected that there would be more repercussions from that gentleman. He cursed himself again for not speaking to Sophia when he'd had the chance, but at the time of his visit as a wedding guest in Harriet's house, he had not found an opportunity to be alone with Sophia and counsel her about her wedding plans. Like many strong men, emotionally he was something of a coward and had decided to let well alone.

Now he'd heard the whole story, he was even more appalled at Baggett's involvement.

'You must have had good reason to act as you did, Sophia. You are not a missish girl to break off a betrothal in any light way, you are a mature and sensible woman who must know her own mind. If Devenish has injured you or insulted you, he will answer to me. As for Baggett . . . that man will bear watching . . .'

153

She thought it prudent not to inflame an already difficult situation and said, 'No, indeed, the fault was mine. I was mistaken in my feelings and felt . . . and felt I was being propelled towards a marriage I . . . I didn't want . . . That is all.

'As for William Baggett's drunken overtures at the Sir John Falstaff, well, at least he seems not to have remembered anything, so least said . . . '

David unclenched his hands deliberately and forced himself to stay calm. He changed the subject. 'I understand we are indebted to Sir Paul Maunders and his mama for showing you such generosity and hospitality.'

'Yes, indeed,' she said coolly. 'Lady Maunders has been all that is kind and I expect to be reunited with dear Fitz tomorrow.'

'Lady Maunders said that you were accompanied by your maid on the journey from Norfolk. Polly is it? I confess I cannot recall her to mind. Is she new?'

Sophia was evasive. 'Yes. She is a country girl and is my personal maid. She is utterly loyal and I know she will not tittletattle to the other servants.'

'It was fortunate indeed that Sir Paul Maunders elected to be your escort, Sophia. I've known him for some years now. He is an out an out gentleman, the devil of a Corinthian. One thing you may be sure of, Sophia, he ain't hanging out for a rich bride. Seems to want to avoid matrimony although he's had any number of caps set at him. The last time I met him, he said that he was like to remain a bachelor until his dying day. Kept his face as straight as a flat iron when he said it, but you know how he laughs with his eyes sometimes when he's gammoning you.'

The very thought of Sir Paul's teasing and the way he had of laughing with his eyes, gave Sophia a sudden pang of longing for their carefree adventure on the journey from Cottleton and she gave a heartfelt sigh.

'I shall say no more of Devenish, Sophia. I always thought it would never answer when Harriet was so determined to match-make and I understand what prompted you to do as you did. I'm in London for a while and will be seeing something of Sir Paul and I shall visit you once you are settled with Fitz. I'm prepared to interview your aunt Harriet on your behalf, but only if you think it would be uncomfortable for you to see her. As for Baggett, should he cause any problems, he'll have me to answer to.'

'Dear David,' she murmured. She was overcome with affection and gratitude for his kindness and was too affected to say more.

He took her hand and kissed it. 'I shall take my leave then, dear Coz. We shall probably meet this evening at Lady Wright's soirée.'

He said his farewells to Lady Maunders and set off for his club. Sophia and her ladyship had a light luncheon and all too soon, Sophia had to make her appearance in Lady Maunders' drawing-room.

Mr William Baggett arrived at two o'clock precisely and was welcomed warmly by Lady Maunders. He bent over Sophia's hand, holding it fractionally too long in his slightly damp palm and said in his high-pitched broken voice, 'Miss Winterton, I declare you are the brightest and best star in all of London.'

Lady Maunders beamed approvingly at this and Sophia resigned herself to the idea of being polite to Mr Baggett for at least half an hour. Correct etiquette would mean that he would surely stay no longer than that. All her pleasure in the ride that morning with Paul had dissipated at what she saw as her bad behaviour and she was convinced that now he would have even less liking and respect for her. All the anticipation and delight she had felt in seeing David again was destroyed at the sight of Baggett's portly figure and fat arrogant stare. She tried to listen politely to the chat between Baggett and her ladyship, but several times found her mind wandering. The harder he tried to be charming, the more he bored and irritated her. She forced herself to remain cool and neutral in her replies, determined to give him no encouragement whatsoever, wishing only that the visit would be over and she could seek the consolation of her own room. He was now congratulating Lady Maunders on the graceful urns that adorned the terrace at Manvers House.

'They add such colour and beauty to the view,' he said rather fulsomely. 'And the terrace looks so cool on such a hot day as this.'

He glanced meaningfully at Lady Maunders. 'Could I be allowed to take a turn on the terrace with two such charming ladies?' He gave Sophia such a knowing smile that she felt a sudden pang of fear at the thought of what mischief he could wring out of the situation.

Lady Maunders smiled approvingly. 'Why, that is a splendid idea, Mr Baggett. But I feel the heat so. Pray excuse me. Perhaps you and Miss Winterton could enjoy a few minutes on the terrace without me.'

Sophia's heart sank, but short of making herself look foolish or causing a scene, she could hardly refuse such a pleasant and open invitation. She was somewhat reassured by

Lady Maunders' approval and by the fact that at all times, they would be visible to her from the windows of the drawing-room. It seemed that there would be no deviation from decorum and she could be agreeable to one of Lady Maunder's guests with complete propriety. She wondered when Paul would be home and was on tenterhooks in case he should return and find that William Baggett had been admitted as a visitor.

But she could hardly refuse to take Baggett's arm when he offered it and they strolled together on the terrace, while he talked inconsequentially of the sun loving flowers and the lack of rain. They sat together on a stone bench and Sophia was careful to keep both her hands clasped on her lap. She became aware that she was clenching her hands tightly, stretching the dainty white kid gloves almost to bursting point and she consciously relaxed them, looking down at them demurely as Mr Baggett continued his stream of small talk, interspersed with his familiar tittering laugh.

One of the guests at the Thorntons', an elderly friend of the family, had told her confidentially that for some time William Baggett had been paying his attentions to a vapid fair-haired young woman whom he knew would bring with her a considerable dowry to her fortunate husband.

'She's very wealthy, you know,' she confided. 'I saw them at Almack's, only last week, my dear, and I must tell you, that she seemed anything but responsive to him. But now that he's met you, dear Miss Winterton, I expect he'll transfer his affections in your direction. He's not even glanced at the Thornton twins this evening. With your sparkling looks and lively personality Mr Baggett is sure to try and fix his interest with you. You outshine every other young lady here tonight.'

She had thrust her raddled old face nearer to Sophia and whispered, 'I knew his father, you know. A devil-may-care charmer and a great gambler to his dying day. He left a load of debts, but dear William has pulled it all round and the family estate has grown prosperous again. A very astute man. Very astute, my dear. I've heard he's wishing to marry and settle down.' She gave Sophia a meaningful look as she said this. Not quite a wink, Sophia thought, but almost as vulgar.

Sophia had smiled politely and ignored the old woman's nods and winks, excusing herself as soon as she could in order to go and join May Thornton and her sister.

Today, Sophia realized that William Baggett had come prepared to put himself out to be

159

pleasant. He seemed more than ready to charm and delight her with a little light flirtation, but was slightly distracted in his efforts by the fact that she kept giving anxious glances over her shoulder, in the direction of the drawing-room window. This was not maidenly modesty on Sophia's part, she was checking whether they were being observed by Lady Maunders and that her ladyship was still within earshot. She was conscious that Baggett knew it was bad form to stay longer than half an hour and was trying to press his suit a little more rapidly.

'Forgive me, Miss Winterton, but ever since we met at Mrs Thornton's, I have longed for an opportunity to be alone with you for a few precious moments. Dare I hope you are also enjoying it?'

She looked away from him in some confusion, but was saved by Polly, who appeared on the terrace carrying Sophia's parasol.

Polly, totally unschooled in the art of being a lady's maid, didn't just present the parasol and bob a curtsy, she beamed at both of them and said, 'Afternoon, madam, afternoon, sir. Wot you wanta sit out for with no shade, miss? Her ladyship's sent your parasol and her wants to see you usin' it, Miss Winterton.'

She unfurled it and handed it to Sophia with a smile and disappeared back into the house, leaving William Baggett looking suddenly thoughtful.

'Your maid is somewhat . . . er . . . unsophisticated, Miss Winterton.'

'Yes, she's a country girl. I met her on the journey from Norfolk,' Sophia said without thinking. Oh no! Why had she mentioned that? He was bound to put two and two together now.

William Baggett was watching her very readable face carefully and his shapeless, almost lipless mouth stretched into the semblance of a smile as he said gloatingly, 'Do you know, Miss Winterton, I have the most uncanny notion that you and I have met before, though where or why, I cannot tell. Most extraordinary.' He gave another of his humourless high-pitched titters.

In spite of the heat of the day, Sophia suddenly felt cold, but answered quickly, 'These feelings of *déjà vu* can be really quite unsettling, can they not, sir? But perhaps we have both been present at social gatherings in Norfolk, before we were introduced at Mrs Thornton's?'

'Just so,' he said, and looking into his face, she was relieved to see that he was satisfied with this and seemed genuinely to suspect nothing. A few moments later, he offered his arm and they walked sedately indoors, where he proceeded to take his leave of Lady Maunders.

As he bowed over her hand and said all that was proper, there was a sound of a disturbance in the hall and Sir Paul Maunders swept in, throwing his whip and driving gloves to one of the footmen. As William Baggett left the drawing-room and the two men came face to face, Mr Baggett's back stiffened, but he said politely, 'Good day, ladies. Your servant, Sir Paul.'

Sir Paul Maunders hated and distrusted William Baggett. He knew him to be an inveterate gambler and womanizer and his mouth tightened into a straight line at the sight of him, but he also bowed slightly and said, 'Good day, sir.'

Only Sophia seemed aware of the hatred underneath the polite exchange between the two men. She begged Lady Maunders to excuse her and fled to her room, hot and bothered and grateful to be alone at last. The fact that William Baggett would be one of the guests this evening cast a damper on her spirits, but then, she thought, there would be plenty of congenial company and she would just have to be vigilant and not allow him to have any more suspicions that they had met on the journey from Norfolk. That reminded her of Mrs Dawkins and she summoned

Polly immediately.

'It is high time you wrote to your parents, Polly,' she said in response to the maid's questioning look. 'But first, my dear, you must decide whether you wish to remain in my employ and live in London, or whether you wish to return to your life at the White Lion. Either way, you must have your parents' agreement in this. Are you happy to remain as a lady's maid, Polly?'

'Ooh yes, Miss Winterton, ma'am. I'm very happy,' Polly said.

'And you're not homesick?'

'No . . . that is, I should like to see Ma and Pa for Christmas, when the church is decorated up and Parson comes round, Miss.'

'I shall make sure you get your wish, Polly,' Sophia promised her. 'And now, you must write to your dear mama and let her know how you go on and whether she agrees to your staying with me.'

With much puffing and blowing and with a great deal of help from Sophia, Polly duly wrote her letter and young Philip took it away to be despatched, leaving Polly happy and contented to be allowed to remain with her beloved Miss Winterton. Both young women knew that this was a significant milestone in their relationship and the start of a very special friendship.

Left alone at last, Sophia lay on the day bed looking at one of Lady Maunders' magazines for ladies and hugged herself with the thought that tonight, her cousin David would be on hand if she needed him and that tomorrow, she would at last be reunited with dear Fitz.

8

Polly was as always, looking forward cheerfully to helping Sophia look her best for the evening ahead. She seemed content to live vicariously through her mistress and, as Sophia half listened to Polly's exclamations and prattle about the choice of slippers, fan and shawl to go with her dress for Lady Wright's party, she marvelled at the young girl's capacity for happiness. If that gift could be bottled without any reliance on laudanum or wine, she reflected, it would make its manufacturer a vast fortune. Polly's round pink face was serious with concentration as she laid out various articles on the bed for Sophia's approval. In recognition of Polly's unfailing support and devotion, Sophia deliberately made choices that she knew would please Polly as well as herself and she was not disappointed with the result. She could tell by the glow in the little maid's eyes as she looked at the shimmering blue evening dress from Madame Justine's, that it was Polly's favourite. She pretended to be undecided, so that choice of satin slippers and dainty fan was made by Polly herself, because she knew it would give the girl such pleasure. By the time everything was laid out in preparation for the evening to come, Polly was radiant with the knowledge that her mistress would be a credit to her and that she would be able to hold her head up in any servants' hall in London.

Lady Maunders was if anything, more enchanted at the prospect of the evening to come, than was Sophia herself and was positively excited on her young friend's behalf, that there was to be dancing.

In the carriage on their way to Lady Wright's, she said wistfully, 'As a more mature lady, I shall not be taking part myself, you understand. I shall sit with the chaperons and exchange some gossip. But in my youth, Sir John and I were enthusiastic dancers and many's the balls and soirées we've put on at Manvers House in the past. My life has changed sadly in the last few years, my dear. Losing Anthony, our elder son so suddenly, affected both our lives and my husband never really recovered from the body blow that fate had dealt us ... Dear Paul has been a great comfort and solace to me of course, but ... But enough of this gloomy talk,' she went on, giving herself a little shake. 'I am enjoying your company, my dear, and mean to make the most of you before you have to go to your godmother.'

'Yes. It will be tomorrow, ma'am.'

'Yes, indeed, tomorrow, Sophie, I hope this will not be the end of our friendship, though. I look forward to making the acquaintance of your dear Miss Fitzpatrick and seeing some more of you while you are in London. Tonight, we're sure to meet several members of the *ton* who will want to become further acquainted with you, my dear and we may even meet Mr Baggett again.'

She gave Sophia a mischievous glance, but Sophia's expression remained demure and she didn't respond. 'Sir Paul has said he *may* look in later, but I know that although he is a very accomplished dancer, he is not very keen and so I don't expect we shall see him this evening.'

Is there any aspect of social life in which Sir Paul Maunders is *not* very accomplished? Sophia thought rebelliously, but then in view of Lady Maunders' obvious pride in her only remaining son, she dismissed the thought and concentrated on looking forward to the evening ahead. There was a whole queue of carriages by the time they arrived at the home of Lord and Lady Wright and when, eventually, they reached their host and hostess, it was almost time for dinner. Miss Cecilia Wright stood with her aunt and uncle waiting to receive the guests and greeted Lady Maunders and Sophia very prettily, assuring them, in reply to their questions, that she was fully recovered from her indisposition and anticipating the evening ahead with the utmost pleasure. She was a tiny little girl with masses of brown hair and huge dark-blue eyes. Her small slender feet in white satin slippers, peeped from under her fashionable gown like little white mice and her whole appearance suggested the delicate fragility of a dainty flower. She looked as though she might blow away on a summer breeze.

What a pretty young lady, Sophia thought. She looks for all the world like a fairy in a child's story book. A flower fairy, she thought. A velvety pansy, in fact. Every aspect of Cecilia's appearance echoed this impression, even her large pansy-coloured velvet eyes, which looked with such serious innocence at every guest presented to her, and her slender white neck, which was like a stalk supporting her flower-like face and clouds of soft dark hair.

The huge dining-room was set for twenty dinner guests and for the time being, Lady Maunders and Sophia were separated. Sophia was pleased that she was seated opposite to Elizabeth Thornton and had Thomas Thornton on one side and Mr Richard Andrews on the other side of her.

Mr Andrews was as attractive as she remembered him and after retaining her hand in a warm clasp said, 'Miss Winterton, how pleasant to meet you again and there is to be dancing later, is there not? I trust you will stand up with me for one or two dances?'

Sophia smiled at him. How charming he was and how handsome. She answered immediately, 'That sounds very pleasant, sir. I shall look forward to it.'

Across the table, she noticed Miss May Thornton staring at her, rather seriously and she nodded and smiled. Thomas Thornton could not but overhear Richard Andrews' request and was quick to put in his own bid for Sophia's attention.

'Lady Wright has planned a very informal dance, Miss Winterton, and Miss Wright has told me that there will be no dance cards, so may I humbly sue on my own account and beg the pleasure of a waltz with you?'

She was amused to notice the schoolboy look of triumph that he darted at Richard Andrews, but she was careful not to show it.

Instead, she gave him her kindest smile and said, 'Of course, Mr Thornton, but dare I suggest it? You must enjoy yourself. There seem to be so many delightful young ladies here that you are going to be completely spoiled for choice and I'm sure that Miss Wright will not lack for partners this evening.'

Sophia looked in the direction of Miss Cecilia Wright who, as guest of honour, was sitting between her aunt and uncle and was gratified that the young man followed the direction of her gaze and that he seemed to notice Miss Wright for the first time. Sophia herself took a quick covert glance around the dinner-table. The soup was being served and various footmen stood in the way of a comprehensive observation of the room, but she could see no sign of William Baggett. Immediately, she relaxed and turned her attention once more to young Mr Thomas Thornton, who was gazing at her with almost puppy-like devotion, waiting for her to notice him again.

He was just as attracted to her as at their first meeting and as ingenuous as before. Sophia realized she would have to deal with him carefully and let him down very gently. Calf love could be just as painful as more mature emotion, she thought bitterly, remembering Sir Paul Maunders' embrace and her shameless desire for him to kiss her. Thomas was speaking now and she made an effort to concentrate.

'I know you will not lack for partners either, this evening, Miss Winterton, but if I have your promise of a waltz, I dare ask for no greater honour.'

She smiled again and said, 'You have my solemn promise, Mr Thornton.' He subsided immediately as one of the footmen stood over him to serve the soup. She smiled to herself as she thought of the young man's efforts to bring her delicacies of food at his mama's dinner party and she nodded graciously to signal to the servant that she would partake of the cream of asparagus. It was then she noticed that Miss Cecilia Wright was gazing in Thomas Thornton's direction with definite interest and admiration in her big pansy-blue eyes and this gave Sophia an idea.

Glancing across at Elizabeth Thornton, she noticed that she and her twin were both seated next to pleasant-looking young men who were naturally unknown to her. The twins both seemed to be very interested in Sophia's polite conversations with Mr Andrews and also in Sophia's cousin David who was talking animatedly to Elizabeth, but as the meal progressed and her wine glass was charged by the young footman, Sophia didn't notice any other details in the pleasure of the meal.

Some of the young ladies present had been presented, but most of them would not be having a come out until the spring. Almost all of them were dressed in the *de rigueur* white dresses of debutantes. No wonder she stood out in Madame Justine's modish creation, she thought. It was silver-blue gauze over an underdress of slipper satin of so pale a blue that the whole effect on her slender straight figure, was of a shaft of moonlight. To do her Aunt Harriet justice, that lady had presented Sophia with her dead mama's jewels as soon as Sophia was eighteen and her Uncle Charles had allowed her to have one very dainty set of blue topaz earrings and a delicate matching pendant, reset, very unusually, in white gold. In spite of her natural preoccupation with the delicious food, all through the dinner, she was aware of various pairs of eyes on her and knew that her unusual and delicate ensemble was much admired. Both the young men sitting near her complimented her on her appearance and it wasn't only the wine which tinged her cheeks with pink and she wished with all her heart that Sir Paul Maunders could be present to add to general approbation. She was also conscious of how often Miss Wright's eyes strayed towards Mr Thomas Thornton, which was natural, she supposed. After all, he was the most good-looking man in the room, his classical features and blond hair giving him the appearance of a mythical Greek god and his smile so engaging, it was guaranteed to melt any young woman's heart.

There was a pause after the dessert and then Lord Wright himself stood up and tapped on his wine glass with a teaspoon to call the company to order.

'Ladies and gentlemen, we are gathered to celebrate the coming out of my dear niece, Miss Cecilia Wright and to wish her the most successful coming out year ever. She is truly our pride and joy, the brightest and best of contemporary young womanhood and Lady Wright and I wish her every happiness as she takes the formidable step of entering into Society, with all its stringent rules and conventions. I am sure she'll be a great triumph. A toast then, to my dear niece, Miss Cecilia Wright,' he said and raised his glass. Everyone responded appropriately and almost immediately, the dancing was announced.

The ballroom proved to be a sad crush, with almost 200 guests and the huge chandeliers adding to the oppressive heat of the summer night. But it was a very happy, informal affair, with young people of both sexes trying out their social wings and enjoying practising both their dance steps and the art of flirtation, with a background of live music. At twenty-four, Sophia was very conscious that she was far more mature than most of the young ladies present, but Lady Wright had wisely included on her guest list several unattached males who were of an age to be seriously looking for a suitable bride.

Her cousin David came over to her to pay his respects. He had not so far had any conversation with her, apart from a smile and a mimed, 'Good evening, Coz,' from across the room. She couldn't help noticing that after the preliminary greetings and compliments, while they were chatting, his eyes constantly strayed towards Elizabeth Thornton, who was never short of a dancing partner and even when she was sitting out a dance, was surrounded by young men.

Even Sir Paul Maunders put in an appearance at 9.30 and from the point of view of several ambitious mamas this set the seal on the success of the evening. Later, Sir Paul sauntered over to Sophia and she could see in his eyes, unqualified admiration. He looked her over critically and surprised her by drawling, 'If ever an admirer of yours considered lavishing jewels on you, Miss Winterton, you must always insist he chooses a set of blue topaz to bring out the colour of your eyes. They are a quite remarkable colour, you know. More than one single colour in fact. They change with your mood.'

'Thank you, sir,' she said gravely. 'If, and it is a big 'if', I should ever manage to acquire an admirer, at my advanced time of life, and if such a one insisted on lavishing jewels on me, I shall bear your advice in mind.'

He knew she was flirting with him and was utterly charmed by her. For once, his smile was open and unaffected as he murmured softly, 'Pooh, Miss Winterton. You are not at your last prayers yet. I have every expectation that it will be many a long day before that situation arises.'

They smiled at each other, taking pleasure in each other's company, their quarrel quite forgotten, but were interrupted almost immediately. Richard Andrews, disengaging himself from a group of Miss Cecilia Wright's young friends bore down on her and said with mock chagrin, 'Now, how could you have escaped me, oh cruel fair one, when I was sure we were engaged for the first dance?'

'Dear me, Mr Andrews,' she returned and cast him a mischievous glance. 'I stand falsely accused. We were engaged for the first cotillion, if you recall and not the first dance of the evening. I'm glad you seem to be enjoying it though and trust that you don't find it too difficult to make a choice among all the lovely young damsels present, this evening.'

'On my honour, it could never be difficult to choose a partner on any occasion which is graced by your exquisite presence.'

He was laughing at himself for making such a flowery speech and Sophia couldn't help but laugh with him. 'I have only one criticism, though,' he continued in the same vein. 'All through dinner, I cherished the hope of standing up with you for the first dance, not merely the first cotillion, you understand. Now I find I was under a misapprehension and furthermore I find myself cut out by Maunders here. Makes a fellow feel like calling him out.'

Sir Paul Maunders frowned. After giving Mr Andrews a curt nod, he was so obviously uninterested in and unimpressed by their nonsense that there was a difficult silence.

Sophia said smilingly, 'Such a circumstance would indeed ruin Miss Wright's party, Mr Andrews. I trust you are going to resist your feelings of disappointment.'

'It isn't a question of feelings, Miss Winterton. Just that Maunders is such a devilish good shot.'

She laughed again and glanced at Sir Paul. He bowed his head slightly and gave a faintly sardonic smile before stepping back politely to allow another young gentleman to approach Miss Winterton and claim her for the waltz, while Richard Andrews went across to May Thornton to beg the pleasure of the next country dance.

Sir Paul strolled away and was next seen having a brief conversation with Lady Wright. He declined to join in any of the card groups that Lady Wright had organized and merely bowed to the lady and her husband without asking anyone to dance. David, she noticed, had no sooner managed to get into the crowd of young fellows surrounding Miss Elizabeth Thornton, than he was begging her humbly for a dance and pretending not to believe her when she protested that she had absolutely no dances to spare.

Sophia's waltz with Thomas Thornton was every bit as enjoyable as she'd hoped and he was a competent and graceful dancer, never hesitating or stumbling as he guided her firmly round the floor. She glanced across his arm towards Sir Paul Maunders who, she noticed, was leaning nonchalantly against a marble pillar, watching her carefully, but with a feigned look of boredom, which didn't deceive her at all. When next she looked at him, she saw him taking his leave of Lord and Lady Wright. By the last twirl of the dance, he'd disappeared altogether, leaving her disappointed and somewhat dejected. David, she noticed was teasing Elizabeth and

Elizabeth was giggling delightedly at him. She had to smile at the young girl's infectious laughter, but then she thought of Sir Paul Maunders and frowned. She was unaccountably infuriated by his behaviour in refusing to join in the party properly and for leaving so soon. It was some time before her anger abated a little and she was able to entertain the idea that perhaps this churlish behaviour on his part sprang from annoyance at her encouragement of Richard Andrews. But why shouldn't I take pleasure in the attentions of nice young men like Richard Andrews and Thomas Thornton? she thought crossly. What a dog-in-the-manger attitude on the part of Sir Paul Maunders. What a selfish arrogant bore, he was. No, not a bore. She had to be honest. He was never that and she amended her opinion hastily as she remembered some of the highlights of their journey from Norfolk. But why couldn't he be pleasant like that all the time? she raged to herself.

She was many times solicited to dance and smilingly stood up with most of those who asked her, not only with Richard Andrews and Thomas Thornton, but several young men who were strangers to her. Gradually, she began to forget her disappointment at Sir Paul's behaviour and for the first time in months, gave herself up to carefree youthful enjoyment.

She managed to have further conversation with David while she was resting on a little gilt chair and fanning herself in an effort to overcome the excessive heat. There was a vacant chair near to her and when she saw David, wandering by a little aimlessly, she beckoned smilingly to him to come and join her.

As soon as he was seated, Sophia began to quiz him gently about his obvious admiration for Elizabeth Thornton. 'You seem to be on friendly terms with Miss Thornton already, Coz,' she smiled. 'And she not even out yet.'

'Yes, she's a very friendly young lady, as well as beautiful,' he added. He spoke quite coolly, but Sophia could sense the feeling behind his apparently casual words.

'She and her twin are both exceptionally good-looking in their different ways,' she went on, fishing a little to test if David would confide in her. She was not disappointed.

'Yes, but to my mind, Elizabeth, Miss Thornton that is, is far more beautiful than her twin. I find her dark good looks very attractive, more so than golden-haired prettiness.'

Sophia thought privately that May's stunning blonde beauty deserved more merit than 'golden-haired prettiness' but she kept her thoughts to herself.

'She is certainly very lovely, David.'

'Yes, but she is not in any way missish, Sophia, she is young and high-spirited. She has a most lively sense of humour you know.'

Sophia smiled teasingly. 'Well, I didn't realize you liked her so extremely.'

David looked surprised and a little startled at this. 'Sophia, I never said that at all,' he protested.

'You didn't need to, dear Coz,' Sophia said, with a wicked smile. 'Your admiration stands out a mile. You seem quite a different person from what you were in Norfolk.'

'Oh yes?' he said recovering his poise and smiling a little. 'In what way, pray?'

'Well you seem calmer and indeed, happier in every way,' she said candidly.

'You mean I'm keeping my temper under stronger rein, now I'm no longer near that woman?' he laughed.

She knew he meant Aunt Harriet, whose constant attempts to interfere with the running of the estate had driven him to distraction.

'And I do so enjoy life in London, even though I love my country estate.' He spoke light-heartedly, smiling all the while but then, was suddenly serious. 'You are a witch, Sophia, to guess my secret. I've not been in

Miss Thornton's company very often, but I must confess to you, Coz, what you obviously already know. As soon as I set eyes on her, I received a leveller from which I'll never recover. Elizabeth Thornton is the girl for me and I shall move heaven and earth to make her mine.'

After so long a speech from the normally reserved David, they were both silent for a while and then Sophia leaned towards him and kissed his cheek. 'Well that was fairly definitive,' she said, and added in a whisper, 'I'm so pleased for you, David. You've been more than a cousin to me over the years. You've been my good friend and the big brother I never had. I hope all goes well for you and that Miss Thornton returns your regard.'

'But I have not yet asked Mr Thornton's permission to pay my addresses, Sophia. Elizabeth is very young, you know and her papa may insist that I should wait until after her come out. Then there is her twin of course. It would be unforgivable to separate them in their coming out year.'

Sophia looked across the room at the beautiful blonde twin who was delightedly enjoying a flirtatious conversation with the handsome Richard Andrews, and she laughed. 'I wouldn't be too concerned about

181

that, David,' she said. 'Deprived of her lovely sister, the younger Miss Thornton is not likely to decline and die.'

He followed her gaze and smiled in return. 'Quite so,' he said. 'And now, I can see yet another of your swains making steps purposefully this way to claim you for a dance.' And he excused himself and walked away.

Most of the young people at the party were known to each other and with so many youthful guests, it was a tribute to Lady Wright's organization and discipline that the dance didn't end up as just another lively romp. Some of the more mature, but still young men seemed to add a more stable influence to the wilder youngsters and the whole atmosphere of the evening was of carefree enjoyment with no hint of licence.

Then, William Baggett arrived. He was immediately shown up to the top of the room where Lady Maunders was sitting with the chaperons. Sophia couldn't help noticing him, moving up the side of the dance floor with his odd mincing walk and suddenly, a cloud descended on the evening. She continued to move among the guests, being polite to each new partner introduced to her and enjoying supper with Thomas Thornton and his sisters as though nothing had happened, but all the while, her brain was seething at the presence of William Baggett. She managed to avoid him for most of the time, by the simple expedient of being constantly in demand for various dances and she lingered in the supper-room with Thomas Thornton until David came to join them.

He and Elizabeth embarked on a light-hearted conversation about the difficulties of eating elegantly at parties when the crab patties were too soft, or the cake too crumbly and Sophia saw a different, more light-hearted aspect of her cousin. Elizabeth was in no way a giddy girl, but Sophia could see that her youthful high spirits and infectious humour entranced her cousin and as they egged each other on to further exaggerations about their experiences of difficult refreshments, Thomas needed no encouragement to join in his sister's hilarious anecdotes. The four of them had a very amusing half-hour, which only ended when David claimed Elizabeth for another dance and she and Thomas were left alone.

They had finished supper and once they'd left the supper-room, Baggett also seemed to disappear. She guessed he was in the card room and was pleased and relieved that he was not in the ballroom and soliciting her hand in a dance. Half an hour later, one of her enthusiastic young partners clumsily stood on the hem of her dress, pulling down part of the last row of the frill and leaving a four-inch tear. His face was so ludicrously aghast at this accident, that Sophia had to take pity on him and assure him that with a minor repair, the dress would be all right, although she knew Madame Justine would consider it ruined.

Amid repeated reassurances to the young man, she sped to the room that was set aside for the ladies' cloakroom. She found Polly ready as always with her needle case and in five minutes, the repair was completed without anyone except her partner, apparently even noticing she was gone . . .

This compounded her shock and surprise when as she emerged once more into the corridor, William Baggett was lurking outside. As soon as she appeared, he sprang forward, surprisingly nimbly for one so plump and caught her arm in a none-too-gentle grasp.

'Miss Winterton,' he said, in his strange cracked voice. 'I thought it was you as I left the card-room. What a pleasure to be alone with you at last. I have been unable to catch anything more than a glimpse of you as you've twirled with your many young partners.'

His face was very near her own and his

breath smelled unpleasantly heavy with all the port he'd drunk, but in spite of the alarmed and rapid beating of her heart, she pretended to be calm.

'Yes, indeed,' she said with a stiff smile. 'It is a most successful evening, is it not?'

She saw his expression of malicious delight as she twisted under his hand, ineffectually trying to get away from him and he gave his effeminate tittering laugh. 'That'll do, my dear,' he said. 'You won't get away from me until I've said what I want to say. I know your secrets, young lady, and my silence comes at a price.'

Still she refused to let him have the satisfaction of seeing her dismay. She kept her voice deliberately calm as she said, 'Indeed? I shall look forward to hearing all about it sometime. But not here, Mr Baggett. This is neither the time nor the place.'

She was frightened at the expression of cold fury on his face. She sensed that he found her pretence of unruffled calm infuriating and she felt that in some subtle way, she'd got the better of him.

'You damned jade,' he hissed. 'You won't get the better of me. I'll show you what fear really is.'

He tightened his grip unbearably and drew her even closer, so that it took all her self-control, not to cry out with the pain. At that moment, Sophia's cousin David came along the corridor with the lovely Elizabeth on his arm and for the same reason as Sophia. She too needed a slight repair to her gown, but David, attracted as he was, had insisted on escorting her.

He took in the situation between Sophia and Baggett at a glance. There was no need to say anything, he merely moved quite languidly towards Sophia's persecutor, one eyebrow raised, questioningly. The fat man shifted uneasily and released Sophia's arm. His confidence collapsed. Like most bullies, he was a coward when confronted by a stronger man. His high-pitched voice was almost inaudible as he said, 'Good evening, ladies. Your servant, Winterton.' He drew back into the shadows and sped down the corridor, the way he had come.

'That fellow bothering you, Coz?' David asked sharply.

'No, indeed, he was a little foxed, that is all. Good evening Miss Thornton. What a splendid party, is it not? I trust you are still enjoying yourself.'

Elizabeth replied shyly that she was and darted into the ladies' room. David escorted Sophia back to the dance and excused himself immediately to await upon Elizabeth's return.

She saw no more of William Baggett and, as she sat out the next dance, she had time to reflect on the situation. She seemed able to avoid him most of the time and although she recognized his veiled threats, she wasn't unduly worried about them. She was far more intrigued and annoyed by Sir Paul's behaviour. She'd been amenable to the idea of flirting with such a personable man, secure in the knowledge that she would soon be in the haven of dear Fitz's home. The horrid suspicion now struck her that a light flirtation was not what Sir Paul Maunders had in mind. She couldn't bring herself to believe that he'd fallen in love with her, but his anger could surely only have been aroused by jealousy. It was most confusing. She had the thought that she must disabuse his mind of the notion that her interest was fixed with any of her admirers, but her next thought was that she didn't care a button for Sir Paul Maunders' notions. She was her own person and having so narrowly escaped Lord Devenish, she was not going to risk parson's mouse trap again.

By the end of the party, all the guests were agreed that it had been a most pleasant evening and before he came to wish her goodnight, Sophia was not surprised to overhear David asking Mrs Thornton's permission to wait on her family and pay his respects. Thomas Thornton, meanwhile, had organized a riding party for the next day and several of the young people, including Miss Wright had promised to meet in the park at ten o'clock.

On the way home, Lady Maunders said, 'Well, dear Sophie, what a very pleasant party and what a capital idea of Lady Wright's to invite all those lovely girls and the young men to be able to get to know each other and practise how to go on before they are pitchforked into the Season. You looked so lovely, my dear, and you were a great success. I congratulate you.'

'Thank you, ma'am. That is praise indeed. I hope you weren't too bored, sitting with the chaperons.'

'Not at all, I was tremendously diverted,' Lady Maunders replied. 'I was intrigued at what made my son take himself off in such a rage, though.'

Sophia blushed in the dim light of the carriage. 'You think he was in a rage, ma'am? I just thought he was merely bored.'

'No, no, my dear. If I know Paul, he was angry with you over something.'

'I don't think we were at outs over anything,' Sophia said mildly.

'But he seemed to be in such a jealous rage

and you know he can have a very bitter and sarcastic tongue,' Lady Maunders said. 'He was my baby and of course, utterly spoilt and since he became the heir, so many caps have been set at him, so many scheming mamas and their daughters have tried to scramble for him, it's no wonder he's so soured with the idea of seeking a bride. I don't despair of him though, my dear. All he needs is marriage to a woman he is in love with.'

'I hadn't thought that love was noticeably lacking from his life,' Sophia said with some asperity.

'Good Lord, Sophie, I'm not talking of the odd opera dancer or any of his bits of muslin,' her ladyship said candidly. 'A man doesn't feel love for them, you know. My son isn't some sort of ramshackle sneaking rascal who would give a carte blanche to a respectable woman. It's my belief that he's ready for the real thing at last. I sincerely hope so, Sophie.'

9

As Polly folded Sophia's clothes and assembled various pairs of slippers and gloves, parasols and fans ready to be packed, she hummed a little tune to herself and Sophia herself was aware that she had that lightness of heart that she knew was entirely due to the prospect of seeing dear Fitz again.

Only Lady Maunders was in the breakfast parlour when she went downstairs, Sir Paul not having put in any appearance as yet. Philip was on hand as usual to serve both ladies and Sophia noticed that although his face was young and smooth, he tried to be impassive and footman-like and serve the two ladies with some dignity.

'I know you are promised for riding this morning, but when you are ready to go to your godmother, my carriage is arranged for whenever you want it, Sophie dear, and John Glover will drive you and Polly to Islington,' her ladyship said with a sigh. 'I trust you will give my felicitations to your dear Miss Fitzpatrick and beg her to join us for the opera this evening. Now that I've found you, I wouldn't like to lose touch with you, dear

Sophie, and I mean to make a friend of your godmother, so that we may meet frequently. Are you all ready? Has Polly done the packing?'

'Yes, indeed,' Sophia laughed. 'She has been up betimes and is as excited as I am myself.'

At precisely ten minutes to ten o'clock, Sophia was ready on the steps of Manvers House and Lady Maunders was waiting to see her off. John Glover brought round the horse for her and she had only just mounted it when Sir Paul Maunders sauntered by, dressed for riding.

'Good morning, Mama, Miss Winterton,' he said pleasantly, and extended his hand to Sophia. 'I trust you will have time to enjoy the ride before you have to leave us for your godmother's house, Miss Winterton, and that we shall see you again at the opera this evening.'

'Yes, thank you, sir,' was all that Sophia could manage and as soon as they reached Hyde Park, she made a point of going up to chat to Cecilia Wright.

This young lady was mounted on a small but spirited chestnut and she seemed to be handling it very well. She was looking quite enchanting in a blue velvet habit with a little feathered hat of the same colour, perched on her soft dark curls. It seemed as though

Thomas Thornton had somehow divined where Sophia was by some invisible force, because in less than two minutes he had joined them and although his admiring gaze was turned most frequently on Sophia, he also paid attention to Miss Wright and even complimented her on the handling of her horse.

Cecilia raised smiling deep-blue eyes set in a little heart-shaped face. She looked at him shyly, but frankly. 'Why, thank you, Mr Thornton. You are most kind,' she said in her gentle voice. 'Bessie and I have known each other for a long time and she is used to me, you see.'

Soon, all the party was assembled and began to advance along one of the main rides in twos and threes. Thomas had attached himself to Sophia and Miss Wright and Sophia noticed that Sir Paul was further back with her cousin David and the Thornton twins.

Suddenly, from nowhere, it seemed, a small dog ran in front of Miss Wright's horse, yapping and whining quite piteously and Bessie began to hesitate and sidle about with nervousness. Miss Wright reined her in and the three of them stopped to look at the little dog, which was no more than a puppy and which now was cowering on the grass, shaking with fright.

'Oh, how sweet,' Miss Wright exclaimed. 'Only see, he is but a puppy, Miss Winterton. Look how he is trembling. Something has frightened him.'

She prepared to dismount and Thomas Thornton hastily went to her aid, grasping her slender waist and swinging her slight girlish body down from the horse in his strong young arms. As soon as he released her, she went immediately to pick up the shivering scrap of golden-brown fur and cradled him protectively in her arms while she looked around for his mother or an owner.

None was forthcoming and Miss Wright's flower-like face, expressed total compassion and concern as she wailed, 'Oh dear, whatever is to be done? I cannot leave the poor little thing all alone.' Tears trembled in her voice and sparkled on the ends of her long eyelashes. She was overcome with concern for the little puppy and Sophia could see plainly that she was not going to relinquish him easily. She looked appealingly first at Sophia and then at Thomas Thornton. Her velvety eyes were drowned by her tears of pity, and yet her beauty was unimpaired. Her tears didn't turn her face blotchy or redden her dainty little nose in the slightest, Sophia thought enviously.

'Oh, what am I to do with him?' she asked again. 'I'm so sorry to be tiresome, but I cannot leave him here. Only look at his little silky ears. This one has a white patch. Oh, what a pretty little thing he is to be sure, he ought to be named Patch.'

The rest of the party had now caught up with them and indeed, Sir Paul and some of the young men had passed them and were trotting on, deliberately ignoring the diversion caused by Miss Wright's sentimental actions over the puppy.

Miss Wright looked appealingly at Sophia.

'Please don't cry, Miss Wright,' Sophia begged her. 'Why, he is so small, I could fit him into my reticule and you could ride with him before you.'

'You don't understand,' Miss Wright said mournfully. 'My aunt and uncle have been so good to me, so kind and have done so much, but they won't countenance a little dog, even one as sweet as Patch. Oh what can I do?'

Her eyes filled up again and Sophia realized that sweet though Miss Wright was, she hadn't an ounce of decision in her. She was content to look beseechingly at Mr Thornton and he responded promptly by striding to her side and gently taking hold of the little hand that was stroking Patch's head.

'Miss Wright, please do not upset yourself

further. I can take Patch with me and keep him until you are ready to return home.'

Miss Wright blushed with pleasure, her tears almost miraculously forgotten.

'Oh will you? Will you really, Mr Thornton? How good you are. How very kind.'

Mr Thornton coloured too and said in a low voice, 'You may trust me to take care of him. I promise you, Patch will be perfectly all right with me and you may see him whenever you want to, of course.'

She lifted her exquisite little face to his. 'Oh, thank you, thank you,' she breathed. 'I know he will feel so safe with you.'

Sophia broke in with, 'Here, Miss Wright, give Patch to me.' She put the tiny scrap into her reticule, leaving it open a little. 'I think we should catch up with the others now.' Miss Wright obediently allowed Mr Thornton to help her back on to her horse. It was obvious that his air of confidence impressed her and she seemed content to leave the details of Patch's fate in his hands. Sophia handed him the reticule with its precious occupant and they rode on to catch up with the rest of the group. Sophia managed only a few brief words from Sir Paul on the way back to Manvers House.

As soon as Sophia and Polly had settled themselves in the carriage, Sir Paul gave a nod to the coachman and they swept round the corner of the house and were off to Islington, leaving Lady Maunders waving a scrap of lace handkerchief until they were out of sight.

The house was identical to the one next door and was as small and contained as Miss Fitzpatrick herself. Like the outside, the inside was as neat as a pin. She was standing at her front door as soon as the coach drew up ready to give Sophia a joyful welcome, her small brown eyes darting everywhere, at the coach, at John Glover, at Polly and at Sophia herself. She ushered them indoors, explaining that she had received the message via her good neighbour, Mrs Soames, and her sister now being up and much improved, she had at last been able to return to her own home.

'And very thankful I am too, my dear Sophia,' she said. 'I was so sorry to have missed you, but delighted you found a haven with Lady Maunders. I'm not personally acquainted with that lady, but received a most civil note from her ladyship, requesting that I should join you at the opera.' Her small bird-like face flushed pink with pleasure. 'What an honour, my dear. She must be very fond of you.'

'And I've grown fond of her,' Sophia smiled. 'She asked if she might call me

Sophie and I agreed. I think it might well be my chosen name from now onwards.' Remembering her last conversation with Lady Maunders, she smiled again and pressed a coin into the driver's hand, thanking him very prettily for his help. He wished them 'good day' very civilly and departed. Polly was made known to Miss Fitzpatrick and immediately went upstairs to do the unpacking and then Sophia's god-mother gave way to her overwhelming curiosity about the sudden breaking of the engagement, the flight from Cottleton, her friendship with Lady Maunders ... until although Sophia was laughing, she was almost dizzy with the questions.

'How long have you been with Lady Maunders?'

'Since Tuesday.'

'And before that?'

'I was travelling from Cottleton with Sir Paul Maunders for three days.'

Miss Fitzpatrick's eyes opened wide. 'Three days, you say? But at least, you had your maid with you?'

'No, Fitz, darling. We met Polly at the White Lion in Bury St Edmunds, but she was with me for two out of the three days and she has proved a treasure.'

There was a significant pause, while this

sank in and then Miss Fitzpatrick said quietly, 'But you were travelling in Sir Paul Maunders' company for three days, my dear?'

'That is correct, ma'am. But Lady Maunders has given countenance to my actions, by offering me hospitality in her home. No one except for Sir Paul Maunders and myself knows the details of my journey to London.'

Fitz looked heavenwards and closed her small bright eyes for a moment 'The servants?' she asked faintly.

'Utterly reliable. Morgan and Polly would never breathe a word of any of it.'

'And Lord Devenish? Your aunt Harriet?'

'I have already written to them, in order to reassure them that I am safe with my respectable godmother and shall not be returning to Cottleton in the near future. Also, that there is no possibility of my renewing my engagement with James Devenish, even if he wanted it, which I doubt. They need not know anything else. It would only distress them.'

The sheer effrontery of this almost took Miss Fitzpatrick's breath away. She gave a gulp and said bravely, 'I expect that is for the best, Sophia . . . Sophie. But now we must make some preparations for this evening.'

The preparations were made to very good

effect. Polly, despite her lack of training, took pride in being a real lady's maid and knew exactly how her mistress liked to have her hair arranged. She had laid out Sophia's most beautiful gown, again chosen by Madame Justine. Madame knew full well the general opinion that ladies with Sophia's colouring should never wear pink, but she chose to ignore it. This was the palest most delicate dusky pink with a light scattering of embroidered rosebuds from one shoulder to the hem, a daring tribute to Sophia's exceptional beauty. Polly echoed the rosebuds in embroidered ribbons for her hair and on her satin slippers.

They were both delighted with the result and Sophia sent Polly to assist Miss Fitzpatrick so that they would both be ready when Lady Maunders' carriage arrived for them. Lady Maunders and her son had gone in Sir Paul's carriage and when Sophia and Miss Fitzpatrick arrived at the theatre, they were already in the box in the company of a male friend of Lady Maunders.

Sir Paul swung his quizzing glass idly and was aware of the hum of conversation from the crowd in the well of the theatre below him. From the quiet of the Maunders' box, he had a perfect view of the whole theatre, which was already filling up rapidly with fashionable members of the *ton*, the ladies in colourful dresses and the gentlemen in the more subdued formality of their evening clothes. Then he saw her and sat up a little straighter. The older woman must be her godmother. As the steward ushered the two ladies into the box, both men stood up and Paul introduced Mr Freddie Ashby and Sophia made her godmother known to the rest of the company. Lady Maunders had ensured that Sophia's place should be at her son's side, herself seated by Mr Ashby and with Miss Fitzpatrick on the other side of her.

'You are in fine bloom, this evening, Miss Winterton,' Sir Paul said softly, and he cast his dark eyes over her in the bold and openly appreciative way that Sophia remembered so well from their journeyings together.

She blushed and glanced quickly at Lady Maunders, wondering if that lady would disapprove of her son's attentions to her, but her unease was over in an instant because Lady Maunders leaned forward to smile. 'Paul is right, my dear. You should always wear that shade. It so becomes your colouring.'

Both Miss Fitzpatrick and Mr Ashby murmured agreement and they settled down agreeably in the privacy of the box and the conductor tapped for silence before the overture started.

Sophia and Miss Fitzpatrick were agreed that *The Marriage of Figaro* was the most entertaining comic opera comedy they had ever heard. In the first interval Sir Paul had organized champagne on ice and as Mr Ashby was putting himself out to be entertaining to the two older ladies, Sophia and Sir Paul had a chance for a little tête-à-tête of their own.

He seemed to have forgotten his ill temper and was sipping his champagne and amusing her by pretending to know the Italian words of Figaro's duet with Susanna.

'I learned a little Italian when I was on the Grand Tour, you see, Miss Winterton,' he said seriously, and at first, Sophia was completely taken in. It only gradually dawned on her as she sipped her own champagne and listened to him respectfully, that he was deliberately reciting words in Italian and making them sound like familiar English words, which made nonsense.

'Sir Paul,' she said indignantly, at last. 'You are bamming me.'

He gave a low laugh and Sophia realized that she had never heard him laugh out loud before. This was quite different from his usual sarcastic smile. He threw his head back and his whole face changed, his eyes crinkling and his mouth curving most attractively.

'How . . . how despicable you are, sir!'

He leaned nearer to her, still smiling so that Sophia could feel the warmth of his breath on her cheek and smell the faint fresh scent of his glossy hair, so close indeed, that Sophia had to resist the impulse to back off a little. Instead, she looked back at him fearlessly, not caring who saw the look they were exchanging, daring him to come even closer.

'Fustian, Miss Winterton,' he whispered. 'I am never despicable to beautiful and elegant women like you.' And he laughed again.

'It is to be hoped that you are speaking the truth, Sir Paul, otherwise I would have to give you the finest set down you have ever had in your life,' Sophia said severely.

In the light of the huge theatre candelabra, she could actually see her smile reflected in his deep dark eyes. 'That would be a very grave mistake, Miss Winterton,' he said with mock seriousness. 'Only recollect, ma'am, although I am never despicable to ladies of quality, I am known for my incivility. I should instantly give you back as good as I get and as you are always so well mannered and ladylike, you would come off the worse. You might then be obliged to call me out and even use your dreaded pistol to wing me.'

The smile that accompanied these words and the merest lightest touch as he stroked her gloved wrist, robbed them of all offence and Lady Maunders gave a sigh as she observed the look that passed between them.

But now, the crowd settled down once more and they were entertained with the diverse fates of Figaro and his love, Susanna, the tragic countess whose errant husband was set on seducing Susanna, and the love pangs of the page, Cherubino, who was in love with every woman he ever met. It was all highly enjoyable and Sophia felt more content than for a long time.

The problem came during the final interval. There had been considerable movement and milling about all evening and many of Lady Maunders' friends had visited the box to pay their respects. Both Sir Paul and Mr Ashby had excused themselves on separate occasions to go and greet their own acquaintances and Sophia had become aware of a dark-haired voluptuous young woman in a box opposite who seemed to be trying to claim Sir Paul's attention. She was very obvious, flashing smiles and comical little grimaces at him and then, positively beckoning him with her fan. When Sir Paul left the box again, she wondered who the lady was and if he were going to join her, but then, while Sir Paul was absent, they had an unexpected visitor in the person of William Baggett. Suddenly, he was in front of her, bowing over her hand and greeting Lady Maunders and Miss Fitzpatrick.

He sat for a few moments in the seat recently vacated by Sir Paul and looked at her so gravely that a little shudder of fear tickled the back of her neck. Her first instinct was to try to escape. Too late. Where was Sir Paul when she needed him? Then she scolded herself mentally for such faint-heartedness. She was in a public place, under the aegis of the formidable dowager Lady Maunders and with the protection of her respectable godmother. There was nothing to fear, she could take care of herself. With a supreme effort of will, Sophia pulled herself together. Baggett was now making himself pleasant to her ladyship and Sophia found herself introducing him to Miss Fitzpatrick. Seeing his sharp observant expression, Sophia had a sinking feeling and now knew for certain that he had recognized her at the inn and that she would be quite undone.

Bows were exchanged and he paused to indulge in a few pleasantries with Miss Fitzpatrick, but at that moment, a couple of

Lady Maunders' friends entered the box and Baggett turned his attention to Sophia. She tried to lean back a little, hoping he would engage in conversation with the others, but it was to no avail.

Miss Fitzpatrick, noticing what she thought was Sophia's unwonted shyness, wondered if this man was her goddaughter's real love. Surely not. His paunchy, dissipated looks and unattractive reedy voice made him an unlikely candidate for a young woman's affections, especially after she'd observed the looks that her dear Sophia had exchanged with the handsome Sir Paul Maunders.

Meanwhile, William Baggett was fulsome in his compliments to Sophia.

'Miss Winterton, you outshine everyone at the opera this evening.' Casually, he laid his arm across the back of her chair and gave her an insolent stare. 'I long to be alone with you. Before I leave here, this evening, I shall beg permission from your godmother to pay my addresses.'

Sophia was so startled at this that she shrank away from him instinctively and stammered, 'No . . . No, sir . . . '

He leaned over her, offensively, so that she was obliged to put up her fan to protect herself.

'Please, Mr Baggett, you have misunderstood my position. I do not wish . . . I have no inclination to — '

'Oh come, Miss Winterton. All young ladies who come to London for the season are looking for a husband. There is no need for any maidenly protest. We both know the truth.'

'The truth, sir? What can you mean?'

Her heart was pounding in her ears and there was a painful knot in her stomach as she looked round desperately, seeking Sir Paul.

He knows. He knows, she thought. He knows it was I whom he grappled with in that unseemly way in the passage way of the Falstaff Arms. He's known all along. What a complete little fool I was to think I could pretend it was not so.

'I mean, my dear, that it is not only young ladies who come to London to seek a marriage partner. I shall call on you in a couple of days.'

She knew he meant what he said. He frightened her. She wondered how he would use his knowledge. He was standing in front of her now, kissing her hand in farewell. 'Good night, Miss Winterton. Ladies,' he said, and was gone, leaving Sophia in a turmoil of agitation and fear.

The final act of *The Marriage of Figaro* was about to commence and Mr Ashby and Sir Paul entered through the door of the box to resume their seats. Sophia had been too distracted to notice whether in fact, Sir Paul had visited the dark lady's box. She composed her face into an expression of untroubled calm as Sir Paul took his place beside her and the curtain went up on the final act, where the count and countess are reconciled, Figaro gets married to his adorable Susanna and all ends happily. If Sir Paul thought she was overly quiet, he gave no sign, but showed Sophia and Miss Fitzpatrick to the carriage and handed them in. He lingered over her hand a little and said, 'Miss Winterton, Mama and I have planned another little riding party for Sunday. Should you care to join us?'

'Why yes, that would be very enjoyable. Yesterday, I managed to commission John Glover, her ladyship's coachman, to visit the sale of Lord Denman's cattle. He knows of a good-tempered little bay and will purchase it on my behalf. I shall have time to get to know my mount before your mama's riding party. John Glover is seeing to the stabling for me.'

'Good. But I could mount you on the same nice-natured horse that you had this morning, if you wish it,' he said quickly.

'I thank you, sir. I shall accept your offer if it should be necessary.'

'We shall meet at eleven,' he said, and then, so as not to lose his place in the busy exodus of vehicles leaving the theatre, he hurried back to his own carriage.

Morgan clicked at the horses and they were off.

Even Miss Fitzpatrick was too sleepy with champagne and too emotionally drained by the scenes of intrigue and romance in the opera, to talk very much and when they arrived back in Islington, Sophia was glad to be in the haven of her own room with only Polly to attend her, before she blew out her candle and sank wearily into bed.

The house felt eerily quiet once she'd settled back on her pillows. Her body was tired as she waited for sleep, but her mind raced desperately, going over the events of the evening, again and again. In the smallest hours, still awake, she thought of Sir Paul Maunders and was forced to acknowledge to herself how attractive she found him. He had only to look at her and she wanted him to kiss her. She was conscious of the rapport between them and the camaraderie they'd enjoyed on that tedious journey from Cottleton. She enjoyed again in her imagination, his smile, his frown, the warmth of his teasing this evening when he'd pretended to speak Italian. She was almost smiling to herself at the memory, except that the one ugly image which kept intruding on her reverie was that of William Baggett and it refused to go away. If he was intent on blackmail, she wondered what chance she would have to hold out against him. He was no callow youth in the throes of calf love like Thomas Thornton. From what Sir Paul had told her, he was a hardened adventurer and was both determined and dangerous. She turned restlessly in her bed, and it was dawn before sleep finally came to give her a few hours of blessed oblivion.

In the morning, all her delight in the opera and all the pleasure of anticipation at the prospect of the riding party, was destroyed by the dread thought of William Baggett's visit. All through breakfast, her heart thudded madly in her breast and she felt her spirits so cast down with anxiety at what was to come when he finally confronted her with the knowledge he had of her flight from Cottleton, that she was too unnerved to do anything except sit alone in Miss Fitzpatrick's small parlour, making a pretence at hemming some handkerchiefs. She found herself wondering what use he would make of both her flight and the fact that she had been in the company of Sir Paul Maunders. That he wanted her in spite of this, she had no doubt; after all, he was after any woman who could offer him pleasure and a decent fortune. He believed she had been Sir Paul's mistress, but she doubted if he cared about that. She was sure that he was fully aware of the fortune she was to inherit and that he would expect her to marry him in exchange for his silence. To her aunt Harriet, he would present as a decent gentleman from a respected old family, prepared to make an honest woman of her, after her disgraceful betrayal of Lord Devenish. She shuddered as she thought of his clutching hands and cloying lips when he'd grappled with her at the Sir John Falstaff Arms. Lost in thought, she was yet aware of the unmistakable sound of Miss Fitzpatrick's brass door knocker. Ten minutes later, Polly tapped on the door to say that Miss Fitzpatrick requested her presence in the drawing-room.

Bracing herself, she entered the room with as much dignity as she could, to find Miss Fitzpatrick pouring out sherry for Mr Baggett and looking quite pink-cheeked and flustered at so important a visitor to her modest home. Miss Fitzpatrick took her by the hand and drew her further into the room.

'Sophia, my dear, look who has honoured

us with a visit this morning,' she said brightly, 'I was just telling Mr Baggett how much we enjoyed the opera last night.'

Sophia curtsied and said, 'Good morning, sir.' Then she went to sit on one of Miss Fitzpatrick's high-backed chairs, deliberately not looking at him.

He'd stood up as she entered and was now lounging by the fireplace with the toe of one of his gleaming hessians resting on the empty grate, his portly belly stuck out, totally at his ease, a man of the world, well used to dominating his environment.

His voice was husky and cracked as he said suavely, 'I too enjoyed the performance, but of course, the highlight for me was the presence of the beautiful Miss Winterton.'

Sophia said nothing, but Miss Fitzpatrick jumped suddenly to her feet at this and said, 'Oh, Sophia, you and Mr Baggett must excuse me for a few moments. Polly has kindly offered to do some mending for me and I must take it to her . . . I must see her about it . . . I shall be back in an instant. Pray excuse me.'

She darted out of the room and Sophia was suddenly left alone with him. He was at her side in an instant. 'Miss Winterton. Sophie. I can't tell you how I have longed to be alone with you.'

She didn't answer but resolutely averted her gaze, praying for Miss Fitzpatrick to come back. Undeterred by her lack of encouragement, he strode over to her chair and sank down on one knee, taking her unwilling hand in his. Once more she felt the panic that had seized her when he'd tried to kiss her at the inn. She tried to remove her hand from his but he gripped it tightly and said confidently, 'Ever since our encounter on the er . . . journey to London, I have thought about you night and day. I am here to make you an offer and as I am a man of the world, Sophie, I need not tell you that your fall from grace does not affect my desire in the slightest.'

'Fall from grace?'

'Well, come, my dear. You cannot pretend the innocent with me. We both know what you were doing at the Sir John Falstaff Arms.'

'This is intolerable, sir. How dare you? Let go of my hand. I wish to ring for my maid.'

He squeezed her hand quite painfully now. 'Oh no, Sophie,' he said softly, his voice positively hoarse. 'You will hear me out. I am here to make you an offer and I shan't be denied.'

At this, Sophia allowed full rein to her pent-up anxiety and anger and rounded on him furiously.

'You must be mad. Why, I would never

marry such as you. You insulted me and assaulted my virtue at the inn and now you are brazen enough to propose marriage, as though this wipes the slate clean. Am I to be pleased and grateful for your insensitive declaration? Kindly unhand me. I tell you now, sir, I would never marry you, even if you were the last man on earth.'

She snatched her hand away from his and stood up, her eyes flashing the green fire of her angry temper. He stood more slowly and languidly brushed away an imaginary speck from his immaculate sleeve. 'You really are most attractive when you are angry, Sophie. Quite magnificent. I shall look forward to having the taming of you, once we are married.'

'That is not going to happen, sir. I have no need to ally myself to a . . . a . . . rogue and blackguard like yourself.'

He seized both her hands now and pulled her roughly towards him, thrusting his face into hers. 'I may be all of those things, madam, but by marrying you, I would be favouring you with my name and giving you some respectability after your little adventure as Maunders' common trollop.'

'How dare you? Sir Paul escorted me to London when I missed the stagecoach, that is all. Nothing untoward occurred. I stayed with Lady Maunders until my godmother returned — '

'Fustian,' he snarled. 'You are asking me to believe that you were with a man like Sir Paul Maunders for three days and nights and nothing occurred? Pigs could fly, madam. I have only to start the merest whisper of what you've done and you'll be ruined. The decision is yours, Sophia. I shall await your answer.'

He reached for the bell pull and when Polly appeared, said calmly, 'Your mistress has the headache and would like to lie down.'

Then, he set off purposefully for 19 Sutton Street and an interview with Marie Baronne.

10

Baggett was whistling soundlessly to himself as Marie's maid opened the door. 'Your mistress is expecting me,' he said in a lordly manner. 'We made the arrangement last evening at the opera. Kindly present her with my card.'

She gave her usual bobbing curtsy and sped off to inform Marie of his arrival. It wasn't necessary. Baggett knew that Marie was fully aware of who and when she had a gentleman visitor. Indeed all her visitors were gentlemen. No lady would dream of calling on Marie Baronne, even ladies of easy virtue like herself. He removed his gloves impatiently and held them in his clenched hand, but the maid reappeared almost immediately and ushered him into Marie's small but elegant drawing-room.

She was seated in a high-backed armchair with her back to the window and very civilly invited him to be seated. The maid placed wine and small ratafia biscuits on the table nearest to the visitor and made herself scarce. Marie looked at him with a calm enquiring expression. He wasn't an attractive man, but she'd been in her chosen profession for long enough to know that you never judged a book by its cover, where wealthy gentlemen were concerned.

Baggett came straight to the point. 'Good morning, Miss Baronne,' he breathed in his sibilant voice. 'Thank you for agreeing to this meeting. As I told you, I think I have information which could be to your advantage. I had only a little time to arrange it with you last night because I had other urgent business.'

She nodded graciously, acknowledging the emphasis that gentlemen must give to any business, urgent or otherwise, and composed her features into an expression of understanding. Baggett kept his eyes on her face as he said, 'I trust you have had time to reflect on last night's little scene in Sir Paul Maunders' box. The beautiful young lady who was with him is the one he has chosen to wed, so you must act quickly if you wish to keep him.'

For a moment, Marie dropped her mask of polite enquiry. She scowled and said quickly, 'How do you know? Who is she?'

'She is Sophia Winterton, an heiress as well as a beauty. She has broken off her engagement to Devenish and she and Maunders have already journeyed from Norfolk together, without the benefit of a

216

proper chaperon. Now that she is about to be established in London Society, he will have every opportunity to court her. You, my dear, will be nowhere.'

His voice was as cold and sibilant as the north wind. Even while she was hating him for the gloating way he delivered his information, yet Marie was aware that she was powerless to influence Sir Paul Maunders' actions without the aid of a man like Baggett.

'Wha . . . what must I do?' she asked him, suddenly shaking at the thought of the chasm which would open up in her life if she could not entice Maunders back to herself. She knew that Devenish had gone abroad and she wouldn't even have the comfort of his protection.

Baggett now began to touch her and stroke her hand in a most offensive and lascivious manner and whispered, 'Just be guided by me, ma'am, and everything will come right for you. First, you must engineer a meeting with Miss Sophia Winterton, who at present resides with her former governess in Islington. I know you are capable of presenting a picture of a respectable young woman who has a close and long-standing friendship with Sir Paul Maunders. Dress discreetly, conduct yourself with dignity and be as convincing as you can.'

She nodded mutely and William Baggett now began to sketch out his plan in detail. He'd overheard Miss Fitzpatrick telling Lady Maunders that dear Sophia wished to go early to the lending library and so would have to go with her maid because, she, Emily Fitzpatrick never ventured out until the afternoon. He told Marie when and where she would bump into Miss Winterton, precisely what she should wear and what she should say. All the while he was taking more and more liberties with her, fondling her body and telling her how he would reward her when she had destroyed her rival. She was mesmerized by his hissing monotonous whispers and could only nod and agree to everything he said, while submitting to his vile caresses. Baggett then hastened off to call upon Harriet Winterton at her West London hotel and to inform her of the latest developments.

Later that day, Sophia herself had a visit from Aunt Harriet, who arrived with the greatest pomp and circumstance in a fine carriage, accompanied by her maid and a footman, and with her groom driving.

There was a peremptory *rat-a-tat-tat* on Miss Fitzpatrick's brass door-knocker and Aunt Harriet swept in and demanded to see

Sophia at once, much to Miss Fitzpatrick's consternation. She was obviously put out and at first tried to avoid a confrontation between Harriet Winterton and her goddaughter. Harriet Winterton wasted no time in preamble. She and Miss Fitzpatrick had met before while Sophia's godmother still lived at Cottleton Hall and she had always treated Fitz in an unpleasantly patronizing way. She was now coldly furious at Sophia's actions and not prepared to either spare any feelings, nor yet hold back her anger at the humiliation her niece's flight had caused her.

'My errand will not take long,' she hissed. 'Kindly summon Sophia at once.'

Emma Fitzpatrick was less than five feet tall and her body was slim as well as petite. Her feet were the tiny feet of a child. Being forced to confront a heavyweight like Harriet Winterton, did not mean any lessening of Miss Fitz's tireless strength or indomitable spirit. She'd been born and brought up in London and was a proverbial Cockney sparrow, bright of eye and sometimes, surprisingly sharp of tongue. She squared up to Sophia's aunt as a veritable David opposing Goliath and denied Harriet from seeing her beloved goddaughter, but eventually even Fitz was defeated in such an unequal contest and she was obliged to send

Polly to request that Sophia should present herself in the drawing-room.

Sophia entered the room quietly and said politely, 'Good day, Aunt Harriet. This is an unexpected pleasure.'

She was determined to stay calm in spite of observing unexpected spots of colour in Aunt Harriet's normally sallow cheeks. As soon as Sophia appeared, she stepped towards her in a very confrontational manner.

'Unexpected I dare say,' she sneered, 'but not unsurprising, I venture to think.' Her voice was full of hatred and Sophia knew Harriet was determined to destroy her by whatever means she could.

Accordingly she answered her with determined politeness. 'No, ma'am, I expect you received my letter explaining that I am now living with my godmother and shall not be returning to Cottleton until later this year when I come into my inheritance.'

'Oh yes, I am sure you wish to keep the whole sorry business of your flight to London with Sir Paul Maunders a secret. And tell me, how much longer do you think you can avoid tittletattle from the censorious world of the *ton*? Once your actions have become common knowledge, the vast majority of the polite world will turn their backs on you. Whatever your inheritance, you will be shunned and totally ostracized. Is that what you want, you little whore?'

Sophia had always suspected that hysteria was only just beneath the surface of Harriet Winterton's twisted personality and now it was confirmed. Aunt Harriet was beside herself. Two spots of saliva appeared at the corners of her mouth and her eyes positively bulged with fury at the humiliation her niece's flight had caused her. She had never been a kind or loving aunt, but now, she'd dropped all pretence of family affection or even common politeness and glared at Sophia as though she could kill her.

'What was your object, Sophia,' she demanded, 'in absconding like that from the wedding that was planned for you? You must know that Lord Devenish has now withdrawn his suit, in view of your disgraceful behaviour, miss. What do you think your reputation is now? I'll tell you,' she went on, as neither Sophia or Miss Fitzpatrick spoke. 'It is that of a common jilt. You will no longer be accepted even in Norfolk society after this, let alone London. I tell you now, Sophia Winterton, that I wash my hands of you completely.'

'And that is a consummation devoutly to be wished,' Sophia muttered to herself, rebelliously.

'Your pardon, miss. I think that is a remark

that you will regret. You will never find an eligible man if you continue with these independent airs. London Society will also be closed to you however wealthy and beautiful you are. Your reputation is ruined. I have been in touch with William Baggett. Your only salvation is to accept Mr Baggett's offer. At least he is prepared to overlook your disgraceful conduct and offer you the protection of his name.'

'Never!' Sophia said darkly. 'You are hysterical, madam.'

Miss Fitzpatrick went pale and said, 'Hear your aunt out, Sophia, I beg you.'

'You will bitterly regret that remark, Sophia. How dare you? It is you who are unreasonable and quite mad. What can you possibly have against Mr Baggett? He is prepared to marry you quietly, by special licence. I never hoped for such a generous offer, given that Lord Devenish is understandably adamant that the betrothal is now over, doomed irrevocably by your foolhardy and irresponsible actions; indeed he has gone abroad, still grieving deeply.'

She said these last words in such a smugly sepulchral voice that Miss Fitzpatrick raised an anxious hand to her forehead and looked about to swoon. With a robustness that she didn't really feel, Sophia said, 'Rubbish! You are mad! He was fully aware before I quitted Cottleton, that our betrothal wouldn't answer. We have both had a fortunate escape. As for Baggett, he is a blackguard and a molester of innocent women. He is ugly, middle-aged and dissipated. I want none of him.'

Without admitting defeat, Aunt Harriet turned to flounce out, her face tight with fury. 'I'm warning you, Sophia. You will rue the day if you stupidly refuse Mr Baggett's generous offer. I promise you that I personally will cause you to regret it. Good day, Miss Fitzpatrick. Good day, Sophia.'

She swept out of the house and into her carriage, leaving Sophia alone with her godmother.

'Perhaps you should consider your aunt's advice, my dear.' Miss Fitzpatrick spoke quietly and Sophia knew that the concern on her godmother's face was sincere and very loving. She must be nearing sixty by now, Sophia reckoned, but she still seemed to have boundless energy and wiry strength. She was infinitely sad that now the planned marriage with Devenish was irrevocably over, her dear Fitz wouldn't be able to help her with any children from their union. Even so, she rejected any idea of an alliance with William Baggett.

'I could never consider her advice nor Mr Baggett's offer, dear Fitz,' she said, appearing more lighthearted than she felt. 'Let us consider tomorrow's riding party instead.'

The next day brought only a note from William Baggett, offering his compliments and suggesting that he should call in a couple of days when she would have had time to consider his proposal. Sophia pushed it into one of the drawers of a small bureau in her bedroom and defiantly requested Polly to put out a green riding habit, which had very smart military-style epaulettes at the shoulders and its own little shako style hat in a darker green. It was a new acquisition and she knew it suited her down to the ground. Both Polly and Miss Fitzpatrick were filled with admiration at such a dashing ensemble and both stood rooted to the spot, gazing at the perfection of her appearance and fussing round her like two mother hens, Polly tweaking the skirt to ease out an imaginary crease and Miss Fitzpatrick saying anxiously, 'Have you your riding gloves, my dear? Oh, here is your whip. Are your boots quite comfortable? Oh, you will be careful, won't you? It wouldn't do for you to take a tumble. Oh, was that the front door, Polly?' She clucked all the way down the stairs.

It was indeed the door. Sir Paul Maunders

was seated on a powerful-looking stallion and Morgan was leading Sophia's own pretty little bay. As she gazed up at him, Sophia wondered irritably why he had to be mounted on such a huge beast of a horse. Because of his military training, she supposed, and so that he could view the world from a commanding height. Both men greeted her pleasantly, then Sophia picked up the skirts of her habit and called her farewells over her shoulder. Sir Paul held her horse and Morgan cupped his hands to help her mount. They gave goodbye salutes to Miss Fitzpatrick and Polly, wheeled the horses and were off, Sir Paul staying solicitously at the side of Sophia and Morgan riding respectfully behind them.

He gave her a sideways glance and said, 'You sit the horse well, Sophie, and if I may say so, she seems perfectly at ease with you. You are in fine fettle yourself today.'

It was the first time since their journey from Cottleton that he had used the shortened form of her name and there was a silence as she registered this and considered telling him that it was unsuitable for him to address her by the pet name used by his mama. She let the thought go immediately, knowing he would take no notice. In any case, she liked the sound of it, coming from his shapely lips and the slight impropriety of

225

it gave her a little thrill of pleasure.

'She's named Moonlight,' she said. 'I don't know why, but as she's so soft and gentle like the moon, I think it suits her.'

She risked a sideways glance at him and found that he was still looking at her, holding her eyes with his. 'Not just in fine fettle,' he continued, his voice low so that Morgan couldn't hear, 'but so ravishingly beautiful, that I want to kiss you, urgently! Now! Immediately!'

Her face flamed. She was completely nonplussed. 'Well, y — you can't. It's impossible,' she said.

'I know it's not possible, here and now,' he said mildly.

'Not ever, sir.'

'If I were a betting man, I might be tempted to wager a considerable sum on the chance that it is both possible and probable. What is more, I want to hold you close and tell you that you are an absolute darling,' he said in a matter-of-fact voice, so that no one who was unable to hear what was being said, would have the slightest idea of the impropriety of his remarks.

She reminded herself of some of the tales that were told about him when she was a girl. No doubt they were true, she told herself. She must resist all his blandishments or attempts at flirtation or it would only end in tears. She spotted the rest of the party at the gates of the park and went before him to meet them, saying over her shoulder, 'Sir, you are incorrigible,' but he could see that she was laughing.

Thomas Thornton and his twin sisters, Lady Wright's niece, Cecilia, and David Winterton, made up the rest of the party and as soon as Sir Paul had reined in his horse and shown his admission ticket, they moved in a friendly group through the gates and trotted companionably into the park. They were joined by Richard Andrews and soon regrouped, some of the young people pairing off and spreading out across the firm green turf. Sir Paul stayed at her side and Thomas Thornton was also close by. Morgan was bringing up the rear, with panniers full of the picnic materials.

No one spoke, but concentrated on guiding the horses towards one of the green and inviting wider rides. Sophia handled the gentle little mare with ease, indeed almost mechanically. The thought of William Baggett's intended visit, still weighed on her mind. She knew she would refuse him. The man repelled her, but she had little idea of what his reaction would be and whether her aunt Harriet was just making hysterical empty threats when she'd said that she would make Sophia sorry.

She drew a deep rather shaky breath, determined to try and forget William Baggett and his unwelcome proposal and think of something more pleasant. Sir Paul Maunders for instance. Today, he seemed to be determined to pay her compliments and make himself pleasant. Why did he seem so changeable? she wondered. He could be so delightfully playful, such wonderful company, so personable and . . . yes . . . handsome and desirable. His other side was so immoderately irritable and impatient. He was gentle and yet so domineering. A creature of contrasts and yet . . . She sighed again. And yet she found him so attractive. Sophia had never been in love and she wondered fleetingly if this was how love was. The desire to be in his company and the feeling of hurt when he seemed insensitive to her own emotions and needs, when she'd wanted his kiss for instance.

Determinedly, she shook herself out of her pensive mood and began to enjoy the ride. There were other riders in the park and even a group of walkers, proceeding sedately and keeping to the shade of the trees. In the distance, she could see a very stylish phaeton bowling along one of the carriageways which criss-crossed the park. Everything was so peaceful, her companions were so pleasant and delightful that she gradually forgot the stresses of the last few days and began at last to feel more relaxed and secure. Thomas Thornton came up on her other side and began to engage her in conversation. For ten minutes or so, Sophia walked the docile little bay around the park, listening politely to Thomas Thornton's small talk, smiling sometimes and occasionally answering him and hardly aware of the silent Sir Paul at her other side. She was so intent on being kind to the poor besotted boy, that when Sir Paul spoke, she jumped slightly and jerked the reins on her mount who immediately jibbed in protest. They were now very close to Miss Cecilia Wright.

'Your mare's restless,' Sir Paul said in a low voice. 'Let's canter for a bit, give her a chance to let off steam.' He immediately spurred his stallion into action and set off across the park with Sophia following closely behind. Surprised at being left alone so suddenly with Miss Wright, Thomas Thornton could do nothing but transfer his attention to Cecilia, who was flatteringly interested in what he was saying, raising her limpid eyes to his and attending to his every word in a very gratifying way.

Now for instance, when she turned her pretty little face towards him and said in her sweet voice, 'Dear Mr Thornton, I must tell you again how pleased and grateful I am that you've been so kind to my little dog. I should never cease to repine, if I hadn't been able to rescue him and I could never have managed it without you . . . '

The word 'you', was breathed rather than said and the pretty little mouth formed such a sweetly seductive shape as she said it that Thomas had a sudden impulse to kiss it. He was surprised at the thought because, ever since he'd met her, he'd been in love with Miss Winterton . . . hadn't he?

Now he was beginning to have doubts and to own the truth, Miss Winterton seemed to be almost impervious to his ardour. She was older than he and was such a strong person, always so pleasant and calm. Sometimes he had the feeling that she was so much above him, so much more mature, whereas Cecilia, Miss Wright, was so young and defenceless. She needed someone to look after her. Her delicate appearance and lack of decisiveness, above all, her trust in him, had made a strong appeal to his chivalrous instincts. From the moment he'd been able to dispel her tears over Patch as if by magic, he'd felt so strong and yes, protective of her.

His sisters never made him feel like this. They laughed at him and teased him and would never think of turning to him for advice over a stray puppy. Miss Wright was different. She was so gentle and kind-hearted. He was surprised that Miss Winterton had dashed off like that, but he was pleased to be out riding with Miss Wright and suddenly, he was content to chat about Patch for as long as she wished.

Sophia meanwhile was now a hundred yards or so from the others and Sir Paul reined in his horse under a group of trees. He immediately jumped down and looped his reins over one of the lower branches of a tree and stood looking up at her. 'Morgan is in a high sweat, carrying the rugs and things,' he said. 'Shall we walk and find a good spot for the picnic?'

He took her firmly by the waist and lifted her down, setting her gently on her feet, the only problem being that once he had her in his hands it was no longer a matter of helping her from her horse, he wanted to hold her close in his arms, to kiss her. Why was she so devilishly changeable, he wondered? If he asked her to marry him, would she let him down flat as she had Devenish? Damn. He was forced to confess to himself that he was deeply, passionately in love with Sophia

Winterton, the most difficult and self-willed woman he had ever met in the whole of his life. And the most beautiful, a still small voice inside his head, added. He was as confused as any young stripling in the throes of a first love affair, wanting to reveal his feelings and yet not wanting to face either her rejection or mockery.

Sophia was acutely conscious of the warmth of his hands at her waist and put her own hands on his. She was aware that Sir Paul Maunders was determined to kiss her and instinctively moved her hands upwards, to clasp him round his neck and tangle her fingers in the glossy hair of his nape. She thought briefly that she most certainly ought to stop this before it went any further, but then his warm persuasive mouth met hers and moved gently over her soft parted lips. Sophia was, all of a sudden, a victim of rapidly increasing and overwhelming need which swiftly overcame any scruples or protestations which she might entertain, and gained complete mastery over both her mind and body. She hadn't the least wish to break away from his demanding mouth. Her whole being was filled with such a glowing joyful languor that she was utterly lost to all sense of propriety or correct behaviour and kissed him back with a passion which matched his own.

They stood there, locked in each other's arms for several seconds until brought back to earth by Morgan's tactful cough. Sophia emerged from her first real experience of masculine passion, dazed and somewhat breathless and moved away from him, confused and shaken. She glanced sideways and saw in the shadow of one of the trees, the dark-haired lady who had been at the opera, but she had no time to find out who or what she was.

'Beggin' pardon, Sir Paul, madam,' Morgan said respectfully. 'Where was you intending for me to put down the picnic things, sir?'

Without speaking, Sir Paul led him round to the other side of the spreading oak tree, where the ground sloped a little. 'Here, I think,' he said impassively, and he and Sophia waited in a constrained silence while Morgan unfastened the panniers and emptied rugs and hampers on to the grass. He spread out the rugs and the young footman took out glasses, china, napkins and cutlery as the rest of the party joined them, at first everyone dismounting while Morgan tethered the ladies' horses and then standing with glasses of wine, chatting cheerfully. When she glanced towards the tree again, the young woman had gone. Sophia was even more disconcerted when Sir Paul drew her unobtrusively to the other side of the tree. He faced her, smiling sardonically and said, 'Well, Sophie. I never thought to see poor old Morgan in the role of duenna. He will be more than miffed to have been cast as a young lady's chaperon.'

'I am mortified that he had to take on any such duty,' she said shamefaced. 'To think I allowed . . . encouraged you to . . . Oh, I am so ashamed. Believe me, it was absolutely alien to my nature.' Sophia was unnerved by what had passed between them and the intensity of her own passion when he'd kissed her. She was still deeply flushed with embarrassment. 'And as for your own behaviour, sir, you are no gentleman.'

There was a silence and then the smile died from his eyes and he said coldly, 'I agree. My conduct was totally reprehensible and quite unworthy of what is expected of a gentleman. I apologize.'

He turned immediately and went to join the other guests. Sophia's instinct told her that only his good breeding prevented him from pointing out that what had passed between them was as much her fault as his own. Far from protesting or struggling, she had actively encouraged and co-operated with him and enjoyed it just as much as he. Chastened, she moved towards the picnic group and the calming effects of social chat, but Sir Paul pointedly ignored her for the rest of the afternoon.

Noticing that Miss Cecilia Wright and Mr Thomas Thornton were both sitting alone, Sophia took a deep breath and said brightly, 'Mr Thornton, Miss Wright, how are you enjoying the riding party?'

'Very much I thank you, Miss Winterton,' Miss Cecilia said.

'It is made even more pleasurable by the presence of so many lovely young ladies,' Thomas Thornton said gallantly.

Sophia knew that he meant her presence, but was determined to deflect the compliment in Miss Wright's direction. She smiled at her and said admiringly, 'You are indeed in your best looks, dear Miss Wright. No wonder Mr Thornton thinks you are lovely.'

Two delicious dimples appeared at the corners of Miss Wright's pretty mouth and she glanced shyly at Thomas Thornton under her long sweeping lashes. Mr Thornton immediately begged to be allowed to help her to a little more game pie. She acquiesced so sweetly that Sophia felt it was not impolite to turn away and chat to the two Thornton twins and her cousin David. Having discovered that Elizabeth Thornton was fond of painting, David was describing a visit he had made to Italy after he'd left Oxford. He was eager to tell her that he was fascinated by Italian antiquities and hopeful of visiting Florence and Rome again. Elizabeth recognized the fire of genuine enthusiasm and warmed to him. She was able to recount some of her father's tales of the wonders he had seen in Europe, when he himself had been on the Grand Tour.

'But I expect with all the turmoil of the struggle with Napoleon, Papa's experiences would have little relevance today, Mr Winterton.'

As Sophia gradually made new acquaintances and renewed her friendship with the twins, she gradually became calmer and in spite of her discomfort over her recent behaviour with Sir Paul, enjoyed the fresh air and company.

Cecilia was full of Lady Wright's plan to organize a rout-party at Vauxhall Gardens with supper and fancy dress. She overcame her shyness sufficiently to chat quite freely to Thomas about the masquerade. She reported that she and her aunt were already planning the guest list. 'For you must know, Mr Thornton, that my aunt likes to be in the first dash of fashion and thinks it a good thing for girls to get used to mixing in company when they are newly out or even before they have their come out. Aunt sees it as an opportunity to invite guests of mixed ages,' she added ingenuously, 'as they will all be wearing disguises, you know.'

Thomas Thornton smiled at her obvious enthusiasm. She was so young and barely out herself and he'd thought his real love was for the more sophisticated Sophia Winterton, but by the time the picnic was finished, there was very little about Cecilia Wright that he didn't know. Although he had two sisters, he had very little experience of other girls. He found the mixture of her child-like innocence and feminine beauty quite out of the ordinary. Without even realizing it, Thomas was beginning to transfer his affections to Miss Cecilia Wright and that young lady was already more than a little in love with him.

And so the afternoon passed pleasantly enough. Sophia was occasionally aware of Morgan's glance, his usually hard-bitten face softening quite paternally as he looked at her. Sir Paul Maunders escorted her to Miss Fitzpatrick's home when the riding party was over and bade her farewell with no softening of his cold expression and Sophia was left feeling unusually flat and depressed.

Both Miss Fitzpatrick and Sophia were quiet that evening. After supper, in answer to Miss Fitzpatrick's questioning, Sophia told her most of what had occurred at the riding party, but finally, noting Sophia's abstracted look, Miss Fitzpatrick said gently, 'Is anything wrong, my dear? Did you not find the picnic enjoyable?'

Her look of loving concern melted Sophia's resolve to keep her cards close to her chest and she felt she must tell her about the note from William Baggett. 'It is nothing more nor less than blackmail, Fitz,' she said despairingly. 'And I can't . . . I won't . . . marry him.'

Miss Fitzpatrick gathered Sophia into a warm and loving hug, stroking the tumbled chestnut curls and murmuring little words of comfort to her goddaughter as she had been wont to do since Sophia was a child. 'There, my dear, please don't fret.' she said softly. Then, very gently, she said, 'Does . . . does Sir Paul Maunders know of Mr Baggett's . . . er . . . proposal?'

'No. No, he doesn't,' Sophia said on a sob. 'And I won't tell him.'

'Sophia. Have you quarrelled with Sir Paul?'

'Yes. Yes, I have. The man is arrogant and impossible!'

She raised her head and set her chin angrily. 'He . . . ' She knew she was as much to blame as Sir Paul for what had happened, but she could hardly tell Miss Fitzpatrick that she had enticed him to kiss her and that she had returned his kiss with willing passion. Instead, she said petulantly, 'He is insufferable!'

11

Well before luncheon the next morning, Miss Fitzpatrick presented Sophia with her subscription card saying, 'You look a little peaky, my dear. Why not go to the library and choose a good book? It might take your mind off . . . er . . . things and will be a pleasant little walk for you and Polly.'

Sophia was glad to agree. The last thing she wanted was to have time to mope around the house, thinking of Sir Paul Maunders. She would choose a book which would provide a topic to discuss with her new friends, Miss Wright and the Thorntons. Fitz was quite right, it would do her good to have a little walk and a book was always an entertaining diversion from real life.

It was a particularly fine morning, but there were few people about as she and Polly turned into Packington Street and headed towards the subscription library. Then, quite out of the blue, a lady carrying a pink parasol came speeding towards them and bumped into Sophia quite violently.

Breathless and almost knocked to the ground, Sophia recovered sufficiently to gasp politely, 'I do beg your pardon, ma'am.' She looked up and saw that the other lady was none other than the dark-haired, voluptuous young woman who had been trying to attract Sir Paul's attention at the opera. And . . . she was sure . . . was the same lady who had spied on them in the park.

'No,' said the young woman. 'It is I who should apologize. So clumsy of me not to look where I am going. I hope you are not hurt, ma'am.'

Sophia was not hurt, only puzzled. The woman had her maid with her. She spoke nicely, was dressed fashionably but modestly and looked a complete lady. And yet . . . there was something about her . . .

Sophia murmured a few polite words and prepared to move on, but the young woman grasped her hand in a friendly manner and said, 'I am Marie Baronne. You must be Miss Winterton. Did I not see you at the opera the other night?'

The two maidservants tactfully moved away a few paces and Sophia answered rather stiffly that she had indeed been at *The Marriage of Figaro*. She wondered how this Marie Baronne knew her name.

'Such an amusing piece,' Marie continued languidly and Sophia agreed, disengaging her hand and feeling a little uncomfortable.

She wondered what was coming next. Marie Baronne presented as a respectable young lady, but when she remembered her antics at the opera, Sophia wasn't so sure and once more made to move on.

This time, Marie caught hold of her arm and went on very chattily, 'You were in Sir Paul's box as I recall.'

When Sophia made no reply to this, she said, 'Sir Paul Maunders and I are dear friends . . . very dear friends. We've been special friends for over a year now. I have my own box, of course, but I am usually to be seen with Paul.'

Her meaning was sickeningly clear and looking at her more closely, Sophia recognized that although the woman looked ladylike, she was in fact wearing some discreet powder and paint. Her dress was very fashionable, but perhaps rather too low cut for a morning's shopping. She was sure this woman must be Paul's mistress.

'He is so charming, don't you think?' Marie gushed. 'Any young lady could be forgiven for being a little in love with him.'

Sophia began to feel a rising tide of panic welling up inside her and she looked round desperately for a means of escape. It was the resourceful Polly who had heard everything, who came to her rescue.

'Ooh, Miss Winterton,' she said anxiously. 'Miss Fitzpatrick says as how the library closes at one o'clock. We should try not to be too late, ma'am.'

'Perhaps we may meet again, Miss Winterton,' Marie Baronne said graciously, and she walked away, swinging her hips. Sophia went through the motions of visiting the subscription library, trying to act normally. She was calm on the outside, but inside, she was screaming, 'No! It isn't true. It can't be true'. But in the silent calm of the library, when she was pretending to choose a book, she knew in her heart, that it was true. Marie Baronne was more than Paul's special friend: she was his mistress. She wondered why she hadn't recognized this on the night of the opera, when he was so pointedly ignoring Marie, while he and Sophia were flirting so charmingly together. How could she have been so foolish as to hope that he could return her love? David Winterton's words came back to her. 'The last time I met him, he said that he was like to remain a bachelor until his dying day . . . ' Whatever Paul said about remaining single, she knew that he would eventually marry and produce an heir, while no doubt keeping a mistress on the side. As the bitter tears threatened, she summoned Polly and they hurried home. She wanted only to be able to go to her own room to grapple with her own melancholy problem, but at the foot of the staircase, Miss Fitzpatrick met her with a pleasant note from Lady Wright. It was a formal invitation to Vauxhall Gardens on Friday week for the masquerade party and Sophia had hardly had time to receive it when there was a further unpleasant encounter with William Baggett. He was preceded by a footman bearing a huge bouquet of hot-house flowers accompanied by a small gilt-edged card with an extremely elaborate and pretentious message to the effect that no flower, however beautiful, could ever compare with his own fair Sophie. Sophia pointedly left them on the hall table, without even bothering to put them in water and forbade both Miss Fitzpatrick and Polly to touch them.

They were the first thing that caught Baggett's eye as soon as he came into the house and it was only the first circumstance to anger him that morning. He stood suave and confident in Miss Fitzpatrick's drawing-room, smiling and holding out both his hands to Sophia, sure of her acceptance of him.

'Well my dearly beloved,' he said fatuously in his thin voice, 'will you name a day for our wedding and put me out of my suspense? Please let it be soon, my own darling.'

She was icily polite. 'I regret, Mr Baggett that my reply must still be the same. I am sensible of the honour you do me but I cannot . . . will not marry you.'

First he tried gentle persuasion. 'I appreciate that a young lady who has already been betrothed, must be overwhelmed at the thought of entering into matrimony with a new partner, especially a young lady who has no mama to guide her, but I am confident I would make you happy, my dearest.'

She didn't respond to this but looked down despairingly at her interlaced fingers. Rather more sharply he said, 'Come now, Sophie. Enough of this maidenly modesty. It is totally uncalled for in view of what we both know of your behaviour.'

At this, she looked up at him, her eyes smouldering, but she said softly, 'Oh yes and what exactly do we know of my behaviour, sir?'

'Oh come,' he said, quite viciously this time. 'Do not play act with me. You are ruined. You spent three days and nights with a well-known rake and had neither chaperon or any male member of your family to accompany you.'

Her voice was dangerously quiet now. 'And who says that I am ruined, sir?'

'Society will say it, miss,' he hissed. 'Once I

have put the word about, everyone will know, even your servants.'

'I'm sorry to disabuse you of your beliefs, sir, but as soon as you put any word about concerning myself, you will hear from my lawyer. I know it has not escaped your attention that I am a very wealthy heiress and can afford to have any 'words that you put about' discredited and your own reputation will be similarly damaged by a law suit. I am persuaded that you do not lack for money, but by the time you have paid costs and damages, you will be much the poorer. Do your worst, sir, but be prepared to take the consequences.'

There was a tense silence. For the first time, Baggett's confidence seemed to waver. Without knowing why, he suddenly felt a shiver of alarm and a feeling of acute apprehension, now that he realized that his bullying tactics had not paid off. Even so, he forced a sarcastic laugh.

'Owing to your youth and sheltered background, you are not familiar with the rules of the *ton* and what it is like to be blackballed and refused entry wherever you go. You will have a rude awakening very shortly.'

'I am afraid you are mistaken, sir. Unless you withdraw your threats of blackmail immediately, it is you and not I who will be blackballed.'

Now he began to splutter angrily and raised his hand as though to strike her, but Sophia held steady and said in a pleasant voice, 'If I hear no more of your stupid threats, I shall merely get my man of affairs to write you a letter of warning. If you continue with your attempts at defamation of my character, I shall sue you. That is my final word, sir, I will not marry you. Ever!'

'Make no mistake,' he snarled. 'You will change your mind, madam. I shall make sure of that. You have not seen the last of me, yet.'

He snatched up his hat and cane, glowering at her. 'I'll bid you good day, madam.'

He departed, but not before he had paused to hurl the bouquet of flowers on to the floor as he passed through the hall.

Sophia was left alone and presently Miss Fitzpatrick came in to see how she did and to cluck over Mr Baggett's proposal once more. 'You know your own heart best, my love, but you must own he has a respectable family and is well off. He is not obliged to marry money and it seems an honourable proposal.'

'Yes. An old and distinguished Norfolk family certainly, but honourable he is not. He is a bully and a lecher, Fitz. That is all.'

Miss Fitzpatrick sighed and went back to

sorting out her linen cupboard, while Sophia remained lost in thought. She was convinced that Baggett and her aunt Harriet were in collusion and were plotting to harm her. She felt tense and threatened. And what of Paul? She felt now that she could never hope for his love and in spite of her self-control, the tears finally spilled over.

When Miss Fitzpatrick had finished the linen cupboard, she went quietly to peep in on Sophia and what she saw prompted her to go and find Polly. She took the unprecedented step of sending a note to Sir Paul Maunders at Manvers House. 'I've ordered a hackney carriage for you, my dear,' she said. 'You will be quite safe and the driver will wait while you deliver my note.'

'There's no reply,' Sir Paul said, when the note was delivered to him, but later that afternoon, he presented himself at Miss Fitzpatrick's house in Islington and was admitted immediately.

'If you would take a seat in the drawing-room, sir, I'm sure Miss Winterton will be with you soon,' Polly said, but Miss Fitzpatrick bustled in within minutes.

'Miss Winterton knows you are here, sir and will be down shortly.' She poured him a glass of sherry from the decanter on the sideboard, but he left it untouched.

* ★ ★ ★

It was on the tip of Sophia's tongue to tell Fitz to deny her, but she overcame the impulse. She dried her eyes and tidied her hair. She had to face him. They were bound to meet socially on a regular basis and she couldn't run away again. She had made up her mind that she must be prepared to meet Paul and to conduct herself when she did so with calm and dignity.

He rose as Sophia entered and she said coolly, 'Sir Paul, I did not think to see you here today.'

'Did you not?' he said softly. 'Your godmother has written to me that you have received an offer from William Baggett and has led me to understand that this is most unwelcome to you. I notice that you paid no attention to my warnings about this man.'

'Yes, I did pay attention,' she said bitterly. 'But my encounter with him at the Sir John Falstaff Arms and the fact that he feels he can reveal the knowledge of our journey to London, encouraged him to propose marriage.'

'Well, no doubt he feels his attentions would be welcomed, whereas mine most certainly would not,' he remarked bitterly.

'His attentions are definitely not welcomed,

sir. He has had no encouragement from me. It is my aunt Harriet's doing. Because she knows my betrothal to Lord Devenish is definitely at an end, she has encouraged him to propose to me and that is why William Baggett has not returned to his home in Norfolk.'

'So, I am to expect an announcement in *The Times*,' he said sarcastically.

Sophia jumped up out of her chair. 'You cannot for one moment think I would accept such as he,' she cried passionately.

He also stood now, taller than Sophia, looming over her, the afternoon sun accentuating the harsh planes of his face. 'So, you have rejected him, then?'

'I . . . yes . . . that is . . . I know he refuses to accept my decision.'

'A difficult choice lies before you, Sophie. Either you accept the obnoxious Baggett, or you tell him to go to hell and marry me. After all, I was responsible for insisting that you should travel to London with me. You could do worse, I assure you. I am in receipt of a goodly fortune, am house trained and, as your husband, would give no trouble.'

His accompanying smile and the implication of his words, conjured up the picture of a future so agreeable, that she almost felt herself weakening. Wanting him and seeing a way out of the dilemma she was in, by being able to rely on his strength, she was almost tempted to accept his offer. Except that it felt so humiliating to accept a proposal where no mention was made of love, or even affection, and where the prospective groom had a voluptuous mistress in tow. She drew herself up proudly.

'I thank you for the honour bestowed on me, sir. But I must decline the offer. I have no intention of exchanging my single state for the shackles of matrimony.'

His smile vanished and his face was rigid with anger, but he merely bowed politely and took his leave of her, leaving Sophia to sink back on to the sofa and shed passionately bitter tears.

To be crossed in his desires was a galling experience for Paul Maunders. Long before his brother died and he came into possession of the Maunders' fortune, he was used to having everything his own way. Even in the army, he was accustomed to people who flattered him and even to downright syco-phants, but it was one thing to despise those sort of people and quite another to be rejected and outfaced by a slip of a girl. Even if she was an heiress and exceptionally beautiful, she was still a country nobody from Norfolk. He had never anticipated this resistance and so had no immediate plans to counter it. He had been surprised and outraged by Sophia Winterton's intransigent attitude to his proposal. His pride had been bruised by her remark about being 'shackled in marriage' and the idea of having his offer refused, when he'd thought she felt attracted to him had rubbed salt into the wound. As he made his way to Manvers House, his thoughts of Sophia Winterton were almost as unkind as the ones she cherished for William Baggett.

As for Sophia, she had plenty of time to reflect on what she'd done. In spite of her bold words about refusing to entertain Baggett's suit, she was worried about the damage he could cause by his spiteful tattling and yet she felt Paul was only prepared to marry her for the sake of her reputation. A marriage of convenience, in fact. She would have respectability, married status and, eventually, children perhaps. Paul would have done the honourable thing. He would have a wife with a considerable fortune and still be able to lead his single life with as many mistresses as he wished. Once he had a son and heir, she would have served her purpose and their marriage would be like so many of those of the *ton*, a loveless, hollow sham. And yet . . . God help her, she loved him. She thought about the rake whose weekend parties had shocked the neighbours when she was younger and whose companion of choice now, was a brazen hussy. Then she remembered the delightful man whose smile still charmed her and would haunt her dreams. It was puzzling to think of them as one and the same person. She reminded herself that charm of manner and an attractive smile must be the stock in trade of the accomplished rake. She was horrified to realize that however disillusioned she was with his tarnished image when she learned of Marie, her love for him hadn't withered and she felt more miserable than she'd ever felt in her life. By the time she had controlled her passionate emotions somewhat, Sophia was even more resolved that she would reject a marriage of empty duty and take the consequences.

It was Polly who came to rescue her from these unhappy thoughts. The unsophisticated country girl was yet able to communicate her love and understanding for her mistress and came uninvited to Sophia's room to put her arms around her and offer wordless comfort as she wiped Sophia's tear-stained cheeks.

'Miss Fitzpatrick is wantin' to do a bit of shopping, ma'am, and she says as how you are looking for some hostess gifts. Why don't we go tomorrow mornin' and forget about thinking of troublesome gents for a while?'

Sophia was even able to smile at the idea of the elegant and top lofty Sir Paul being named 'a troublesome gent', by a young serving maid and she agreed immediately.

She was receiving much kindness and generosity from the close circle of Lady Maunders' friends and so far had not returned their hospitality. When all this unpleasantness with Baggett was at an end and she had got over her infatuation for Sir Paul Maunders, she promised herself that she would organize a little party on her own account. Her lawyer could sort out any tangles with Baggett and Aunt Harriet. After all, she would soon be mistress of her own destiny and need not give a fig for such people.

It was another fine sunny day, when they set out and both ladies carried parasols and Sophia was still lost in thought as they waited for the hackney to drive them to Bond Street. Miss Fitzpatrick's garden was separated from the one belonging to Mrs Soames by a mellow brick wall and it supported several old-fashioned species of roses which flowered in profusion. As they paused to admire one particular climber with tiny pale-pink double flowers, for some reason, she knew not why, Sophia felt compelled to glance upwards. The heavy coping stones atop the wall, looked secure enough, but one was loose and had a fine sprinkling of dust around it. Before she was even aware what was happening, she heard a grating sound as if bricks were being rubbed against mortar. She instinctively leapt backwards, holding her parasol sideways as if to protect Miss Fitzpatrick, who was standing behind her. The heavy shaped stone missed her by inches and cracked into the gravel path, scattering little pebbles and sending up a small cloud of grey debris as the edges splintered and chipped.

Her thoughts rudely interrupted, for a few moments, Sophia stood rigid with shock and fear. Behind her, she heard Miss Fitzpatrick gasp and then she dropped her parasol and clasped Sophia to her, concern and terror shaking her slight body and making her cheerful little face look suddenly grey and old.

'Oh my dear . . . Oh Sophie. What a dreadful thing! A few more inches and . . . Oh! . . . I must get the rest of the wall checked. I never thought that such a thing could happen. I feel so terrible about it and especially while you are my guest. Do you wish to retire back indoors, my dear? We can cancel our shopping if you wish.'

Sophia looked dazedly at her companion

for a moment and then, collecting her thoughts, raised her chin and said, 'No, Fitz darling. It was a mere chance and not your fault at all. A weakened cope stone, nothing more. It will be easy to get it repaired.'

The hackney arrived at that precise moment and if the jarvey noticed anything amiss, he gave no sign, but set off to Bond Street with no further delay.

It was only later, when Sophia had time to reflect upon it that the full implication of her brush with death really came home to her. Two inches nearer to the wall, two seconds later before looking up and seeing the danger, would have made the difference between life and death. She shuddered. It didn't bear thinking about. She'd had to make light of it for Miss Fitzpatrick's sake, but she went to sleep that night thankful to still be alive.

She had heard no more, good or evil, from William Baggett for which she was profoundly thankful and when Lady Maunders sent word that she had obtained vouchers for her for Almack's, Sophia was pleased and was conscious of a lightening of her spirits after the problems of the last few days. Now she would see how it would feel to be accepted by the ton and not rejected as Baggett had forecast, and she would test her resolution to forget her love for Sir Paul Maunders.

Excitedly she shared with Fitz her limited knowledge of this famous institution. She had heard so much of the patronesses, the dances and the rules and the fact that Almack's was considered something of a marriage mart, that she was curious to see it for herself.

It was less than a week before the Masquerade and she had occasion to go into town to order a new dress and decided to make the excursion include a visit to her lawyer. It would soon be her dear Fitz's birthday and Sophia knew that her ex-governess would like to choose a book as a birthday present. Miss Fitzpatrick had once been a very educated and accomplished young lady, able to sing and play on the pianoforte as well as being proficient in French and Italian. But her papa had died suddenly, deeply in debt, and Miss Fitzpatrick's gentle, ineffectual mama had died soon afterwards. There were relatives, but none of them was prepared to help, so Emma Fitzpatrick, alone in the world, used her father's meagre assets, which consisted mainly of the family home and the silver, with one or two good oil paintings, to pay off the tradesmen's bills. There was enough left after the sale of the house and other possessions, for the family's man of business to advise her to buy a small annuity and Miss Fitzpatrick, who was the godmother to young Sophia Winterton, had found a position as a governess, first with a succession of difficult brats and over-protective mamas, but finally, joyfully, with Sophia Winterton, the little 10-year-old orphan who was her beloved godchild and whom Miss Fitzpatrick loved with all her heart. From the start Sophia had been a thin, nervous child, unable to take in or understand the absence of her parents. However patiently and gently her aunt and uncle had explained the meaning of death to her, she was still unable to comprehend why she would never see her mama and papa again. For many months, she was tormented by the idea that it was all her own fault, that she'd done something wicked and unforgivable. She became even thinner and started to chew the inside of her lip nervously in an effort to concentrate on the reason why her parents were dead. The lively confident little girl, who had been doted on by an adoring mother and father, became a nervous wraith, silent and never smiling. In spite of her aunt and uncle's loving care, it was only Miss Fitzpatrick's genius at understanding young children, which gradually brought about a change for the better in Sophia.

Fitz had so many tales and poems, such a ready understanding and so many interesting activities that were attractive to a young and lonely child, that Sophia gradually became reconciled to the terrifying idea that though her parents were now dead, her aunt and uncle loved her, and would take care of her until she was grown up. All her doubts and fears, her bad dreams and sadness at her loss, were always taken to Fitz and discussed calmly until Sophia was reassured and began to lose her nervous habits and she became a tall, sturdy child, like her cousin David. She and he were both only children and it was natural that they should be like brother and sister, sharing ideas and adventures and building a lifelong friendship, cemented by the kind and caring influence of their beloved Fitz. Now, Sophia knew she had the means to repay Fitz's kindness somewhat and make her declining years happy and she was determined she would make her former governess comfortable and contented for the rest of her life.

Miss Fitzpatrick had expressed a desire to accompany Sophia into Town, saying that she would have the rare pleasure and indulgence to browse in various bookshops and choose the birthday present that Sophia wished to give her and that they could meet at one of the respectable coffee houses and come home in a hackney.

Meanwhile, Sophia would be able to visit Mr Shaw, who, since her parents' death, had acted for her over the legacy involved, her uncle's guardianship of her, the regular delivery of her very generous allowance and all the bewildering and complicated details of her financial affairs. She had never been to visit him in his office before, he had always in the past travelled to Cottleton twice a year and put up at the Eight Bells in order to discharge his duties as executor of her father's estate. Mr Joseph Shaw had been more than her financial adviser over the years, he had been a true friend, explaining her father's will, the duties and obligations of her guardians even when she was but a little girl of ten and finally, the safeguards that were in place to protect her finances from such as Aunt Harriet.

He would surely advise her sensibly about the problem of William Baggett. She had been obliged to think long and hard about how to explain the hold this evil rogue had over her in respect of her flight from the marriage with Lord Devenish and her journey to London with Sir Paul Maunders. Finally, she had decided on a carefully edited version of the truth. Without wishing to deceive Mr Shaw, she wanted to explain the circumstances tactfully without being too shockingly explicit.

Joseph Shaw was a small, rubicund man in his late fifties, with thinning hair and an expanding waistline. Fine wines played a big part in his day-to-day existence and in spite of his gout and increasing breathlessness, he enjoyed his life to the full. His four children were long since married and he was completely happy and comfortable with his placid, loving little wife of thirty years. He looked benignly at Sophia when she was ushered into his presence by the office boy, Master Nick, who was himself all of seventy years old.

'Miss Winterton,' he beamed, and moved round to her side of the desk. He took both her hands in his soft workshy palms and kissed them. 'What a pleasure, my dear. How well you are looking. And to think that you will be attaining your majority in less than three months. Shall you still be needing your poor old Mr Joe any more?'

'Of course,' Sophia said, and smiled at him as she took the chair that was offered. Master Nick poured out two glasses of sherry and bowed himself out of the room, leaving the two of them alone.

Joseph Shaw took a sip from his glass and then said gently, 'And how may I help you, my dear? The last time we met, I was busy drawing up the marriage contract. I take it that the betrothal was not an unqualified success?'

Sophia took refuge for a few moments in her own glass, but said finally, 'It was a very unhappy experience, sir, and the engagement is at an end.'

He took up his glass again and twisted it in his short white fingers. 'But at the time, it seemed set to be such a triumph, my dear.'

'Perhaps. Unfortunately I discovered that my fiancé was not what he seemed and I was ... was obliged to ... escape my aunt's wrath and I ran away.'

The small bright blue eyes set in his jolly pink face opened wide in amused surprise. 'Ran away?'

'Yes. I escaped from the whole situation and am now residing with my former governess and godmother, Miss Fitzpatrick.'

'I see.'

'Unfortunately, on my journey to London, I was importuned by a rogue and a blackguard, namely William Baggett. Since then, he has sought me out and has pressed his unwelcome attentions on me and been ... thoroughly unpleasant.'

Joseph Shaw made a castle with his fingers. 'Understandable, my dear,' he murmured, but his eyes were twinkling.

'You see,' she said earnestly 'Unfortunately I missed the stagecoach to London, but was offered a ride by Sir Paul Maunders, a friend of my cousin David's.'

'I see.'

'I was obliged to stay with Sir Paul's mother until my godmother returned to her home in Islington. Since he arrived in London, this Baggett person has . . . threatened me and . . . tried to blackmail me into marrying him.'

'On what grounds, my dear?'

'On the grounds that . . . for part of the journey, at least, I was unchaperoned, and thinking I was alone, he attempted to make an attack on my virtue at one of the coaching inns. I assure you, Mr Shaw, everything between Sir Paul Maunders and myself was strictly honourable and above board, of course,' she added hastily.

'Of course. So, how may I help you, child?'

'I would like Baggett to be warned about spreading untrue stories about me and defaming my character, but I know that he is a hardened rake and a gambler and perhaps I might even offer some . . . some recompense for . . . for the expense and inconvenience of his fruitless courtship?'

'Buy him off, you mean? That could be arranged,' Joseph Shaw said calmly. 'But he is not without money. I doubt it would make any difference to a man like him. Furthermore, I might point out, Miss Winterton, that you are under no obligation to offer any such recompense. Quite the reverse in fact. I would strongly advise against such a step. However, leave it with me, my dear. I shall give it some thought and will know how best to proceed. Meanwhile, if you are set on buying in London when you come into your inheritance, I know of some reliable agents who could negotiate for a suitable property on your behalf.'

After pleasant enquiries as to how Mr Shaw's wife and children were and how the first of the Shaw grandchildren did, Master Nick was summoned into the office and instructed to show Miss Winterton out.

Sophia and Miss Fitzpatrick stood arm in arm, outside Mr Shaw's office waiting for the hackney which Master Nick had summoned for them. The street was fairly quiet, but a couple passed them, both in nondescript clothes, both wearing hats. The woman wore a bonnet shading her face, the man was in a slouch hat, pulled well down over his eyes. Neither Miss Fitzpatrick or Sophia took much note of them because before they'd had time to go by, a curricle and pair came charging round the corner, cutting it off most dangerously and while the two ladies were taking this in and gasping at the sight of such dangerous driving, Sophia received a violent push in the middle of her back and was thrust suddenly forward into the path of the powerful black horses. As she staggered and began to pitch forward, small, brave Miss Fitzpatrick, clasped her round the waist and with the superhuman energy which is only granted in such life-threatening situations, she heaved the tall, strong Sophia sideways, pulling her back so vigorously that Sophia fell over. Both ladies landed in an undignified heap on the ground, shaken but unhurt. By the time they'd gathered themselves together, the curricle had sped onwards and the two people had disappeared completely. It was all over in seconds. Sophia and her godmother were left to straighten their clothes and try to compose themselves before the hackney appeared to take them home.

They were silent on the brief journey to Islington, too stunned by the incident to discuss it, but once inside the little house, with Polly to fuss over them and serve dinner, Sophia realized what a shock the experience had been for both of them. Later, as Miss Fitzpatrick sat in her big armchair, alternately blowing and sipping at her tea, Sophia looked at her carefully. She always looked so small and doll-like in that comfortable chair but now, Sophia thought, that she looked even smaller and slighter than usual. Her normally fresh face seemed pinched and grey. She held her cup in both hands and her small fine-boned fingers trembled slightly.

Sophia tried to make light of the incident, comparing it to the fallen coping stone. 'We must both have a charmed existence, Fitz,' she said jokily. 'Perhaps we shall have nine lives like a cat. Let us just hope these alarms don't go in threes.'

Miss Fitzpatrick shuddered and said nothing and it was suddenly brought home to Sophia that her seemingly vibrant young godmother was no longer what she had once been. When had she grown old and fearful? I don't recall her being older, she thought. Perhaps age had crept up, like a thief in the night, making her body seem shrunken and her pleasant little face, thin and shrivelled. Looking at her now, Sophia was overwhelmed with feelings of tenderness and affection for the governess who had always been there for her, for as long as she could remember. Strong, humorous, kind, is how she would describe dear Fitz. Loving, certainly, protective and nurturing to the lonely anxious little girl that Sophia had once been, undoubtedly. For the first time, it was brought home to her, how vulnerable Miss Fitzpatrick now was. She must avoid any jokes about accidents and alarms; it was obvious that dear Fitz's nerves wouldn't stand it. Miss Fitzpatrick declared quietly that she was certain the couple were a man and a woman. She hadn't actually seen either of them push Sophia, but she believed Sophia when she said that this is what had happened, otherwise Sophia would not have been pitchforked into the road.

'But it all happened so quickly, Sophia, dear. Oh, if only I'd had the wit to take more careful note of the curricle, I might have been able to identify it.'

'Don't reproach yourself, dear Fitz,' Sophia begged her. 'If it hadn't been for your brave action, I would be dead.'

Fitz shuddered and put a hand to her head, saying she had a headache and thought she would go to bed early, if dear Sophia would excuse her.

Later, in the quiet of her own room when she had time to reflect on it, Sophia wondered who the mysterious couple were and who the driver of the curricle was. She agreed with Fitz that it was almost certainly a man and a woman who had passed her, yet could it have been that one of them was merely dressed as a woman? Most of those sort of vehicles were driven by gentlemen. It would be usual after such a near miss for the driver to stop and enquire after the victim's safety and well-being. She had seen in that quick glimpse that it was a single driver. She knew that she hadn't imagined the sensation of that vigorous push in the middle of her back, and yet . . . and yet . . . Who would deliberately do such a thing? In view of the seemingly planned nature of the street attack, could the incident with the loose coping stone also have been a deliberate attempt on her life? Who hated her so much as to want her dead?

The logical answer was Lord Devenish. But what would it profit him if she were to die? All his hopes of matrimony were destroyed anyway, with the humiliation of the broken engagement. William Baggett would surely not have had time to plan such a deed. After Mr Shaw had organized a lawyer's letter warning him to keep away from her, then perhaps Baggett might seek revenge, but to deliberately plan to have someone killed seemed extreme, even for Baggett. He would not benefit financially by her death. She must surely have been mistaken in thinking that the incidents were deliberate. Both the falling coping stone and someone stumbling against her must have been accidents. Mustn't they? To Sophia, one of the worst aspects of this unnerving situation was poor Fitz's distress and anxiety. Her godmother had done nothing to deserve such disruption to her quiet retirement. Sophia was ashamed that she had landed so unexpectedly on Miss Fitzpatrick, totally uninvited and had now embroiled the poor lady in such trouble.

She put her book aside and leaned back and closed her eyes. And what of Sir Paul? She had neither seen nor heard from him since her refusal of his offer. She had a sudden vision of him laughing and carefree and then a different picture of him entirely, white to the lips and glaring with fury at her when she had thwarted him. She wondered briefly if he would seek her out at Lady Wright's masquerade. She hoped not. In spite of her defiant stance about ignoring what had passed between them, she realized that the first time they were together in company, it could be a difficult situation for her. Not for him, though, she thought bitterly, he had so many opportunities for dalliance, he probably never gave her a thought, now that she had refused his offer.

The next morning, Lady Maunders called to see if Miss Fitzpatrick and Miss Winterton were at home to visitors and she was full of the gracious condescension displayed by Mrs Drummond-Burrell in the granting of the vouchers for her young friend. The three ladies sat together in Miss Fitzpatrick's drawing-room and, as if by mutual consent, Sophia and her godmother took care not to mention the two accidents that had so unnerved them in the last few days.

Lady Maunders was quick to mention that an old friend of hers, with a granddaughter who was recently out, would also be attending. 'Mrs Carleton is a very young grandmama, Sophie, and dear Lavinia is the apple of her eye. Although we shall both sit out the dances and chat together, I know that you and Miss Carleton will not lack for partners and it should be a chance for both of you to extend your acquaintance with the . . . um . . . opposite sex, in the most select and refined circumstances. I have even managed to prevail upon Paul to put in an appearance. He is so depressingly disparaging of Almack's usually and says that it is just a roomful of old tabbies sipping weak orgeat and gazing at the parade of hopeful virgins in a veritable meat market atmosphere.'

Miss Fitzpatrick looked shocked at this, but Lady Maunders, observing Sophia's flushed cheeks and downcast eyes, could see that the girl was looking forward to it. She felt a sudden impatient irritation with her son. Why on earth hadn't he managed to become betrothed to Sophie? It was so obvious that they were in love with each other. There was no reason for him to hold back. He had money and position, he had met the love of his life, and there was no one else who had ever engaged his affections like this girl. As for Sophie, she was an heiress, young, beautiful and deeply in love with Mary Maunders' beloved son. They had absolutely no reason to delay what could be the society wedding of the year.

She said nothing of these thoughts, but continued to chat in the same light-hearted way for the next ten minutes or so. 'He reckons to find the company insipid and the play at the tables mere chicken stakes. He chafes at being obliged to wear dress uniform or knee breeches and mutters about the doors being shut at eleven. I reminded him that greater personages than himself have been obliged to abide by the rules. Why, when the female despots turned away his hero, Wellington, for wearing trousers, the great man himself meekly obeyed orders and left. The ladies in charge are very disciplined, so although he might jib at it, I warrant that he will also fall in with the rules.'

Sophia said nothing but smiled at Lady Maunders and thanked her very prettily for the trouble she'd taken on her behalf. She was in a turmoil of anticipation and yet dread at the idea of seeing him again. Supposing he asked her to dance? Supposing he didn't ask her to dance, but cut her dead? She probably deserved it, she thought, after the way she had so ungraciously refused him. She responded to the rest of Lady Maunders' conversation with a polite, 'Yes', 'Mm' or 'No' and was relieved when her ladyship took her leave with Sophia's grateful thanks ringing in her ears.

Joseph Shaw, as promised, had sent a warning letter to William Baggett. The man was well known to him and most of Mr Shaw's associates were aware of his evil reputation. Master Nick delivered it by hand and though couched in circumspect lawyers' language, it was clear in its intention to deter Baggett from spreading vile defamation about Miss Winterton. As soon as Master Nick had departed, Baggett tore it into small pieces and ground it under his heel, cursing Sophia Winterton and Sir Paul Maunders in equal measure.

12

Lady Maunders came in her carriage the next night to accompany Fitz and Sophia to Almack's. It was obvious to her godmother that Sophia's enjoyment was her ladyship's first concern and she was pleased about this. She knew that Sophia's life in the last few years had not been very happy and just as she had been willing to try and help her when she was a child, she was still very wishful of promoting her goddaughter's success and well being.

They arrived somewhat early at Almack's and not many people were there, but Lady Maunders spotted her friend almost immediately and was able to introduce them to Mrs Carleton and Lavinia before the rooms filled up and while they were still able to hear themselves speak.

Miss Lavinia Carleton was a dark-haired rather doll-like creature who had little confidence and next to no conversation. She was obviously doted on by her grandmama, who had lavished every luxury that money could buy to make Miss Carleton's come out a great success and secure her a suitable husband in her first London season. Sophia and Miss Fitzpatrick were able to introduce her to Lady Wright and her niece, Cecilia, and later, to Mr Thomas Thornton and his friends. Both Mrs Carleton and Lady Maunders were obviously delighted to see such a group of personable partners around their young protégées. In no time at all, they and Miss Fitzpatrick were seated together, remarking and exclaiming on the confidence and beauty of young ladies nowadays and how fortunate they were that the prevailing fashions were so flattering, especially to the young and slender.

'Why, I mind when the fashion was for hooped skirts, just the management of them when we were presented, was so taxing,' Mrs Carleton said.

'I know what you mean,' Lady Maunders replied, 'but you cannot possibly be old enough to remember such archaic fashions, ma'am.'

Mrs Carleton was pleased to deny this, but she did it in such a charming way that even Miss Fitzpatrick admitted to having once worn a most unbecoming gown of an unattractive shade of puce which indeed had a hooped skirt, and was at the time, all the rage.

'But it was so terribly unflattering to me

when I was but seventeen,' she confessed. The other two smiled sympathetically and then, all three turned their attention to the young men who were soliciting the hands of their three darlings for the first dance. They all seemed to be filling their dance cards in a way that was very gratifying to the ladies who were observing.

They watched the three of them chatting together and fanning themselves as the rooms gradually became crowded and their dance partners sought them out. Sophia was engaged to dance the quadrille with Thomas Thornton and, as she accepted his proffered hand and they joined the set, she noticed Miss Wright was following his tall figure with her soft large eyes, even though Richard Andrews was bending over her hand to claim the first dance.

'How pretty Miss Wright is looking this evening,' she said to Thomas. 'She always shows such taste in her dress and the way she has her hair arranged, I am sure she is going to have a very successful year. How are you managing with Patch?'

'Well, I thank you,' he smiled. He looked consideringly at Cecilia Wright, who did indeed look extremely pretty and was obviously being admired by other young blades who were without partners. 'Miss

Wright has been very keen to observe his progress and has visited on two or three occasions,' he went on. 'She is very gentle with him and I fear is out to spoil him.'

He didn't mention that the last time Miss Wright had visited Patch, she had been utterly irresistible. Thomas Thornton's mama had come to the library to ask a favour of him before he'd even had time to go for a drive in his new curricle. Well, it was fairly new he supposed. A present from one of his doting grandmamas for his twenty-first birthday. He'd still not got over the thrill of possession, the overwhelming sensation of pride of ownership and the confidence and dash that the vehicle inspired in him.

Mrs Thornton had not come straight to the point about what favour it was that she was seeking, but had talked round it for a few minutes. 'Papa,' she had said to him, 'is persuaded that you would not have the least objection or you may be sure, my darling boy, that I would not even have ventured to ask you. And he is sure you would wish to oblige me in this.'

She'd paused for a moment and gazed doubtfully up at the darling boy. It couldn't have been said that his incredibly handsome face bore the expression of one delighted to oblige his dear mama in anything, yet he listened politely enough and she was encouraged to plunge quickly into an explanation.

'You see, my dear, Papa has been obliged to accompany Elizabeth and May to see your Aunt Emily. Just a courtesy visit you understand, but a request from his sister cannot well be refused when she is godmother to both our dear twins.'

'And your point, Mama?'

'Well, my dear, Miss Wright has sent word that she would like to come and see how her little dog fares. Of course, with the groom missing, there will be no one to see to it, apart from the stable lads, that is. You have taken such an interest in the little creature, she is bound to be grateful if you could spare a few minutes to fetch, Spot, is it? from the stables.'

'Patch,' Mr Thornton had corrected her.

'Patch?'

'It's his name, but why I should be called upon . . . ?'

'Well, you did agree that you would be responsible for Miss Wright's puppy, Thomas.'

He scowled but said, 'Have no fear, ma'am, I will not discharge my duties toward the puppy until such time as Miss Wright is able to take him home.'

Mrs Thornton sighed with relief. 'You are such a good boy, Thomas. Never one to cause trouble. Always so conscientious. No mother could have a better son . . . '

'That's enough, Mama,' he said hastily. 'What time will Miss Wright arrive to view her pet?'

'In about ten minutes,' his mama said calmly. 'Thank you so much, Thomas. It is so very good of you to put aside your own plans like this in order to entertain Miss Wright.'

He was hardly entertaining Miss Wright, he'd thought moodily. It was more in the line of a tedious duty, since he'd been so rash as to promise the young lady that he would care for the wretched puppy. He walked out to tell the stable lad not to bring the curricle round for another ten minutes or so, as he was sure to be delayed. But he was a kind and good-natured young man and quickly over-came his mood of irritation, especially when the object of his thoughts came tripping round the corner at that precise moment, carrying a dainty little parasol and accompanied by her maid.

He was obliged to return her smile. She looked so fresh and pretty and the little face that was tilted up to his own wore a smile that was beguiling enough to melt away the blackest of moods.

Encouraged by his pleasant manner, Miss Wright plunged into a torrent of breathless speech. 'It is very obliging of you, Mr Thornton. The notion of visiting dear little Patch only came into my head when Mrs Thornton mentioned that the twins were to visit their aunt and, of course, that meant I would be able to spend some time with Patch . . . and, oh . . . Mr Thornton, I do hope he has been a good little dog and has not done anything to vex you.'

Her little face was suddenly anxious and her smile disappeared at the thought of Patch vexing kind Mr Thornton.

'On the contrary,' he said. 'It so happens that the stable lads have found him very amenable and he is taking his food and water very willingly.'

The whole of Miss Wright's slight body had visibly relaxed at this and her smile returned with all the brilliance of bright sunshine after a shower. Mr Thornton's mood lifted as he walked round to the stables with her. To view the reunion between Miss Wright and her little dog was to see enacted a scene of truly touching sentiment. Mr Thornton had to smile at her delight in her little pet and the rapture of the puppy's response.

The stable lad, obeying Thomas Thornton's instructions to the letter, then led the curricle round and Miss Wright stood upright and, still cradling Patch protectively, gazed admiringly at Mr Thornton's smart vehicle.

As if in a dream, Thomas had been beguiled by a pair of sweet violet eyes, into taking Miss Wright up, just for a little spin in the park, while the stable lad returned Patch to his kennel and Miss Wright's maid was left to wait for their return.

Now, as the figures of the dance continued, his eyes followed Cecilia as she smiled politely at Richard Andrews as he claimed her for the first dance. Thomas bowed to Sophia and they took their places for the quadrille. As they danced, his thoughts returned once more to Cecilia's visit. He still had no idea how he had been cajoled so easily into taking Miss Wright for a ride in his new curricle.

All he remembered was that as soon as they'd arrived in the park, Miss Wright had said, with innocent admiration, 'What a good driver you are, Mr Thornton. Why, I believe you could even teach me how to drive.'

She looked away for a moment and then said, shyly, 'Do you think I might take the ribbons for a while, Mr Thornton?'

Thomas was aghast. Dash it, the last thing a chap wanted was to have his precious equipage put at risk by the clumsy mishandling of a silly young girl.

'I don't care to entrust my horses to anyone else, except the groom,' he said rather pompously.

Miss Wright's face fell and she blushed. 'Of course, I do understand,' she said, and looked wistful, her beautiful eyes downcast and her pretty mouth, drooping a little.

So, in a moment of madness, Thomas Thornton had helped her to change places with him. He had carefully placed her little hands in their dainty lace mittens on the reins in the correct hold and had disposed of the parasol on to the floor of the curricle. Leaning close to her, he had gently guided her through the intricacies of her first driving lesson, just as if he were a kind old grandfather rather than a fashionable young blood, he thought disbelievingly.

She had laughed with delight and thanked him so prettily when she'd finally relinquished the reins and they returned to the house, that he was utterly enchanted.

As he danced almost mechanically with Sophia Winterton, it didn't escape her attention that his eyes were straying more and more often to Cecilia Wright and that he seemed a little absent. As for Sophia, she was content to watch all the young ladies chatting to each other while they kept an eye on the best-looking young men and wielded their fans so flirtatiously, as the rooms gradually filled and became warmer. These wide-eyed young ladies were mostly debutantes and were as anxious as their mamas to create a good impression and net themselves a wealthy husband. As the dance ended and Thomas Thornton escorted her back to her seat, Sophia was able to smile to herself as she reflected that she had no such ambitions and could enjoy the evening for what it was. She was content to sit near Miss Carleton and watch the dancers.

'I wonder what is amusing you, Miss Winterton? I could offer you the proverbial penny for your thoughts, they seem so interesting.' He spoke in his distinctive low voice behind her, and she gave a start of surprise but recovered herself quickly.

'Alas, not worth a penny,' she said with a pretence at regret, and looked up at him, her hazel eyes serious. 'I was merely considering how very youthful some of the young ladies look.'

'And you in your dotage, positively ancient,' he said jokingly. 'I wonder you are not sitting with the chaperons this evening and wearing a suitable lace cap as befits your great age.'

'Sir! You are odious,' she said, but with an irrepressible smile at the corners of her mouth.

As he teased her and looked with mock commiseration at her elderly status, he found it hard to imagine Sophia Winterton anything other than young and beautiful. The creamy skin of her face was smooth and flawless, her brow high and serene. He lowered his gaze to her full lips and Sophia was so caught by the admiration in his dark eyes that they were both silent. He was lost in his own thoughts of the bitter disappointment he'd felt when she'd refused his proposal and, as for Sophia, she was thinking regretfully that if only Paul Maunders had not been saddled with a demanding mistress, he might have mentioned love and affection when he'd proposed to her and she mightn't have been so quick to refuse him.

The next dance was a waltz and he said softly, 'Should you care to dance, Sophia?'

She tore her thoughts back from his proposal and hesitated. 'One must have approval from the patronesses in order to waltz.'

Mrs Drummond-Burrell, who had been watching the little scene between the two of them, materialized from nowhere and said helpfully, 'Sir Paul, may I present Miss Winterton to you, as a suitable partner for this dance?'

He flashed her his devastating white smile

and Sophia curtsied to Mrs Drummond-Burrell. Watched with envy by the younger girls and their ambitious mamas, Sophia went into his arms and let him guide her skilfully through the other dancers on the floor. Well at least, she thought, there seemed no obvious awkwardness at this, their first meeting since she had so determinedly rejected him. He appeared to have got over his initial fury and was now being charming. She was very conscious of his physical nearness and concentrated hard on the steps so as not to make a mistake or stumble. His arm felt so strong and comforting about her waist, that she found herself telling him of the two accidents which had so nearly befallen Fitz and herself. He took the incidents seriously and urged her to be vigilant and in spite of her determined stance against marriage, the feel of his hard strength next to her made Sophia aware of the advantages of having a regular partner, reliable and supportive. Someone to protect her from danger, someone to love and cherish her when things went wrong, someone like Sir Paul Maunders, for instance? But he didn't love her; Marie Baronne was proof of that. His proposal was entirely out of duty because he felt he had compromised her reputation.

She gave a little impatient shake of her

head, of which he was fully aware. Indeed, Sir Paul Maunders was aware of every sensuous movement of her body, of the warm rhythm of her pulse and the way the little curls at her brow quivered when he breathed near them. He was tormented by his acute awareness of her and his desire to kiss her.

She was silent and finally, he observed lightly, 'You are not speaking and are shaking your head over me, Miss Winterton. Am I not forgiven then for my earlier remarks about your age and decrepitude? Am I consigned forever to suffer your disapproval? Must I be prepared to get me to a nunnery, or even a monastery, whichever is appropriate, because I had the temerity to ask for your hand in marriage? Is there no help for me?'

Startled, her eyes sought his, but immediately she summoned up a laugh and said, 'You are quite incorrigible. I can do nothing with you.'

'You could marry me,' he said very softly against her ears, and she drew back, blushing furiously. She was appalled to find that she was unable to look away. She was compelled to look at him. She felt breathless. This was ridiculous. It was the second time he'd mentioned marriage. Had he no shame after she'd so crushingly refused him? The normally spirited and verbal Sophia Winterton could think of absolutely nothing to say and they continued the waltz in silence.

Both Miss Fitzpatrick and Lady Maunders had watched with interest while Paul and Sophia danced the waltz and although they couldn't hear a word of what was being said, they had exchanged the merest flicker of a glance when they'd both noticed the shake of Sophia's head and the way that she had drawn back when he'd suggested she could marry him. Both of them were left to wonder whether the romance was going to flourish between the two of them or whether it was not.

When the dance ended, he escorted her back to her seat and asked humbly if he might solicit her hand in another waltz. She went through the motions of pretending to consult her card, but as she had only just received approval for a waltz, they both knew it was only a formality and Sophia curtsied and agreed, letting him take the card and scribble his name.

Thomas Thornton's friend, George Sinclair was her partner for the next country dance and she did her best to be friendly and entertaining. He was her own age and so a little more acceptable in her eyes than some of the younger men.

She so enjoyed talking to him, that when he asked if he might escort her into supper, she was about to accept, but then just past his shoulder, she saw Sir Paul Maunders, who said with the greatest panache and confidence, 'Miss Winterton, we are engaged to go into supper together, are we not?'

This was a blatant untruth, but for some reason she felt unwilling to refute it and said gently, 'Mr Sinclair, I have so enjoyed our conversation, but I am promised to Sir Paul for supper. Perhaps we may enjoy a dance later?'

He bowed politely and withdrew and Sophia took Sir Paul's proffered arm and went with him into the supper-room. As she did so, she was aware that her heart was beating a rapid tattoo inside her chest and that she felt a quite ignoble pleasure in the fact that several young ladies and their mamas were looking at her with ill-concealed envy because she had the company and attention of one of the most handsome and eligible men in the room.

As always, it was very plain food at Almack's and she was forced to smile at his grimace as he looked at the lemonade and plain sponge cake which were on offer.

'One must take care to dine substantially before coming here,' he said with the sardonic smile that she knew so well. 'You and I have had much better fare,' he said thoughtfully. 'It doesn't do to long for better food when dining at Almack's, yet I recall vividly that al fresco meal on our journey from Norfolk and the mouth watering meat pie prepared by Polly's mother.'

Immediately, he realized what he had said and the compromising situation they'd been in when they'd enjoyed that particular picnic. Sophia blushed to the very roots of her hair and looked down at her plate.

'Miss Winterton — Sophia,' he said, and ignoring the curious glances of several of the starchy dowagers, he seized both her hands and raised them to his lips. 'I do beg your pardon. I have quite put you to the blush. Forgive me.'

'You, sir, are always putting me to the blush, every time we meet,' she said indignantly. 'I suppose I should be accustomed to it by now.' She tried to free her hands, but he refused to relinquish them.

'It is my fondest hope that you will become even more used to it,' he said softly. 'And you used to call me Paul when we travelled from Norfolk.'

She blushed again, not knowing how to answer him and he let go of her hands and turned to greet a friend of his mama's who had four single daughters and was a notorious husband hunter. He kept his bow to one of strict formality and his smile to one of mere politeness, so that even his mama's determined friend blenched a little and didn't pause to chat.

'Oh Lord, thank heavens she has gone,' he groaned. 'The last thing I want is the pleasure of a dance with one of Mrs Watson's girls. This is the first time I have been to Almack's for a few years, and now I can remember why.'

'A pointless exercise, if you have no pleasure in it,' Sophia said coolly. 'I wonder how Lady Maunders was able to persuade you to attend at all, this evening.'

His dark gaze met hers with an uncomfortable intensity. 'Oh yes you do, Sophia,' he whispered. 'You know very well I was persuaded to attend by your presence and for no other reason.'

She was thrown into such confusion by this remark and the look which accompanied it, that all she managed to say was 'Sir!'

She pressed her lips together, determined not to say any more, but she was still flushed and her mind was still filled with the memory of his proposal and his anger when she'd refused him.

For a moment she had been startled by the

openly passionate glow in his dark eyes, the sincerity in his voice and his caressing smile. Then, just as she was thinking, this won't do! he assumed his most polite and bland expression and spoke only of banalities, until her embarrassment faded.

His behaviour from then on was above reproach and once more he was the congenial friend and companion that she remembered and she began to feel more at ease with him again. She found his mind so very similar to hers that she was not obliged to explain her own particular blend of humour, or guard her tongue for fear of offending him The rest of the supper interval passed pleasantly and he was attentive to her needs without behaving in any lover-like way, so that she was reassured and relaxed, enjoying the evening. She danced with both George and Robert Sinclair and with Thomas Thornton who, a little later in the evening, had occasion to come to the rescue of Miss Cecilia Wright, when she caught her foot in the hem of her dress and fell heavily, twisting her ankle very painfully. While Miss Wright's partner stood looking on rather helplessly, both Thomas and Sophia went to Miss Wright's assistance and it was obvious from the young lady's soft adoring eyes that Thomas was her knight in shining armour. She winced with pain as

Sophia tried to help her up and it was clear that she couldn't put any weight on her foot.

Immediately, Thomas Thornton scooped her up in his arms and said quietly to Sophia, 'Show me to the ladies' retiring-room, if you please, Miss Winterton, so that Miss Wright may rest a little and recover.'

He was all concern, inspecting the swollen ankle with the utmost gentleness and sending one of the abigails to bring her aunt to attend her. He was much moved by her bravery when the little satin slipper had to be removed from the injured foot and although her beautiful soft lips quivered and her huge eyes were flooded with unshed tears, Miss Wright remained as brave as ever. Seeing the look of admiration on Thomas Thornton's face and the innocent trust on Miss Wright's as they gazed at each other, Sophia left her to the maid and retired from the room, well pleased.

Sir Paul came to claim Sophia later on for another waltz and this time she felt no constraint at all, but chattered and laughed with the utmost naturalness, so that he was utterly enchanted all over again and determined now that whatever happened, he wouldn't take her 'no' for an answer or ever let her go.

'I suppose I must make the most of you,

Miss Winterton,' he said with mock gravity. 'Even though the esteemed patroness has given you permission to waltz, it would be frowned upon if you were to dance with me for a third time.'

She smiled up at him. 'Is that a polite way of telling me that you do not wish to dance with me again, sir?'

'No. It is a polite way of telling you that you are absolutely irresistible and adorable.' His voice was low and he lifted the hand that he was clasping to his lips and kissed it lightly.

The words were spoken before he could stop himself and with such feeling that Sophia immediately stiffened and replaced her hand in the correct position for waltzing. All her unhappiness and doubts came flooding back again and she realized with a pang, how foolish she was being to lower her guard like this.

'What is it? What is troubling you?' he asked gently.

'Nothing.'

'Is it that villain Baggett? Has he been bothering you again?'

'No. Nothing is troubling me.'

As she continued to look downcast, trying not to respond, he said, 'Please don't fob me off. Something is making you unhappy. What is it? Is it because I've offered for you before you were ready? Was it too soon after . . . after Devenish, perhaps?'

'No. Really. It is nothing.'

How could you ask a man if he had a mistress called Marie Baronne? It was impossible. Besides, even if it were true, he could deny it and such was her love for him, she would long with all her heart to believe him. Women were such fools in love and she was no exception. These thoughts strengthened Sophia's resolution and she said in a stronger voice, 'I assure you, sir, nothing is troubling me.'

She turned her head away from him and he fixed his eyes on her profile. Then he said, 'Don't you think you might reconsider my offer? I . . . I can't think you are as indifferent to me as you would have me believe.'

She flushed. 'If I have led you to think I felt more than liking for you, please forgive me . . . I . . . '

He smiled ruefully at this and whispered, 'My dear girl, you have never led me to think anything of the kind, *au contraire*, you have always been the most antagonistic, combative, difficult female I ever met in my life. You have consistently held me at arm's length, argued against everything I say or do, and have generally been most infuriating. You have even gone so far as to threaten me with your pistol! These are not the actions of a young lady who is expressing more than mere liking for a fellow! And yet . . . and yet . . . there has been a look in your eyes . . . I am not a callow youth . . . I couldn't mistake it.'

'Yes, I am sure you have had a lot of experience with women,' she said bitterly. 'But even if I wished to be married, it would not be to a man whose morals . . . whose way of life . . . is . . . is so different from my own.'

So that was it, he thought. He suspected Marie's handiwork in all this. That whore. She was even more devious than he thought.

They were both silent now, but Paul held her a little closer for the rest of the dance and Sophia did nothing to prevent him, finding comfort in the clasp of his hand and the warmth of his arm around her waist. All of this was noticed by Lady Maunders and Miss Fitzpatrick, but by the time he'd escorted her back to her seat the flush on her face had faded and she was calm and composed again.

'May I hope to see you at Lady Wright's masquerade at Vauxhall on Friday?' he said, as he bowed his farewell.

'Yes, I expect to be there,' was all Sophia said.

With that, Sir Paul departed and went to

his club where the first person he saw was William Baggett, surrounded by some of his cronies. As soon as those gentlemen met the hard level gaze of Sir Paul Maunders, they melted away discreetly to the various club rooms and Baggett himself, trapped where he was, tried to look away and cut him dead, but with only a slightly raised black eyebrow, Sir Paul gave him no option but to hear him out.

'It has come to my attention, Baggett,' he said quietly and almost conversationally, 'that you are indulging in a little evil blackmail against someone who is very dear to me.'

Baggett's dissipated face went first red and then deathly white as he faced his enemy. His small wet mouth was pinched and white with anger, but there was fear in his eyes as he muttered, 'I have no idea what you mean.'

'Oh yes you have,' Sir Paul said. 'You observed a certain young lady and myself on our journey from Norfolk and you made insulting assumptions about the situation. This is my warning to you, Baggett. Cease your importuning of Miss Winterton. She and I are betrothed and are to be married. If you do not desist forthwith from your pestering, you will have me to reckon with.'

Baggett recovered enough poise to say sneeringly in his reedy cracked voice, 'Oh really, Maunders? Will it be pistols at dawn or will you resort to your famous fisticuffs? Either way, it will do the lady's reputation no good at all. Your threats are as ineffective as your so-called *protection* of her. The last time I met her, she was betrothed to no one.'

There were now no gentlemen in the ante-room. Most were engaged at the faro tables or chatting over brandies in the various card-rooms. Acting on an irrational, passionate impulse, Sir Paul grasped William Baggett by the immaculate reveres of his black evening jacket and dragged him forcibly towards him, saying between clenched teeth, 'I give you fair warning, Baggett. Get back to Cottleton where you belong and leave Sophia Winterton alone, or it will be the worse for you!'

William Baggett was tall, but not as tall as Sir Paul. He was strong, but gazing so closely into those uncompromising black eyes, almost feral in their fierce antagonism, there was no contest. When Sir Paul released him, he stepped backwards a little and adjusted his cravat sulkily, his podgy hands trembling. After a quick glance around him to ascertain that no one had noticed their ungentlemanly exchange, he turned away and stalked angrily into the card-room, leaving Sir Paul still glaring at his retreating back.

David Winterton had entered the club at

that very moment and although he hadn't heard Paul's declaration that he was betrothed to Sophia, or seen Baggett's humiliation, he was in time to see him stalk away, angry and chagrined, and to observe Sir Paul's furious scowl.

They greeted each other politely and Paul stopped scowling to chat affably to Sophia's cousin. He'd told Sophia that he and David Winterton were old friends, but in reality he was an acquaintance of long standing, rather than a close friend. They were members of the same clubs and when David was in London, they both practised boxing with a former bruiser turned coach. Paul liked what he saw of David Winterton and knew him to be a gentleman. Furthermore, he was Sophia's much-loved cousin, her brother, in all but name, so when David suggested a quiet glass of brandy, he agreed and led the way into one of the lounges. Here there were no card games or billiards to distract them and they could settle down comfortably together.

'You seem to be extending your visit to the City, Winterton,' Paul smiled.

'Yes indeed,' David replied. 'My cousin has never had occasion to visit London before and I am keen to be around should she need me for anything.'

There was a short pause and then he said quietly, 'Sophia and I are very much obliged to you and your mother for the kindness you've shown her. It . . . it was not the happiest circumstance when she ran away like that . . . set us all about the ears, I can tell you. Aunt Harriet has still not come down from the boughs.'

'That's understandable,' Paul murmured. 'Miss Winterton is . . . um . . . a very spirited lady. It is not to be expected that she could bear to be leg-shackled to an old fortune-hunter like Devenish.'

'That's true,' David agreed, looking serious. Then he grinned suddenly. 'But, oh my God! You should have seen the uproar when she ran off. It was devilish decent of you and your mama to care for her as you did. She's such a firebrand you know, Maunders. There's no dealing with her at times and yet . . . at the same time . . . she's so . . . so . . . '

'Adorable,' Sir Paul Maunders said firmly. 'I know.'

David looked at him in some surprise. 'Yes. I suppose she is,' he said slowly. 'But don't you find her maddening, old fellow?'

'Yes, but you see I fell in love with her the moment I saw her running along the road, although of course I didn't realize it at the time,' Paul said, with the utmost simplicity.

He smiled as David's jaw dropped. 'I wasn't just being altruistic in protecting your cousin, you know. If she would accept me, I'd be the happiest man on earth.'

He said it so matter-of-factly and sincerely that David was at a loss for words. 'I see,' was all he could say and thinking of his own feelings in connection with the delightful Elizabeth Thornton, he raised his glass and said, 'Well, here's good luck to you, Maunders. For my part, I would have no objection to your paying your addresses to my cousin. Good health, sir.'

The two men toasted each other gravely and then smiled.

More seriously, Sir Paul flicked his head in the direction of the card-room, indicating Baggett. 'She has another admirer now and he's by way of being an infernal nuisance. I've had to warn him off. A pity he ever left Norfolk. Sophia won't have him, though.' He forbore to mention that he himself had been turned down in no uncertain terms by the beautiful Sophia Winterton. Instead, he asked David if Miss Winterton had mentioned the two near fatal accidents that had recently endangered her life. David had not heard of this and was very concerned for Sophia's safety.

'I don't mind telling you, old fellow, that

I'm dashed worried myself,' Sir Paul said. 'Neither Miss Fitzpatrick or Miss Winterton have any idea of who could wish her harm, or indeed whether both incidents were purely accidental. I am in touch with a retired army batman who works part time as a Bow Street officer. If you agree, I could get him to keep a discreet eye on Sophia and Miss Fitzpatrick, as well as that rogue Baggett and ascertain whether she is in danger and from whom.'

David was only too pleased to agree to this and the two men promised to meet at the Vauxhall Gardens Masquerade. Paul left the club on very amicable terms with Sophia's cousin and David was left alone. He was not on his own for long however. As he sat with the last of his brandy, he thought deeply of this new turn of events. If Sophia and Sir Paul Maunders were to make a match of it, he would be pleased and delighted. He couldn't wish for a better man to love and care for Sophia in marriage and it might be that his own courtship would be successful.

Lost in his thoughts, he didn't at first notice Baggett sidling up to him and was less than civil when Baggett greeted him and asked after Harriet Winterton and his cousin Sophia. 'Dashed fine girl, your cousin,' he said. 'Some might find her recent behaviour hard to stomach, but I tell you, Winterton, I'd be prepared to overlook that if you was to look favourably on me as her husband.'

David almost laughed at this and said scathingly, 'My cousin is not for the likes of you, Baggett.'

William Baggett glared. 'Could do worse,' he said. 'And I'd be willing to keep quiet over her escapade with Maunders. It would save her reputation. If I told what I knew, your family name would be ruined.'

David didn't even bother to answer this, but turned away contemptuously, before he gave way to the temptation to land Baggett a facer. Baggett himself left shortly afterwards and made his way to 19 Sutton Street.

13

The day before Lady Wright's party, the event was announced in the social columns of the newspaper and as Sophia and Miss Fitzpatrick enjoyed a leisurely breakfast in the sunny little dining parlour, Miss Fitzpatrick read out various items of interest to Sophia and then silently handed her the newspaper which she had folded open at a page largely devoted to carefully phrased gossip about members of the *ton*. It stated that Lady Wright, aunt to the beautiful Miss Cecilia Wright, and famous for her soirées and social gatherings, was entertaining various high-ranking members of London Society to a masquerade party in Vauxhall Gardens. The illustrious guest list included Miss Sophia Winterton, Miss Lavinia Carleton, the beautiful twin daughters of Mr and Mrs Thornton and other persons of consequence such as Sir Paul Maunders and the Dowager Lady Maunders as well as a recent visitor to London, Mr William Baggett. The writer of the paragraph added coyly that several beautiful young debutantes and well-connected young men had received invitations, so perhaps further interesting announcements might be expected.

This item was very gratifying to Miss Fitzpatrick, but Sophia was not so impressed and merely said that newspapers were always full of such trivia. Even so, she gave a little shiver of excitement at the prospect of the evening to come.

Someone else had also read the announcement. Marie Baronne lounging in her boudoir with William Baggett, rang the bell languidly and ordered more hot chocolate for them both. When the paper arrived, she flicked the announcements page with one carefully manicured finger and said, 'Look at this.'

'Yes, the opportunity we need,' Baggett said. They both whispered, thinking that the maid could return any time. Baggett thrust his unpleasant wet lips into Marie's naked shoulder and felt her flinch slightly.

'Seize the moment,' he said, his reedy voice almost falsetto. 'You did well when you arranged your encounter with Sophia Winterton and destroyed her illusions of romance with Maunders. But at Vauxhall Gardens, there's more to play for and no room for mistakes. Once Harriet Winterton is rid of Sophie, you could win back Maunders and I could be evens with that stiff-necked jade,

Sophia Winterton and her top-lofty cousin. You must attend the party, but no Helen of Troy or Queen Bess costume for you, my girl. You must dress as a humble flower-seller and then you'll get to wear a bonnet and shawl and carry a basket. Both good means of concealment.'

Marie moved away from him slightly and asked, 'And what of you, sir? What is your costume of choice?'

'Why, Nero of course, the omnipotent emperor.' He gave his characteristic high-pitched titter.

The maid entered the room with the chocolate and Baggett waited until she departed before he outlined his plan to Marie Baronne.

On the day of the masquerade the sun had almost disappeared behind the clouds and for the first time, there was an almost autumnal feel to the air, but Sophia hardly felt it. She and Miss Fitzpatrick had chosen their costumes with care and were both convinced that no one would be able to recognize them. There was to be a prize for the most baffling disguise of the evening and she was looking forward to seeing the costumes of her new young friends.

'I shall go as a humble shepherdess, not a Marie Antoinette pastiche of the character,' declared Miss Fitzpatrick. 'I have fashioned my crook from garden bamboo and ribbon. After all, my love, there will be any number of Marie Antoinettes and stately queens of England at Vauxhall this evening. What about you, Sophie? You are tall for a woman. Do you think you could be some more antique heroine perhaps?'

'Something like that, Fitz. I thought of Cleopatra. Although the costume is, of necessity, rather flimsy, she would also have a cloak and an asp, of course. With the wig and the painted lines on my eyes and the mask, my disguise should be a good one.'

'A stroke of inspiration on your part,' Miss Fitzpatrick said. Then she smiled mischievously and added, 'I wonder how many Mark Anthonys and Julius Caesars there will be this evening, my dear?'

Some of Lady Wright's guests were taking sculls from Westminster to cross the river and were to be accompanied by a boat with a small chamber ensemble to entertain them. Miss Fitzpatrick was enchanted at this idea and almost wished they were in that particular party, but Sophia was content with the coach and John Glover, the reliable coachman. They were to meet Lady Maunders and Sir Paul inside Vauxhall itself and had exchanged confidences about their disguises. Sir Paul was going as Othello and her ladyship was dressed as a very dignified Britannia, complete with trident and shield.

The evening was fine and although not yet dusk, all the walks were lit by golden globes of light, burning with a myriad of lanterns and lamps, as the two ladies made for the centre of the pleasure gardens. Lady Wright had reserved a number of booths for her party, all draped with pink and white muslin and all named with place settings for her guests. The whole scene had a magical sparkle and an atmosphere of party gaiety; light spilled out of every booth and flowed from the open entry of every secluded walk as they made their way towards one of Lady Wright's footmen. They presented their cards and were immediately caught up in a flood of costumed bodies struggling to find their places.

In the middle was a large open pavilion where the orchestra was playing for the dancing and more punctual guests in fancy dress and wearing masks strolled about to greet friends and to show off their costumes.

They were met almost immediately by Lady Maunders, who was already finding the accessories to her costume a bit of a nuisance.

'Paul has blacked his face and is trying out

his disguise in front of some of Lady Wright's other guests,' she said. 'But I'm finding these so tedious,' she added, as she dropped her trident and shield inside their box. 'I feel much better now that I haven't those horrid things to carry. I am going to have a stroll round, my dear. Should you and Miss Fitzpatrick care to keep me company?'

'Why yes, ma'am, but equally, I like to watch the world and his wife go by. Perhaps Miss Fitzpatrick may care to go with you and I . . . I shall catch up with you later.'

She knew she was looking her best as Cleopatra, the most beautiful woman in the world and was hoping that Sir Paul would present himself to her, but he didn't appear, so she settled herself in the box and surveyed the passing throng through her velvet mask.

Miss Fitzpatrick was only too delighted to tuck Lady Maunders' arm in hers and commence a leisurely stroll to look at the superb fountains and cascades for which the gardens were justly famous. Sophia accepted a glass of ratafia from one of Lady Wright's hired waiters and enjoyed sitting back and looking at everything.

The scene was a strange mixture of the elegant and the grotesque. Some, like the graceful black and white Harlequin and the equally elegant dainty Columbine, in her stiffly starched skirts and white stockings and pumps, were almost unreal in their grace and beauty. Others, including a large, grossly corpulent man, who was dressed to represent Falstaff and his equally portly partner unsuitably dressed as Maid Marian, could never be described as elegant, even if they lived to be a hundred.

She still held her dark-blue velvet mask quite high and with the headdress and dark wig of the famous Cleopatra, she was sure that none would recognize her. She enjoyed identifying first, Thomas Thornton as the Harlequin, in his bold chequered costume and black mask and then almost immediately, she realized that the exquisitely small dainty Columbine must be Miss Cecilia Wright. Soul mates, she thought to herself. Even their disguises matched each other.

'And do you really have an asp?' came a voice behind her, and Sophia turned to see a studious Will Shakespeare, complete with small pointed beard and quill pen with a roll of ancient parchment. She recognized the voice of her cousin David and smiled behind her concealing mask.

'No, indeed, Mr Shakespeare. It is merely a model made of paper and paste.'

He lowered his voice a little. 'With so many guests and all in fancy dress, it is hard to recognize who is friend and who is foe, Coz.'

His words caused a momentary shiver the length of Sophia's spine. She wondered what disguise the hateful William Baggett had adopted and studied her cousin's masked face in some alarm.

'What can you mean, David?'

'I mean,' he said, 'that although many people here appear as total strangers, yet there are those who will be determined to guess your identity however impenetrable your disguise. Be careful, Sophia,' he said more quietly still. 'Don't let yourself be alone without Fitz or some of the others in your party. That is all.' He bowed and kissed her hand, then left her. She looked about her carefully and observed a very military-looking Roman soldier in a leather kilt and metal helmet and carrying a short sword, strolling by in a most unmilitary fashion. She became aware that quite unconsciously, she was scanning the ranks of soldiers, sailors and famous kings, wondering which one would be William Baggett.

She rose to her feet, hoping she might follow Thomas Thornton and Miss Wright. She could catch them up and walk with them to join Lady Maunders along one of the main walks, but at that moment, the Roman soldier appeared and begged for the honour of a dance with her. She smiled as she recognized him. Richard Andrews, she thought and accepted graciously. She took his proffered arm and he led her on to the dance floor. He danced gracefully in spite of the leather panels of his kilt and the restraints of the helmet.

'Well, are you enjoying it, Miss Winterton?' he asked and smiled at her.

'Why, yes,' she said. 'But . . . but . . . How did you know?'

'Your name? Easy, Miss Winterton. You are the most beautiful young lady in London. Cleopatra was the most famous beauty in the world. You have disguised your glorious hair and are wearing a mask, but you're not able to hide your upright graceful posture, the beauty and fluidity of your walk Oh . . . a hundred clues, Miss Winterton . . . ' He stammered to a halt as though embarrassed that he had said so much. 'And then there is your attractive speaking voice,' he went on. 'So distinctive and lovely. But you also seemed quick to penetrate my own disguise.'

'Yes, it wasn't too difficult. Your voice mainly, but also your eyes even under the helmet and the mask. I suppose these are clues by which even the lowliest of animals may recognize a friend.'

He was much struck by this observation

and inclined to pursue it further, but conversation was gradually becoming more difficult. It was almost impossible to hear anything in such a throng. After a full half-hour, by mutual consent, they made their way to the vast tent which housed a sumptuous supper of cold chicken, buttered prawns and the usual standby of society hostesses with a crowd to feed, white soup. All of it was delightful. The ratafia cakes were delicious, but Sophia felt a little pang at the thought that she had neglected to seek out her other friends and she wondered where Fitz might be.

'I should like to return to our box, if I may,' she said. 'Lady Maunders and Miss Fitz-patrick will be wondering what has happened to me.'

'Of course,' he said, and led her back to the booth where Lady Maunders had left her trident and helmet and politely took his leave of her. Contrary to her expectations, there was no Fitz or Lady Maunders and after a few minutes of scanning the passing crowd in vain, she set off to seek them out. Ahead of her, she thought she spotted Harlequin and Columbine and hurried in pursuit of them. As she followed them, they turned down one of the more secluded narrow alleys and she had a sudden feeling that the lights had dimmed somewhat. At that moment, she lost sight of Harlequin and Columbine and cast about, somewhat confused, wondering how they had so suddenly disappeared and where on earth Lady Maunders and Fitz had got to.

Harlequin and Columbine had turned along a quiet pathway, pleased to be away from the crowd and they now slowed to a saunter. Miss Wright was saying in her soft and gentle voice, 'I never cared anything for driving before I met you, Mr Thornton. That is, I have always loved riding my own dear little Bessie, but I so enjoyed my driving lesson the other day.'

'I confess I find it very exciting,' Thomas Thornton said very enthusiastically. 'But it is different for young ladies, naturally. They do not seem so keen on it.'

'But I am very keen,' Miss Wright said eagerly. 'I also find it exciting and would be delighted to try it again.'

Without meaning to, she stretched out her hand to him as she spoke and immediately he stood still and took her little hand in his looking at her with such kind and loving eyes that her heart began to race.

'Dear Miss Wright . . . Cecilia . . . You are so beautiful. I do love you,' he said.

'Oh,' she gasped and the next moment she was in his arms, whispering that she had loved him from the moment he had first held dear little Patch and taken charge of him. 'I knew then that one so kind and strong as you, must have my heart,' she said confidingly.

'Cecilia, you are so sweet, so gentle,' Thomas said. 'I couldn't help but love you when I saw the tender concern you had for the little dog.'

The next few minutes were spent in kissing and murmured endearments as the two young lovers exchanged more confidences about their feelings for each other before strolling on down the path.

'But I thought you were Miss Winterton's beau?' Miss Wright said at last, very innocently.

'No, not at all,' Thomas disclaimed. 'A man may sometimes be attracted to a vivacious female such as Miss Winterton, but it's you I love, darling Cecilia. I have loved you from the first and I mean to marry you.'

Neither of them thought it worth wondering what Cecilia's aunt and uncle or indeed her parents would say to this declaration, but merely strolled on, both lost in a dream of love.

David Winterton meanwhile, had set off to meet with Sir Paul, by prior arrangement. He knew that Sir Paul would be disguised as Othello and he'd informed Sir Paul that he himself was to be William Shakespeare. He had a good pair of legs and was very attractive in doublet and hose and with part of his face concealed by a false Elizabethan beard. He appeared at the agreed time in the nearest arbour to the Grand Fountain and was surprised to see Sir Paul in company with a small stocky man who stood silently in the shadows.

'And who might this be?' he asked, when they'd greeted each other.

'This,' said Sir Paul gravely, 'is Mr John Sawyer from Bow Street. He has my complete confidence. It's Mr Sawyer's belief and mine also, that the two near fatal accidents recently sustained by your cousin, were not accidents at all, but serious attempts on her life.'

'So, what are you and Sawyer planning?'

'Mr Sawyer has already spent some time keeping Miss Winterton under surveillance and — '

'If you want to put someone under surveillance, Sawyer,' David Winterton growled, 'it should be that damnable Baggett. I met him the other night at White's and the dog threatened me. Threatened me ! Said if I didn't look favourably on his courtship of Sophia, my family name would be ruined. I tell you Maunders, I ain't in the habit of taking that sort of talk easily.'

Looking at David Winterton's angry expression and flashing eyes, so like his dear Sophia's, Sir Paul was in no doubt of that.

'Let me assure you, sir,' he said calmly, 'that there is not the slightest danger of such a thing. Sophia — Miss Winterton — that is, has rejected him in no uncertain terms and Sawyer here has been keeping an eye on William Baggett.'

Mr Sawyer coughed behind his hand. 'Beggin' parding, gentlemen,' he said. 'One of my men has been watching the said Baggett and has reported as how he's taken up with a Marie Baronne, sir.'

Paul looked startled at this and muttered, 'The devil he has. And what sort of mischief are the two of them hatching, I wonder?'

'As to that, I don't know, sir, but both parties is present here tonight. Miss Winterton may be in danger at this very moment. I think you should stay close to her.'

David Winterton was obviously concerned at this and gazed questioningly at Sir Paul.

'My thoughts are that you, Winterton, should keep Baggett under close surveillance for the whole of the evening. I myself shall go to my mother's booth and stay with Sophia. Sawyer's is the most difficult role. Please patrol all the time and look out for suspicious characters, but keep within shouting distance in case we shall need you. We'll meet up at this place at the end of the evening or if for some reason, we lose each other.'

David Winterton nodded and went in search of Baggett. Paul stood thinking for a moment and then said, almost to himself, 'I am determined to settle this business with the rogues responsible for trying to harm Sophia and then I shall claim her as my wife.'

To John Sawyer he said, 'Any surveillance we do tonight must carry with it a certain risk. I'm glad I'll have you and Winterton as my aides because we'll need to catch the villains before they can harm her. I'll go and seek out Miss Winterton now, old fellow. Keep your eyes and ears open and stay reasonably close. Don't forget, if we lose contact with each other, we shall return to this spot.'

He set off towards the main pavilion where the dancing was in progress and lounged casually around the perimeter of the dance floor, his roving eyes belying the studied relaxation of his movements. John Sawyer, equally alert, blended in with the crowds strolling round the area. Paul took himself unobtrusively to Lady Wright's box but saw only her ladyship and Miss Carleton sipping wine and fanning themselves. The twins and their brother were on the dance floor but neither Sophia or his mother were to be seen.

Puzzled by the disappearance of Fitz and Lady Maunders, Sophia continued down the smaller alley where she'd last seen them. There were still many people about on the main walks, but the particular path she was treading seemed strangely deserted. She resolved to quicken her pace a little in order to catch up with Lady Maunders and Fitz and as she hurried along, distracted by her own thoughts, she almost bumped into a flower-seller, whose basket full of nosegays and sweet smelling blooms, fetched her a painful blow on the shin. The woman let the basket fall and stood barring her way. She was dressed in a concealing bonnet and had a shawl covering her arms and neck. It was impossible to see what sort of woman she was, except that as she moved nearer to Sophia, something about her swaying sensual movements, seemed oddly familiar. The woman was silent, but Sophia's way forward was now effectively blocked and she looked round helplessly for another pathway. There was a narrow path to her right, but now she noticed a large and corpulent Nero, with a traditional toga and crown of laurels, standing four square across it.

Thoroughly alarmed, she spun round again

looking for a way out, but there behind her, was the sinister figure of Guy Fawkes, dressed in a dark cloak and a slouch hat. It seemed now as though she were trapped.

The bloated-looking Nero now stepped forward and said, 'Stay where you are, Miss Winterton.'

With a shiver of alarm, she recognized immediately that distinctive thin and sibilant voice. He stood under one of the ornamental lanterns, which lit up his face clearly.

She stared at him in silence. Ever since their encounter at the Sir John Falstaff Arms, he had always frightened her and the lantern light revealed his cold eyes and the bulbous nose over-hanging his hideous wet mouth. His sparse hair was scraped under the crown of laurels and revealed the mean cruel face beneath it.

The thin mouth twitched into an evil grin 'Cleopatra,' he said. 'The most beautiful woman in the world.'

It was cold, so cold that Sophia became aware that she was shivering uncontrollably. She had never before known this fear. It was as cold as ice. She knew that Baggett meant more than mischief. She was going to have to pay for all the humiliation that he had suffered. There was nothing she could say or do. She became aware that Guy Fawkes had crept up a little nearer, but she ignored him. She looked again at Baggett's pitiless face. There was no point in begging him to let her go, this would only delight him all the more. She was on her own, without a soul in sight and the other two were there, ready to trip her up, if she decided to make a run for it. In any case, she felt suddenly weak. She had no strength to run and any resistance on her part would either make him laugh or anger him so much that he would kill her. Then, with dreadful clarity, she realized that killing her was not the only thing on his mind. He would enjoy himself first and take his revenge on the proud Miss Winterton who had rejected him so disrespectfully.

She refused to cry or beg for mercy, but tried to play for time. She said perfectly calmly, 'Since you are here, Mr Baggett, and Guy Fawkes too, of course, you can satisfy my curiosity about the mysterious accidents that have befallen me recently.'

He probably thought she'd run mad. She was sure he intended to attack her virtue as brutally as possible and then kill her. Yet here she was, looking him in the eye and making conversation. His voice was an indignant squeak as he said, 'So you want to know, do you? Well my assistant arranged for the wall to collapse on you, my dear, she knows a jack

319

of all trades in Islington, who worked it loose for us and then it only needed a gentle push. The carriage accident was a joint effort, only that interfering old woman, Emma Fitzpatrick, intervened.'

He seemed lost in his own thoughts for a moment and Sophia was silent also. So, Guy Fawkes was a woman. What sort of woman would go to such lengths to try and harm a fellow human being? She could think of no answer and once more, was overcome by terror.

The pause became longer and then he said, 'And now, I'm going to deal with you, Miss high and mighty Winterton and let me tell you, you won't live to enjoy your inheritance.'

As he advanced towards her, she knew that it was all over. There was no path or way of escape open to her. She decided that she would shut her eyes and not resist, but would pray that it would soon be ended and she would be dead. She'd almost forgotten the one behind her, but at that moment became aware that Guy Fawkes had stepped forward and raised an arm holding a heavy club. As it came down forcefully, Sophia dodged to one side and received a blow on her shoulder that felled her to the ground.

The flower-seller gave a startled shriek, then turned and fled.

14

David Winterton set off with cool determination to search methodically for Baggett among the main walks of the gardens, but with no success. The moon had now risen and away from the bright light of the lanterns, the trees and shrubs loomed in dark massed shapes silhouetted against the night sky. He trod silently, gazing at every group of guests as they passed him, but there was no sign of Baggett. It wasn't until almost midnight that he passed once more across the path near the arbour where he'd met Sir Paul Maunders earlier. It was darker here now and in the gloom, he discerned a figure sitting alone in the shadows.

It was John Sawyer, who was sitting on the stone bench and nursing his shoulder.

'Sawyer! What the deuce has happened?'

'Winged by a stab wound from Guy Fawkes hisself, no less,' he said with a rueful grin. 'He was gone in a flash. Just a cut, sir. One of my patrol was able to help me and bind it up. I'm just about to find Sir Paul.'

David returned his grin and said, 'And I'm off to have a quiet talk with our friend

Baggett, when I can find him that is.'

He nodded to Sawyer and strode on, methodically traversing every single path and alley once more, but it was a good twenty minutes before he espied a bulky man with the peculiar mincing walk which immediately identified him as the evil fat Baggett. He was still dressed as Nero, complete with the crown of laurels and a voluminous flowing toga and, as though sensing David's approach, he glanced nervously over one shoulder. When he realized he was being followed, he gave a convulsive start and let out a strangled high-pitched shriek as he tried to quicken his pace.

It was useless. David Winterton put an arm like an iron bar round his throat and clapped his free hand over Baggett's mouth. 'Quiet,' he said, between his teeth. 'Don't dare make a sound, or it'll be the last you ever make.'

Baggett rolled his eyes frantically, indicating that he would remain silent and began to shake like a jelly. His eyes were still rolling alarmingly as he attempted to glimpse his attacker, his hands scrabbling ineffectually in the air as he tried to claw away the vice-like grip on his throat.

'No noise,' David warned him again. 'I shall remove my hand and if you make a sound I promise you I shall break your neck.'

Baggett, his vocal chords crushed, was physically unable to speak and could only roll his eyes more than ever as he tried to nod his head, his large plump body ready to collapse with fear. He was unable to nod his head even when David's cruel grip was loosened somewhat and he was quite incapable of crying out. He could only wheeze as he gasped for breath, still with David's iron hand on the back of his neck.

'Who are you and what do you want?' he whispered hoarsely, still trying to get a look at the elegant Will Shakespeare who had accosted him. 'If you're trying to rob me . . .'

'You know me well, I'm Sophia Winterton's cousin and no, I do not wish to rob you. Listen to me, Baggett, I want a truthful answer and do not raise your voice or it will be the worse for you. Understand?'

'Yes, yes,' Baggett muttered, totally incapable of raising his voice above a whisper. 'Please, I beg you . . .' His voice, from being hoarse and strained, had now become a desperate soft squeak and seeing David's hand descend threateningly, he started to cough. David waited with uncharacteristic patience as Baggett coughed for some seconds and then wailed, 'Wh — what do you want of me, Winterton?'

David curbed his impulse to do Baggett a serious injury and said between clenched teeth, 'You are fully aware that Sophia Winterton is missing and you know what has happened to her. You can tell me where she is.'

'No, no, I haven't seen her. I've no idea what costume she wears or where she is,' Baggett squeaked, his fat face white to the lips.

'You're lying. Someone has been attempting to take Sophia's life and you, Baggett, are the prime suspect.' Once more, he tightened his grip viciously until Baggett seemed about to swoon and his eyes disappeared, revealing only the whites as he gasped and fought for breath. 'No, no, I swear it was nothing to do with me . . . ' His weak squeaky voice now failed him completely.

'Fustian. The other night you attempted to blackmail me and declared your intention of pressing your unwelcome attentions on Sophia.'

'I'd . . . shot the cat, Winterton. My apologies . . . I would not . . . c — could not threaten you.'

'And the matter of attempting to kill a Bow Street Runner?'

'No, no, on my honour . . . I had no hand in any such attempt.'

'Your honour?' David hissed contemptuously. 'What honour? Let me inform you, Baggett, that I have just left John Sawyer and he has been stabbed. He will be able to prosecute whoever has attacked him and you, Baggett, will have to persuade a jury that it was not you who thrust a knife into him and left him for dead.'

'No, no, believe me,' Baggett croaked, still trying to keep his tone hushed. 'It wasn't me. As God is my witness, you must believe me!'

'Believe a gallows cheat' David said derisively. 'I'll live to see you jerk and twist at the end of a rope, Baggett. You'll be doing the morris dance on Tyburn before very long. Your only hope now, is to tell me what you have done with Sophia.'

'Nothing. I have done nothing. It wasn't me who . . . who — '

'Who what?'

'Who wanted . . . '

'Who wanted what?'

'Who wanted her . . . dead.'

Baggett looked ghastly now, unable to stop trembling, his voice reduced to a broken whimper.

'Where is my cousin, now?'

A shudder ran through Baggett's corpulent body and he tried to pull away from his tormentor. 'Dead,' he said, in a despairing croak.

'Dead?' In his fury, David tightened his grip mercilessly until Baggett's face changed from white to puce.

'Who's killed her?'

Baggett sagged in his arms and David thought he was going to have a seizure, but still he didn't release him. He was dangerously close to losing his temper completely and finishing Baggett off.

'Who has killed her?'

'Not I, Winterton. The one in the cloak. G — Guy Fawkes in the black m — mask.'

He gave a moan and suddenly became limp, his legs sagging, unable to support him. With an angry oath, David thrust him away in disgust and Baggett, his crown of laurels a mangled mess, sank to the ground at the side of the path, groaning. Whatever Baggett had or had not done, David thought, he was now clearly no threat to Sophia.

He strode back to the meeting point and found Sir Paul and John Sawyer about to search the gardens once more in their quest to find Sophia. They were silent while David reported on his encounter with William Baggett.

'We'll keep together and comb each main path and all the smaller ones in every direction,' Paul said finally. 'So far, I have had absolutely no sighting of Sophia. We must find Guy Fawkes, urgently. When we apprehend him, Sawyer here can summon his patrol and have him arrested on the spot. It shouldn't be difficult to pick up Baggett and take him into custody. Do you have a pistol, Sawyer?'

The Runner nodded. As well as managing to have his wound seen to, Sawyer had also acquired a lantern and he lit it and walked at the back of the other two, the beam fixed steadily on the path before them. Sir Paul walked as swiftly as he could, conscious that finding Sophia was now a matter of urgency. They were going along one of the less frequented paths and ahead of them loomed dense darkness. He could hear Sawyer's laboured breathing and realized that his wound must be paining him. Glancing at David Winterton he saw his anger and anxiety, by the set of his pugnacious jaw, in sharp relief with the lantern shining behind him. Inside his head, he prayed desperately that they would find Sophia soon.

They came across her suddenly, seeing at first only what looked like a heap of clothes lying slightly to one side of the path and partially hidden under a laurel bush. Lying nearby was an overturned basket of flowers and the black Cleopatra wig which had disguised her so effectively. But not well enough to deceive the murderer, Paul thought.

'Bring the lantern nearer,' he ordered, his voice hoarse with emotion. There was another silence as all three men dropped to the ground to examine what they recognized as the body of Sophia Winterton. She was unconscious and deathly pale, but still breathing.

'Thank God,' Paul breathed. 'Here, Winterton, give me a hand. Gently now. Leave the lantern, Sawyer, and go and get the carriage brought round to the main entrance.'

They lifted her with the utmost care and Sir Paul gathered her up in his arms. 'We'll get her to the carriage as quickly as possible,' he said. He drew a deep breath and sighed. 'I hope we don't get caught up in the crowds trying to leave.'

The journey to Sir Paul's carriage was accomplished slowly and safely. Along the way, all of David Winterton's frequent offers to relieve Sir Paul of his precious burden, were courteously refused and both men were thankful when they finally reached the carriage and were able to lift Sophia inside and settle her comfortably against the cushions.

John Sawyer had seen Miss Fitzpatrick and Lady Maunders, waiting for John Glover. They'd assumed that Sophia was with other young people in the party and would be meeting them at the coach for their homeward journey. He told them briefly that Miss Sophia had met with an accident and was being taken home by her cousin and Sir Paul Maunders.

The normally calm Miss Fitzpatrick was all of a twitter at this. 'Oh my goodness, we must make all haste to return home and prepare ... I shall have to send for Dr Humphreys. Oh, it is so late. What can have happened to the poor child? She was in my care! How could I have been so negligent? Oh dear, oh dear, how did this all come about?'

'We don't rightly know as yet, ma'am,' John Sawyer said stolidly. 'But she's injured, ma'am, and will definitely need the doctor. That's all as I knows at the moment.'

Late as it was, he nodded to the ladies and returned to his search for the mysterious Guy Fawkes.

All the way to her house, Fitz kept up her anxious speculations as to what might have happened to her dear goddaughter and, to Lady Maunder's credit, she remained calm and reassuring throughout it all and even stayed on to help poor Miss Fitzpatrick to prepare for the injured girl. John Glover was dispatched to knock up the good doctor and request his presence urgently.

Not ten minutes after this, Sir Paul and David arrived with Sophia who had briefly recovered consciousness on the way home and had whispered that she'd been stopped by a flower-seller and by William Baggett, dressed as Nero. Guy Fawkes had indeed struck her but she had been unable to recognize him, behind the disguise. She was speedily put into bed and Dr Humphreys duly arrived and listened patiently to Lady Maunders' explanations and Miss Fitzpatrick's tearful recriminations against herself and her folly in leaving her dear Sophia unattended.

Gently but firmly, he cleared the room of all visitors and carers except for Miss Fitzpatrick. Then Dr Humphreys carefully and expertly felt her injured shoulder and declared that it was not fractured and her arm was not broken and, in spite of having fallen heavily, no ribs were damaged. 'Mercifully, she is still unconscious so I can strap up her shoulder, ma'am,' he said. 'I shall wait until she comes round before I administer any medicine. Meanwhile, bathe her temples with lavender water and I shall prepare a sleeping draught for her to make sure she has a comfortable night.'

Over the next few days, flowers, fruit and several magnificent bouquets gave silent testimony to the love and affection of her young friends and also to the devotion of Lady Maunders and her son. They visited daily to enquire how she did and Dr Humphreys gave the same reply to every concerned questioner.

'She is young and strong. I am certain she will recover. She is sleeping at the moment and although I can administer cordials and medicines to help her, nature must be allowed time to heal her. I am in no doubt that Miss Winterton will sleep herself better. Whoever has done this to her deserves to be hanged.'

Sir Paul Maunders was of the same opinion, but no amount of enquiries by John Sawyer met with any success whatsoever, except that early the following morning, the costume of the legendary Guy Fawkes had been found near the river by one of the stewards hired for Lady Wright's party.

Miss Fitzpatrick was on duty every night, giving Sophia Dr Humphreys' medicine and bathing her temples after he had been to check on the progress of her shoulder, but it was left to young Polly to guard her mistress from taxing visitors during the day and to take up Sophia's lemonade and barley water, to tidy her hair and straighten the bed, causing as little discomfort and pain to her mistress as she could.

By Wednesday, Sophia was allowed to sit up for half an hour, supported by a mountain of pillows and sustained by a strong painkilling draught from the doctor who left the house full of confidence that she was at last on the mend and with a promise to return as usual the next day. Miss Fitzpatrick was persuaded by Dr Humphreys to have a lie down and Polly sat sewing by Sophia's bed, talking to her in a soft voice.

It was at that precise moment that Sophia's Aunt Harriet chose to visit, just as the invalid was beginning to sit up against the pillows and take notice. Without using Miss Fitzpatrick's polished brass knocker, she strode in and went straight up the stairs to Sophia's bedroom and entered after the briefest of knocks. Sophia, propped up on her pillows looked up at her aunt and tried to smile, 'Why, Aunt Harriet,' she said in a low voice. 'This is a surprise.'

'Yes, isn't it?' her aunt said. 'I heard about your . . . accident and came to see how you did.'

She stood at the bottom of Sophia's bed and Polly was so flustered, she didn't even offer her a chair. Sophia noticed with some puzzlement that unusually for such a mild day, her aunt was wearing a cloak, with the hood cast back on to her shoulders. As she gazed at her, trying to think of something pleasant to say, Sophia's mind was jolted into sudden activity by the memory of the pair who had pushed her towards the carriage and of the Guy Fawkes wearing a black cloak and mask who had dealt her such a blow in Vauxhall Gardens. She had the haziest recollection that Baggett had referred to his assistant as 'she'. Aunt Harriet's eyes were now rolling a little wildly and Sophia recognized with sudden insight, that Harriet Winterton was now utterly divorced from reality and meant to do her further harm in spite of the presence of Polly. And she is convinced she'll get away with it, she thought, and started up in sudden alarm.

The tense silence was rudely interrupted by a thunderous knocking on the front door and with a hasty, 'Please excuse me, ma'am,' Polly went to answer it, nervous in case poor Miss Fitzpatrick should be disturbed from her well-earned rest.

Opening the door, Polly discovered it to be Sir Paul Maunders and said politely that Miss Winterton was not able to receive visitors. Miss Winterton was still unwell and was not allowed to leave her room.

'I know that,' Sir Paul said brusquely. 'Take my card up if you please and say that I wish to speak with her.'

Polly took the card nervously as though it would bite her and said, 'Very well, sir. At once, sir. Please bear with me. I shall convey it to Miss Winterton immediately.'

'Don't keep me waiting on the doorstep, girl,' he said gruffly, and poor Polly was nonplussed. She knew Dr Humphreys had said no visitors. She knew Mrs Winterton was at present with her young mistress and she also knew that there would be the devil to pay when Miss Fitzpatrick got up and discovered that the patient was defying doctor's orders and entertaining people in her room.

'Sir. Please,' she said desperately. 'Please, sir. You'm not allowed to see her, today. Miss is only allowed to sit up on the pillows for half an hour. Please, sir. I shall lose my place, so I shall.' She was wringing her hands in an agony of anxiety. 'You must understand, you can't see her, sir. Please! She's not allowed visitors. I'll tell Miss Winterton as you called, so I shall.'

'No, I don't understand that I can't see her,' Sir Paul said brutally. 'And see her I shall.' He made as if to stride past her and she dodged him hurriedly as he went purposefully towards the stairs.

Polly followed him more slowly, wondering whether her new-found happiness and contentment in the employ of a lady of Miss Winterton's quality would soon be at an end, after she'd committed such a grave social solecism. When she reached Sophia's room, Sophia who had been lying back with her eyes half-closed when she'd left her, now had them opened fully and was gazing at her aunt Harriet in horror. Her aunt was standing very stiffly, still wearing her cloak with the hood thrown back on her shoulders and now for the first time, Sophia saw that she was holding the very same pistol that her uncle had given her and that she thought had been lost. Harriet was now holding it and pointing it with a deadly purpose, at Sophia's head.

'Aunt Harriet,' she whispered, 'wha-what has happened?'

'Nothing, dear Niece,' Aunt Harriet said in a honeyed voice. 'A slight misjudgement on my part at the Vauxhall Gardens the other night. That fool, Baggett was too lily-livered to carry out his part in the accident I'd planned for you.'

'Accident?'

'Yes, you little fool. You must have known that the *accidents* which had befallen you were not accidents at all?'

'Not accidents?' Sophia then remembered the encounter with Baggett and her attempt to divert him by asking him questions. She tried to gather her wits together and take in what her aunt was saying to her, but the pain in her shoulder, which had dulled somewhat with the medication she had taken, now returned and was shooting up violently into the back of her head, making coherent thought almost impossible. She tried to concentrate on what her aunt was saying, but her head was swimming and she began to feel curiously unreal and far away.

'No, they were not accidents, my dear,' her aunt said vindictively. 'Merely failed attempts to have my dear niece done away with. But there will be no failure this time, my dear. Definitely no failure.'

She raised the pistol and pointed it at Sophia. 'Close your eyes,' she said. 'Go back to sleep.'

She took aim and, at that moment, Sir Paul burst unceremoniously into the room and seized both Aunt Harriet's arms, pulling them back and holding her in an iron grip. There was a terribly loud bang as the gun went off and a smell of powder as the bullet lodged itself above the lintel of the window, making Polly scream.

'Aunt Harriet,' Sophia said again and promptly fainted.

Then everything happened at once. John Sawyer entered the room with Miss Fitzpatrick and fastened Harriet's wrists together and sat her on the day bed with Sir Paul Maunders to guard her while he picked up the gun and placed it in his bag as evidence. Dr Humphreys arrived and both men then turned their attention to Sophia who was a deathly shade of pale and appeared to still be in a deep swoon.

Miss Fitzpatrick began to bathe her temples and wafted a vinaigrette under her nostrils, while Dr Humphreys checked her pulse. Sir Paul sent Polly to direct his groom to take John Sawyer and his prisoner to Bow Street immediately. John Sawyer kept stern and unrelenting guard over Harriet Winterton and Sophia, her eyelids fluttering, gradually regained consciousness. Her eyes were still filled with terror and horror, but she was also conscious of Sir Paul's strong presence.

Harriet Winterton was taken away to be questioned by the magistrate and, as soon as Sophia was once more settled comfortably, Dr Humphreys also left, leaving Sophia and Sir Paul alone. It was Polly's turn to rest for a while and Miss Fitzpatrick busied herself tidying up the room, putting things away, straightening the curtains at Sophia's window and generally trying to be tactful as Sir Paul sat holding Sophia's hand and gazing with concern at the still quiet face which was usually so bright and alive.

At nine o'clock, Miss Fitzpatrick touched him gently on the shoulder.

'Miss Winterton is ready to sleep now, Sir Paul. I must ask you to leave her for tonight. She will be in very safe hands, I assure you.'

'I know,' he said, and smiled somewhat wearily and took his leave.

15

Sir Paul visited Sophia every day for the next few days and while she was lying so ill, he was admitted without question. Gradually, however, she became much better and more able to say who she would receive and who not. Then, one morning when she had only just been allowed to get up out of her bed, Polly met him with the announcement that Miss Winterton was not at home to visitors.

Miss Fitzpatrick had been obliged to make a hasty visit to the subscription library to replenish Sophia's stock of books which, not surprisingly, was much reduced by her enforced inactivity and Polly took her responsibilities as the guardian of Sophia's peace and quiet as well as her virtue, very seriously.

'I am not a visitor,' he declared firmly. 'I am her betrothed and demand to see her at once.'

'I don't know about that, sir, but if you would care to wait in the drawing-room, I'll ask Miss Sophia if she's prepared to see you.'

She sped away and he hadn't long to wait before she returned saying, 'Miss Winterton will receive you now, sir,' but as she paused on the landing, she said in a low voice, 'Miss Winterton is not well, sir. She is still very pulled down with the injury to her shoulder. I beg you will not agitate her or upset her in any way.'

'I promise I will not,' he said gravely, and Polly opened the door of Miss Winterton's bedroom and ushered him in.

When Polly had carried the news of Sir Paul's visit to Sophia, her mistress had indeed appeared agitated. She had pulled herself up painfully from the day bed and said, 'Oh no! Not Sir Paul. I cannot receive him when I am looking so dragged down and ghastly. I do not wish to see anyone, Polly. I am such a fright and I feel like an utter frump.'

'Well, miss,' Polly said doubtfully. 'I could say you're not receiving anyone, but if he's that way intended, ma'am, he'll pay it no heed. He'll come pushing his way in, anyway. He's very demanding, Miss Winterton.'

'I know,' Sophia sighed. 'What a difficult man. But for a start, you may remove this horrid rug from my knees. I will not meet him lying on the couch like some languishing lily in a Gothic novel.'

When Sir Paul entered, he found her sitting up at one end of the day bed, wearing a soft satin dressing-gown, her shoulder still strapped up, but all her injuries hidden from view. She greeted him calmly, saying, 'Good day, Sir Paul. I am so sorry not to receive you in the drawing-room, but my godmother is out and I am not allowed to leave my room.'

She attempted to stand up but the enforced bed rest had weakened her and she staggered and would have fallen had not Sir Paul grasped her in his strong arms and gently helped her to sit down again. He sat down beside her and still kept one arm around her. Sophia, to her own surprise, made no protest at this.

Not even the most daring of her admirers had ever been so bold as to do more than kiss her hand. None had ever attempted anything as indiscreet as an arm around her slender waist and she herself had begun to wonder if it was some fault within her own make-up that made her find the idea of kissing any gentleman intimately, utterly distasteful. To be sure, her former fiancé had pressed her hand, offered a chaste kiss to her cheek, but that was all. Yet, each time Sir Paul Maunders had taken her into his arms she had found it anything but distasteful and admitted to herself that any protest would just be for form's sake. His arm tightened round her just as someone tapped at the door.

It was Miss Fitzpatrick, her hands full of

books and her bright eyes calmly taking in the scene before her. 'Dear me, you are only supposed to be out of bed for half an hour, my dear,' she said sternly. 'What will Dr Humphreys say when he knows you have been jauntering about the room, instead of resting?'

'He has said that I might try all everyday activities that I can manage,' Sophia said demurely, her colour high and her eyes bright. 'The strapping must stay on, but I may be as active as I can.'

She shot a mischievous look at her godmother, who said firmly, 'Sir Paul, you must leave now and Sophia must rest.'

He went with a good grace, kissing her hand before he left and promising to visit again the next day.

Noticing that Sophia was now looking very peaky and tired, Miss Fitzpatrick said, 'I think that's enough excitement for one day. I shall leave you with Polly now. Let her help you to get undressed and back into bed. Have a little rest, my dear, and if you feel better later on, I will come and have supper with you.'

Sophia nodded her agreement. She admitted to herself that she had been tired by Paul's visit and was still confused by her feelings for him. She was grateful to be helped back into the cool fresh bed as her anxious godmother closed the door quietly behind her. In spite of her troubled thoughts of Aunt Harriet and Sir Paul Maunders, she succeeded in sleeping until supper-time and then she and Fitz ate from a small occasional table.

'You're looking so much better, Sophia,' her godmother said happily. 'It will be so nice when you're out and about again. David has been every day and your friends are obviously missing you, my dear. We have been inundated with flowers and quite a few of your visitors came in person today.'

She asked Polly to bring up the various cards that had arrived and as Sophia read them, Miss Fitz was pleased to see her face relax and her pale cheeks once more become tinged with a little colour.

'Dr Humphreys will call in the morning, so I would like you to have a good night's rest. He's said that after his call, you may have visitors whenever you feel up to it.'

'Fitz dear,' Sophia protested, 'I cannot possibly sleep just yet. Bring your sewing and keep me company while I look at the books you have brought for me.'

They sat in silence, Fitz busy with her needlework and Sophia making a pretence of reading the books her godmother had brought, her mind occupied with Sir Paul Maunders. If only everything were straight-forward, she thought. If only she had not allowed herself to be persuaded to become engaged to Lord Devenish; there would have been no need to run away. If only she had met Sir Paul Maunders first and he had asked in the conventional way for her hand, she might now ... she might now have been ... the happiest woman on earth, she acknowledged to herself and sighed, but this sort of 'if only' thinking could not help her.

Miss Fitzpatrick, who had taken note of Sophia's restlessness and lack of interest in the library books, said gently, 'I heard some distressing news today, my dear. Your aunt Harriet who, as you know, was apprehended for attempted murder, was found dead. She died by her own hand, Sophie dear, and, of course, the funeral cannot be held on consecrated ground, even if you and David should have wished it. She had no one else in the world, Sophie, but maybe that is for the best. Her evil life and her wicked end are best forgotten.'

Sophia thought of her kind and loving uncle. How on earth did he come to marry a woman such as Aunt Harriet? Perhaps he'd been lonely, been attracted by her strength and the obvious care she took over their house. Sophia knew he wanted to ensure that Harriet had a comfortable home for as long as she needed it and Harriet had taken care never to let the pretence of caring for her niece drop, while he was alive.

Miss Fitzpatrick noticed her shudder and went on, 'William Baggett was found dead the day after Lady Wright's masquerade. It seemed he suffered some sort of seizure. At the last, he obviously repented of his liaison with Harriet Winterton and regretted his involvement in making attempts on your life. I just hope it can now be a chapter closed and that you will be able to live your life in peace, when you are stronger.'

The next morning, Dr Humphreys came early and bustled in just as Sophia had finished her breakfast. He talked softly and reassuringly, not pausing for a reply and not expecting one.

'Good. You're eating well,' he said when he saw her empty plate. 'And you're looking a lot better, child.' He beamed at her. 'How are you sleeping? Does the noise from the street bother you? I can leave a sleeping draught if you wish.'

He pulled out a large old-fashioned watch and took her pulse. 'I shall remove the strapping and you can get dressed today,' he said, 'and tomorrow you can go downstairs for an hour or two. Do not overdo things, my dear. I know what you young ladies are like as soon as you feel a touch better, wanting to gad about and shop and so on. Take life at a steady pace, dear Miss Winterton, and you will soon be fully recovered. Unless I am needed, I shall not visit until next week.'

He patted her hand in his fatherly way. 'Good day, my dear. Good day, Miss Fitzpatrick. I shall see myself out, ladies.'

In spite of Dr Humphreys' reassurances, Sophia found the process of dressing slow and painful, even with Polly's help and she was glad to recline on the day bed and read.

Meanwhile, her cousin David and her friends and admirers were just as assiduous in their attentions, and various gentlemen, including Thomas Thornton and Richard Andrews, sent flowers, bouquets, sweetmeats, books and cards, all expressing hopes for her recovery.

Sophia was glad to be downstairs and the next day, sat alone in Miss Fitzpatrick's tiny courtyard garden, reading one of the books by Miss Austen that her godmother had brought for her and enjoying the last of the September sunshine. She was pleased that Dr Humphreys had finally removed the strapping but her spirits were still at a low ebb.

Even through the length of the narrow

Georgian house, she heard the sound of Fitz's brass door knocker and wondered idly if it could be Paul.

Sure enough, Polly appeared looking flustered and said, apologetically, 'I didn't rightly know what to do, miss, you didn't give any instructions about if you was at home.'

The door opened with enough force to send it banging against the wall of the house and Polly, muttering something inarticulate, rushed back inside, closing the door behind her. Sophia put down her book with trembling fingers as he stood with his back to the door for a long moment, ignoring Polly's protests and gazing at Sophia as though he'd never seen her before. His look was gentle and loving as he walked towards her and crouched by the side of the stone bench. In her precarious emotional state, she was overcome by the tenderness in his voice and had to blink back tears of utter weakness.

His voice was soft as he said, 'I was sorry to hear of your aunt's death; I hope you are not grieving unduly. She was wickedly misguided, but I fear that she was also mentally unhinged and not responsible for her actions.'

'I know,' Sophia said regretfully. 'I am trying hard not to think about her. Both David and I were obliged to accept her, but in truth, there was no emotional tie. She was

'. . . she was . . . my uncle's wife, that is all. I tried to love her but . . . '

'But it is still very distressing for you. It is wonderful to see you out of your sick bed, though. How are you feeling, now? Has the doctor been today?'

'No. He's hardly had time, I think. We're not used to such unfashionably early social calls.'

She tried to speak lightly, but he heard the tremor in her low voice and noticed the slight trembling of her lower lip as she looked down at her hands, clasped tightly on her lap. 'But I am feeling much more myself. I shall soon be completely well, I thank you.'

'But you look so sad,' he said even more softly.

'It is a sad thought that there were two people in London who wished me . . . wished me . . . dead,' she said almost inaudibly and her beautiful head drooped disconsolately. Then with a brief return to her usual spirited self, she said firmly, 'They were the only two people who were able to blackmail me over our journey from Cottleton, so there is no need for you now to feel that you have to marry me.'

His brows met in the well-remembered black scowl. 'Oh yes there is. Quite regardless of Baggett's evil plots, I have ruined your reputation and I will marry you.'

'Rubbish!' Sophia exclaimed. 'I am in no way ruined. I do not give a fig for what Society thinks. I am about to attain my majority. I am an independent woman and shall soon have my own establishment.'

'Independent or not, Sophie, you are a woman, and I will not let you overrule me in this. My honour is at stake. I must and will marry you. I warn you, Sophia, do not try to run away from me as you did Devenish. He and I are very different animals. I shall call on you every day until you agree.'

'I will not. I will not,' she said defiantly, and beat her fists against the stone bench as he turned on his heel and strode away. Then she burst into tears.

Sir Paul Maunders was sufficiently experienced with women to know that Sophia didn't find his advances repugnant. He'd registered her innocent but passionate response to his kisses and knew that she returned his ardour. True to his word, he did visit every day and made himself so civil and pleasant to both Sophia and her godmother, that the thought of marriage to him became more and more attractive. His behaviour was completely correct for a man fixing his interest with the woman of his choice. Having received David's permission to ask for

Sophia's hand, he acted with the utmost propriety. He made no attempt to kiss her again and with the perversity of a woman in love, Sophia now wished that he *would* kiss her and repeat his proposal.

Then, Sir Paul was obliged to visit his country seat in Cottleton and Sophia heard nothing from him for five interminably long days. She was now almost in full health and spirits and Dr Humphreys had urged her to take gentle exercise during the rest of the healing process and go walking in the fresh air while the weather was so pleasant.

It was on the sixth day that the weather changed and became a little more unsettled. With his usual disregard for the niceties of convention, Sir Paul arrived almost immediately after breakfast, before Sophia and Miss Fitzpatrick had managed to gather themselves together and organize their activities for the day.

Polly showed him into the drawing-room and he greeted both ladies courteously, but without any preamble, said abruptly to Sophia, 'I thought you might care for a drive, now that you are so obviously improved and feeling better.'

Her spirits lightened and she agreed. Miss Fitzpatrick clucked about the weather turning inclement. 'It might be unwise in an open carriage, my dear. Suppose it came on to rain? Dr Humphreys — '

Sophia said determinedly, 'I will take care, dear Fitz. My cloak has a hood and I will have my shawl also.'

Sir Paul's usually saturnine expression was lightened by an unexpectedly sweet smile as he looked down at Miss Fitzpatrick's anxious little face and said, 'You may swathe her in quantities of shawls, ma'am. Believe me, she will be quite safe. Try not to worry, ma'am, I shall take great care of her. If it comes on to rain, we can seek shelter, you know.'

'Very well. Put on your bonnet, my dear, and enjoy your drive.'

A few minutes later, she was waving farewell to them on the doorstep and Sir Paul settled Sophia in and they set off at a smart pace. She glanced at him sideways from under the brim of her bonnet and said demurely, 'How lovely it is to be out in the air after being confined to my room for such a long time.'

He kept his eyes on the horses, but said, with mock seriousness, 'I only hope that the good doctor may not call on you today and find no patient.'

'But you will not keep me out too long, will you?'

'No. I will not keep you out too long,' he promised.

This meekness on his part was so unexpected, that she looked at him in some surprise and this time he was looking at her fully, meeting her questioning gaze openly.

'I shall only keep you out long enough for all normal purposes,' he said, and smiled at her.

'Oh? And what might that mean, exactly?' She glanced suddenly at the countryside and noticed that they had turned on to the coach road leading to St Albans. 'Oh my goodness, where are we going?'

'Bury St Edmunds,' he said briefly.

She laughed, disbelieving him. 'But we are going on a gentle drive, you said, to have some fresh air and will be back in case the doctor calls later this morning.'

'No,' he said seriously, 'we are not going to be back by then.'

'Stop bamming me, Paul,' she said. 'We cannot possibly be going to Bury St Edmunds in an open curricle.'

'No, we shall stop at St Albans and pick up my chaise which is waiting for us at the Sir John Falstaff.' He registered the fact that she had used his first name and his dark eyes glowed with pleasure and satisfaction.

'This must be a joke. And what will happen

when we reach Bury St Edmunds, pray?'

'This is no joke, I assure you. I have a special licence and we are going to be married.'

Still only half believing him she said, 'This is nonsense. I positively cannot, will not, elope with you. Take me back at once.'

'No,' he said, quietly but firmly, 'I am not eloping with you. This is far too serious for that. I am abducting you and am going to marry you, Sophia. I will brook no argument.'

This so took her breath away, that she was torn between anger and laughter. 'Odious man! Take me back at once. Dear Fitz will wonder what has happened. She will think I have run mad to agree to such a havey-cavey plan.'

'You don't need to agree to it. An abduction is not something you agree to; it is forced upon you and you are obliged to acquiesce.'

'But I don't acquiesce. I won't . . . I cannot exchange one cage for another. I thought you knew that. Besides, what about . . . ?'

She felt too humiliated to say, 'what about your mistress?' but Paul recognised the unspoken question immediately.

He slowed the horses so that they ambled along at the side of the road.

'Oh, Marie, you mean? God knows,

Sophia, I am no saint. I've sowed my wild oats and had the money to commit the usual youthful indiscretions with gambling and women, but I don't think I am more of a sinner than any other man. It was all over with Marie before I asked you to marry me, Sophia. Believe me, I would never play false with my wedding vows. All I know is that I love you and I am going to marry you. If I really thought that you did not wish it I would not demand it of you.'

'You . . . love me . . . and you have finished with . . . that woman?'

'Yes. She has fled abroad with Devenish,' he said, his expression forbidding further discussion.

Sophia registered this and chose to accept it, but still felt moved to protest about the abduction.

'But the disgrace. The scandal. Cousin David. Poor dear Fitz.'

His smile reached his eyes in the attractive well-remembered way. 'As soon as we are married, they will be reconciled to the situation and offer their felicitations. It is human nature.'

'But, this is too ridiculous, Paul. Please take me back.'

'No. Not until we are married.'

'But I have no bride clothes, no abigail, no

toothbrush,' she wailed.

'We can get all those in St Albans,' he said mildly. He tried to look penitent, but she was not deceived and she was obliged to laugh. It was the laugh that he'd heard on their journey from Norfolk, exuberant and joyous, the laugh he had longed to hear again.

'You are no gentleman, sir, and I have not consented to marry you,' she said, but she was still smiling.

He stopped the coach and turned to her, so that she was obliged to meet his eyes and he spoke with mock seriousness. 'Let me inform you, Sophia Winterton, I am not a loose screw who would keep a mistress when I am a married man, and I will listen to no more of your arguments.'

He softened his words by putting an arm round her and saying, 'Only tell me that you return my love, Sophia . . . tell me.'

He was truly serious now. The dark compelling eyes blazed into hers so fiercely that what she saw made her drop her own. 'Yes, I do love you,' she whispered. 'I have loved you ever since our journey from Norfolk.'

He needed no further prompting, but drew her into his arms and kissed her with infinite tenderness, having remembered, rather belatedly, her injured shoulder.

We do hope that you have enjoyed reading this large print book.

Did you know that all of our titles are available for purchase?

We publish a wide range of high quality large print books including:
Romances, Mysteries, Classics
General Fiction
Non Fiction and Westerns

Special interest titles available in large print are:
The Little Oxford Dictionary
Music Book
Song Book
Hymn Book
Service Book

Also available from us courtesy of Oxford University Press:
Young Readers' Dictionary
(large print edition)
Young Readers' Thesaurus
(large print edition)

For further information or a free brochure, please contact us at:
Ulverscroft Large Print Books Ltd.,
The Green, Bradgate Road, Anstey,
Leicester, LE7 7FU, England.
Tel: (00 44) **0116 236 4325**
Fax: (00 44) **0116 234 0205**

Other titles published by
The House of Ulverscroft:

DANGEROUS LEGACY

Shirley Smith

When Sir Thomas Capley inherits a fortune from his great-uncle, he returns to Wintham determined to restore the family seat to its former glory. In somewhat unusual circumstances, he meets the proud and beautiful heiress, Miss Helena Steer, who has decided never to marry and, instead, devotes herself to her widowed father and her two young sisters. However, aided by Thomas's mischievous grandmother, the couple fall in love. There are many dangerous adventures for both of them, but will Helena find happiness with the passionate Sir Thomas?

DEAR MISS GREY

Shirley Smith

When beautiful Lucy Grey and her brother, William, become orphans, their futures are organized by hard-nosed Aunt Esther. Whilst Will is sent to Oxford University, Lucy is found a post in London as governess to Lord Hallburgh's two motherless children. However, Lucy soon senses a strange and threatening atmosphere in the household, run by Edmund Hallburgh's much older sister, the autocratic Honourable Caroline Hallburgh, who is physically disabled. She sees the growing friendship between Lucy and Edmund as a threat to her own position and is determined to break Lucy Grey . . .

THE UNCONVENTIONAL MISS WALTERS

Fenella-Jane Miller

Eleanor Walters is obliged, by the terms of her aunt's will, to marry a man she dislikes: the irascible, but attractive, Lord Leo Upminster . . . Leo finds Eleanor's unconventional behaviour infuriating, her beauty irresistible and their agreement not to consummate the union increasingly impossible. It is only when he allows his frustration and jealousy to drive her away that he realizes what he has lost . . . Meanwhile, in her self-imposed exile on a neglected country estate, Eleanor becomes embroiled in riots and treachery. In a desperate race, can Leo save both her life and their marriage?

THE ADVENTURESS

Ann Barker

Florence Browne lives in poverty with her miserly father, but seeking adventure, she goes to Bath under the assumed name Lady Firenza Le Grey. But there, she meets a man calling himself Sir Vittorio Le Grey, who accuses her of being an adventuress. When her previous suitor, Gilbert Stapleton, visits Bath, Florence is plagued by doubts. Is Sir Vittorio the wicked Italian he appears to be? Are Mr Stapleton's professions of love sincere? And how can she accept an offer of marriage from anyone while she is still living a lie?